TURBULENT
DESIRES

TURBULENT DESIRES

A Billionaire Aviator Novel

MELODY ANNE

Montlake
Romance

Published by Montlake Romance, Seattle

www.apub.com

Amazon, the Amazon logo, and Montlake Romance are trademarks of Amazon.com, Inc., or its affiliates.

ISBN-13: 9781503940758
ISBN-10: 1503940756

Cover design by Eileen Carey

Cover photography by Regina Wamba of MaeIDesign.com

Printed in the United States of America

This book is dedicated to Patrick Falk. You are the epitome of the confident, sexy pilot, and you always make me laugh. Ladies, beware. ☺

PROLOGUE

Rubbing her eyes, Lindsey Helm slowly stood up from her post at the nurses' station in the hospital and walked down the quiet hallway to the back room to organize supplies. Most nights, she loved the quietness of the calm hospital. This wasn't one of them.

She was carrying a full course load to finish her nursing degree and working forty hours a week, and it was beginning to catch up with her. She couldn't remember the last time she'd had a night out on the town, seen her best friend, Stormy, or done something as luxurious as take a long bath.

But it would all be worth it in the end. She'd inherited her family's work ethic, and growing up, her parents had taught her that the only way to succeed in life was to put in one hundred percent effort no matter the situation. She'd been taught to work hard, and she wasn't going to start complaining now. Lindsey would never be happy being handed something for free. It meant nothing unless she'd earned it.

Her brothers—her wonderful, amazing, over-protective brothers—always tried to help her, to carry her along, but that wasn't what she wanted. They'd managed to better their lives, just as her parents had wanted, and she needed to prove she could do the same.

Though her family hadn't had a lot of money while she was growing up, they had always provided ample love. Even though the finances had changed, thanks to the hard work of her brothers, the love remained as strong as ever.

Leaning against the dim storage wall, she rubbed her temples. Was it terrible of her to hope for a trauma just so she could stay alert? Yeah, that probably wasn't the best thing to hope for.

Another lesson her mother had always taught her was to be careful what you wished for.

A loud crashing noise, followed by the echoing shout of a male voice, snapped Lindsey into high alert. She took a step toward the door and a chill ran down her spine. This wasn't the sound of EMTs barreling into the ER.

An uneasy fear gripped her. She tried to tell herself that it was nothing more than a violent patient whom the staff was trying to restrain. Still, something didn't feel right, which left her frozen where she stood instead of rushing ahead. Even though, normally, she would be in professional mode, she felt as if she should stay exactly where she was.

Ridiculous.

A scream sounded and prisms of fear shot through Lindsey's entire body. Moving away from the door, she found a wrapped scalpel, grabbed it, took off the covering, and stuck the unsheathed blade in her scrub pocket. She couldn't just continue to hide in the closet, though. It was three in the morning, and there was only minimal staff in the ER. They would need her in there.

Her coworkers were out there. Patients needed her, and she had a responsibility to help. She was trained for this and didn't have time to panic. Gathering every ounce of courage, she cracked open the door.

She couldn't see anything, but she could hear cries from down the hallway.

Leaning against the wall, Lindsey slowly made her way toward the nurses' station, listening for further sound. There was nothing. The lack of noise had her more worried than the scream she'd heard not long ago.

When she reached the end of the hallway she peeked around the corner, but didn't see a single person. It was okay, she assured herself as she moved a little quicker to go down the next hallway, which led to the ER doors.

She was sure her friend Sandy was in there helping Dr. Stamos with an unruly patient. The paramedics who had most likely brought the patient in must have already had the situation fully under control since she'd taken too long in the supply closet.

Pushing open the ER door, she didn't immediately see the crew. Her worry was for nothing, she assured herself.

"Dr. Stamos," she called out.

The ER door slammed shut behind her, taking her breath away and causing her to jump at least a foot in the air.

"Hmm. What do we have here?" A man in desperate need of a haircut and shave took his time perusing her body from head to toe with beady eyes as he shifted from foot to foot in front of her. "Had I known such hot doctors were in this hospital, I woulda come in a whole lot sooner."

Lindsey took a few seconds to assess the situation. The man was obviously high on something, or more likely, many somethings. She didn't want to be within grabbing distance of him. Taking a couple of side steps, she scooted away, trying to nonchalantly put much-needed distance between them.

He wasn't necessarily acting violently at this point, but she almost felt naked with the way he was staring at her, as if he could see her body through the loose scrubs. Where in the hell were the paramedics and the doctor? And where was Sandy?

"What are you doing in here?" Lindsey asked him with as much calmness as she could muster.

His scabbed lips went up in a grin. "I need some medical care, doc," he said, taking a step closer to her. She shifted sideways and backward.

"I'm not a doctor, but I can get one for you," she said, wanting to get away from this man and to a phone where she could call for reinforcements.

His laugh sent a chill through her. "This place seems like a ghost town to me, lil' doc," he told her.

Lindsey weighed her odds of getting through the door she'd just come in, but the man was nearer to it than she was. Plus, she wasn't sure where Dr. Stamos or Sandy were and she felt like an animal in a small cage.

"There are plenty of staff here, sir. If you just sit down over there, I'll get someone to help you right away," she said with bravado.

"I think you're telling me a lie, lil' doc. I have a feeling you're all by your lonesome in here. Now, that just don't seem right," he told her as he continued to box her in. "Matter of fact, I bet we have us at least a good hour or so before we get more docs coming to your aid."

His meaning was clear, and Lindsey had to swallow the bile in her throat. She'd grown up with four brothers, and this man wasn't going to take her down easily. The problem was that she didn't know where Sandy or Dr. Stamos were or when anyone else would enter the hospital. She needed to get help.

The man took another step toward her and her fear was almost all-consuming. Fight or flight had most certainly kicked in and she was ready to knee this guy as hard as she could and then run for help as he flopped on the ground like the weasel he obviously was.

"You're wrong. There are plenty of people in the halls, but more importantly, the ambulance will be here any second now," she bluffed. If only her voice was stronger. Even in her own ears, it sounded weak and pathetic.

There was a light of victory shining in the man's eyes that told her that her bluff wasn't working. He knew they were virtually alone, and he held a royal flush in his hands. It was her strength against his, and though he wasn't a big man, he was bigger than she was.

Just as she decided to run, a pained scream sounded from the only other emergency room. She twisted her head for only a moment to gaze in that direction.

That moment was all her attacker needed. He pounced much faster than she would have believed possible. Before she had a chance to defend herself, he wrapped one arm around her waist from behind and the other reached up and gripped her neck, making it instantly difficult to breathe.

"Was that one of the other staff members you were talking about?" he whispered cruelly in her ear.

Lindsey couldn't help the pain rolling through her heart. He had at least one accomplice, and it appeared as if they'd already found Sandy, and most likely Dr. Stamos as well.

The door opened, and Lindsey stopped struggling against thug number one as a new man entered the room, this one far larger than the guy holding her. She knew her chances of getting away from him were slim to none.

Why hadn't she just called 911 immediately when she'd gotten the bad feeling? Wouldn't it have been better to beg for forgiveness if she'd been wrong? Maybe she could have saved her coworker and friend if she had trusted her instincts.

"You found a new one," the large man said as he took his time examining her.

"Yep, appears she wanted to join our little party in here," the smaller man holding her said with a laugh. "I just wanted some easy drugs, but this is so much better. Remind me to thank Pete again for the recommendation. He said last week the night shift was a skeleton crew. Guess he knew his shit."

"Yes, Pete's pretty damn smart," the larger man said as he stepped right in front of her and ran a filthy finger down the side of her cheek and then over one breast. "I prefer bigger, but she'll do. She's feisty. That makes up for her lack of size."

Lindsey jerked back against the man holding her, but his vice-like grip didn't loosen at all. He just laughed as he stepped back and leaned against a counter as if he had all day. The longer these men took, the more chance of someone arriving.

"Hey! You got the last one. This one's mine," the small man behind her snarled.

The good humor on the large man's face vanished as he shot a look at the man holding her. Another chill traveled through her because she had no doubt who the boss was in this relationship. The man behind her shut up.

"No. They are *all* mine first," the large man said almost pleasantly.

The man behind her let go of her throat and she sucked in a much-needed breath before it was knocked back out of her when he pushed her forward hard enough to drop her to her knees on the hard floor.

The large man gripped her arm and yanked her back to her feet, sending shooting pain arrowing through her shoulder before smashing her to his chest. Up close, she could see dents in his face, and missing teeth from years of drug use.

Fighting tears, she tried to plead with him. "Please, just let us go."

Leaning back, he smiled before his fist came out and knocked her in the side of the head, making her see stars for a moment. She almost wished blackness would overtake her vision just to free her from the hell she was in.

"If I want you to open your mouth, I'll let you know when and how wide," he told her. "We're going to have a good time here, and then you're going to unlock these nice pretty cabinets with drugs in them."

The man's stinky spit splashed her in the face, making her shut her eyes for a brief second as she tried to regain her bearings.

"I don't have access to any of that," she told him. That was partially true. The sort of drugs they wanted had to come from the doctors.

The man slapped her again for her less-than-satisfactory answer. She tasted copper in her mouth and couldn't help the whimper of fear and pain that escaped. It was exactly what he wanted, but she still couldn't help herself.

He shook her for a moment before a gleam returned to his eyes. "I'll just have to get you a bit more relaxed and then you can give me what I came for."

"Where's Sandy?" Her voice was a bit stronger this time, but still not as forceful as she would have liked.

"Me and Sandy had a good time a few minutes ago. If you're a real nice girl, then both of you will get to walk away from this. Do you understand?" he said. He then began pulling her toward a curtained room.

"I get her next then?" the first man hollered as the giant continued moving.

"Don't worry. I'll get her nice and prepared for you," he replied back.

"Fine. I'm gonna search this place then." The first man stomped out of the ER.

Pushing Lindsey down on a hospital bed, her attacker leaned close as he pointed his disgusting finger in her face and smiled, his rotten teeth showing.

"We're gonna have us a good time, sweetness. If you cooperate and do what you're told to do, then no one gets hurt. If you fight me, then I'm going to carve you up into so many pieces they won't be able to identify your body unless they're real good with puzzles," he told her.

Then to make sure she understood he was serious, he took out a huge knife and stabbed it into the bed only a foot from her face.

"Where is Sandy?" she asked. The more she kept him talking, the more time she was giving herself.

"She's tied up at the moment," he said with a chuckle, standing there, admiring her. In that moment, Lindsey had a sick feeling that her friend was gone. He'd done what he'd wanted with Sandy, and then disposed of her like he was planning on doing to Lindsey.

"Please don't hurt me," she begged. She hadn't given up, but the situation seemed so hopeless.

He backed up a bit and Lindsey knew she had to try something. She lunged for the door. But she made it no more than a foot when his meaty hand wrapped around her arm and swung her back to him before shoving her face first into the mattress.

Time stopped having meaning as he yanked at the tie in her hair. When it was loose, he pulled the long strands while he pushed up against her behind. She choked back sobs and bile as he struggled to undo the drawstring on her pants.

If he got them off, the battle would be over. She continued fighting against him, but she knew she was losing. Tears streamed down her cheeks as the struggle continued. She could hear his belt buckle jingle and felt him fidgeting with his own pants. The sounds of his grunts and her whimpers mixed through the air. Then she could feel that he'd gotten his pants down and only her scrubs barred him from violating her.

"That feels good now, doesn't it, princess?" he jeered as he pressed himself against her.

As he struggled again to get her pants undone, Lindsey remembered the scalpel in her pocket. Reaching down, she managed to pull it out, and then she struck without giving it a second thought.

With all her might, she swung her arm backward, aiming as high on his leg as she could go, hoping to hit his femoral artery. God willing, he'd be too busy bleeding out to retaliate. Then she could call for help.

Lindsey knew she hit something, because his howl of pain and rage assaulted her ears before she managed to pull the blade out and push him away.

He stumbled back and Lindsey turned around, trying to decide whether to stab him again or make a run for it. He made the decision for her when he lunged back into her face, his cruel eyes completely arctic now.

His hands circled her neck, and instantly her vision blurred as he looked into her eyes with vengeful hatred. She knew if she lived through the night, that look would haunt her for years to come. Lifting her arm again, she stabbed him once more, this time in the side.

The man let go of her neck and punched her hard enough that the room went black. When she became aware again, she felt deep pain in her abdomen, and then felt the stickiness of blood as it trickled down her side.

Lindsey felt a tear slip as she realized she was going to die. There was nothing she could do to stop this man. It was over. The last thoughts were of the pain her family was going to go through. Her mother and father would be devastated. Her brothers would seek revenge. So much pain was going to be caused by this evil man, and she'd been too weak to stop it.

Devastation consumed her.

"I warned you to play nice, you stupid whore." He screamed obscenities at her as he lifted the scalpel and sliced her again. The pain stopped and she knew that was bad—knew that meant her time was almost up. She just hoped they caught this bastard before he could ever harm another person again.

As his arm lifted to administer the final blow, a gleam of victory in his eyes, his clear intent to go for her throat, a banging sound echoed off the ER walls.

Everything slowed down as she watched disbelief enter the man's eyes for the briefest of moments, and then his arm dropped and he fell on top of her, pinning her to the bed beneath his lifeless body.

The next few minutes were a blur as his weight was lifted and a torrent of activity overtook the room. Lindsey knew if she did make it through the night, her life would never be the same again. She came in and out of consciousness as she was lifted, her clothes removed, a needle painfully stuck in her arm—and then the lights went out.

CHAPTER ONE

Sitting in the corner of the pew, Lindsey kept her large bag beside her so no one would sit too close. Even with that layer of protection, her body was pressed uncomfortably hard into the wall as she stared straight ahead, not wanting to make eye contact—not wanting anyone to speak to her.

She hadn't told anyone she was coming to the funeral of Doctor Ted Stamos, but she couldn't miss it even though her injuries weren't remotely close to being healed.

It had been only a week since the stabbing, since the moment she'd nearly lost her life. The doctor had told Lindsey she was lucky she'd been assaulted in a hospital; otherwise, there wouldn't have been time to stop the bleeding.

Rubbing her fingers beneath her silk shirt, she felt the bandages on her lower abdomen and grimaced. *Lucky* wouldn't exactly be the word she would use.

Lucky wouldn't be a word she would ever use again. Luck had nothing to do with her coming out of that horrible event while two colleagues, two friends, had died. It had been the timing of the police force. But if she'd made a call when she'd initially had the bad feeling, then today she might be sitting around the cafeteria table sharing a laugh with the charismatic doctor instead of sitting in a church, crushed against a wall, while she fought back tears as people said their final good-byes.

Clenching her fingers into a tight fist, Lindsey took shallow breaths as she tried to tell herself she was safe. Her side ached where she'd been stitched back together, and her head throbbed because she'd refused to take her pain meds on this particular day.

Lindsey wanted to feel the pain of survival. She wanted the reminder that she'd lived while two other good people had died. It wasn't fair. None of it was fair. But even so, she didn't want to be dead either. She was just dealing with some major survivor's guilt.

The temperature in the room seemed to suddenly heat up, and there was a shift in the air that Lindsey couldn't possibly explain. But without turning her head, she knew who was next to her, knew who would dare sit so close when everything about her screamed that she wanted to be left alone.

She said nothing, her body ramrod straight, her shoulder aching as she pushed it even harder against the wall as she tried to move farther away. She was barely able to hold herself together, and this wouldn't help her at all.

Her shallow breaths became tiny little pants as her vision blurred, little black dots sparking in front of her. If she didn't pull it together fast, she was going to pass out. That was the last thing she wanted. Who knew what would happen?

"You need to breathe, Lindsey."

His low voice was meant to be soothing, but his words only made her panic escalate. She bit her lip, and instead of taking a much-needed deep breath, she stopped breathing altogether, and those flashing black dots became larger as her head began spinning.

"Seriously, you have to breathe," Maverick told her.

She felt his fingers settle against her leg and a small squeak escaped her tight throat as she felt darkness trying to pull her under. Before she sank into the abyss, though, Maverick's strong fingers were gripping her shoulders, turning her toward him, and shaking her.

The motion caused her to take in a deep breath and her gaze unintentionally locked on his worried eyes. The spots that had been dancing in front of her cleared, and she couldn't turn away.

He said nothing else as he waited for her to process what was going on. The worry she saw in him helped clear up her muddled brain. Still, it took a few more moments before she was able to open her lips.

"Don't touch me," she said, her words a harsh whisper.

"You need to be touched, Lindsey. You're falling apart," he told her.

The words weren't said cruelly, more matter-of-factly, but that didn't stop the wince she felt through her entire body.

"You know nothing about me, Maverick. Just because the two of us had one night together at my best friend's wedding doesn't give you the right to try and analyze me."

She needed to get away from this man and get away fast. She *was* falling apart. Coming to the funeral had been a mistake.

"This has nothing to do with our night together," he said, his eyes narrowing the tiniest bit. He obviously hadn't liked that comment.

"I just want to be left alone," she told him. She needed to go, but she was trapped between the wall and Maverick.

Twisting her head, she looked behind her. No one was there. She was in the last row of seats. She could vault over it and run through the doors, probably without anyone even noticing.

"That's what you keep telling everyone, Lins, but I think remaining alone is the worst thing you can possibly do," he said, his fingers moving against her shoulders in what she assumed he thought was a comforting gesture. It was anything but.

"I needed to say good-bye to Ted. But I've done that. I want to go now. Please let me leave," she said, hating her pleading tone.

Surprisingly, Maverick let her go, but he didn't scoot away.

"He was a friend of mine too. But I came here to find you since you've refused to see me. I want to help you, Lins."

The sincerity in his voice couldn't possibly be faked. She wouldn't claim to know this man, not after only a single night—a very passionate night, but still, only a single night with him.

It was just too complicated. Even before the attack, it had been too complicated. Now it was impossible. Lindsey was broken. She knew she would never be the same again. And being around Maverick, who had more energy and life flowing through him than anyone else she'd ever met, hurt her so much more than the stab wounds that had been inflicted upon her body.

"There is no helping me," she told him, quiet resignation in her tone.

He winced as if her words were causing him physical pain.

Lindsey couldn't sit there and keep talking to him. She decided to make a break for it. Grabbing her purse, she stood up, her head going a little light again at the speed with which she did it. But before she could launch herself over the back of the pew, Maverick was standing next to her, his hand once again gripping her arm.

"I'll walk you out."

He didn't let go. He led her from the church just as the organ music began to let the patrons know the funeral was about to start. Maverick said nothing as they exited the giant doorway and then moved to the parking lot.

"Let me go," she said to him again. He just ignored her as he moved toward his truck and opened the passenger door.

"I need to make sure you get home safely," he said as he held out a hand, indicating he wanted her to get in.

"I'm not your responsibility," she said, her anger rising.

She was thrilled at the anger. It was so much better than the constant emotional pain she'd been feeling since the attack. But as soon as it engulfed her, it fizzled back out, leaving her feeling even more empty than she'd felt before.

He didn't say anything more to her, just waited. And Lindsey was suddenly too tired to keep fighting this man. She climbed into his truck and sat down, her body pressed against the side of the door as soon as he shut it.

Maverick tried talking to her more on the drive back to her place, but she didn't respond. The day had been too exhausting and she had nothing left in her.

When they reached her apartment, she didn't even question the fact that he knew where she lived. It had been nearly a year since Stormy's wedding to Maverick's brother Cooper.

Lindsey had fallen hard for Maverick and had spent an amazingly passionate night making love to the man. He could really make love like nobody's business. It had been the greatest night of her life. But she'd known in the morning that it couldn't continue.

Stormy was like a sister to her and Lindsey would see Maverick at too many social gatherings for them to have a casual affair or, even worse, get in a relationship that could end very badly.

So even though the man had pursued her, she'd resisted. Now, she didn't want anyone in her life—ever again.

"Lindsey—"

"Please just respect me enough to leave me alone," Lindsey told him as they reached her front door.

A flash of different emotions ran through Maverick's eyes, but Lindsey was relieved when resignation settled on his face.

"I'll give you some time. But I know you need me. I'll be back."

He stood there as she entered her empty apartment and shut the door. She leaned against the door as his footsteps retreated. Lindsey sank to the floor as the day settled in on her, and she wept into her hands.

Time would do nothing for her. Lindsey didn't think there was anything that would ever sew up the wounds in her soul—not even Maverick Armstrong.

CHAPTER TWO

One year later

Lindsey knew she needed to move. She couldn't allow fear to define her. But even knowing this, she sat in the bright window seat as the sun continued to rise higher in the sky, its piercing summer rays mocking her dark mood.

Soon she would find joy in life again. She'd had plenty of time to recover, but the thought of just going on as if nothing had ever happened didn't appeal at all. She wasn't yet ready to face the real world. Heck, she could barely face the guesthouse and the hospital she dreaded going to. Even after a year had passed, each night before bed she roamed the small cottage triple checking that all the locks were securely in place before she attempted to fall asleep. The lights were never turned off.

She wanted—needed—to feel normal again, but she wasn't quite sure how she was supposed to accomplish that. Trusting people and venturing back out was something she knew she needed to do, but she couldn't quite manage to talk herself into living life normally again.

There was a knock on her door before she heard the key in the lock and then watched as the knob turned. Even though she knew it was Stormy, since she was the only other person to have a key to the cottage, her heart still thundered as she watched her barrier against the world begin to push open.

"I have donuts, coffee, and homemade granola bars just to add a healthy kick to the meal," Stormy said as she walked into the room carrying a tray.

Her heart still thundering, Lindsey gave her best friend a smile, or at least the shadow of a smile, which she hoped was at least somewhat convincing. She slowly began to calm down.

"Thanks, Stormy. You know you don't need to keep waiting on me hand and foot," Lindsey told her as she accepted the cup of coffee and curled her legs up under her on the window seat.

"Showing up with snacks isn't waiting on you. It's being a good friend," Stormy assured her as she settled on the next cushion.

"Well, you do bring good snacks, but I feel bad when I take you away from the baby so much," Lindsey said with a sigh.

"I love having you here, and you never take away time from my family because you are a part of it," Stormy told her. "And I'm trying to give you space. You know I would much rather you stayed in the main house, but at least you're close enough that I can sleep at night," Stormy continued as she reached out to pat her hand.

Without meaning to, Lindsey flinched back, instantly feeling terrible when her best friend's eyes shone with hurt, yet understanding.

"I'm sorry," Lindsey mumbled.

"Don't apologize. I get it," Stormy said.

But the reality was that no one could understand what she was going through. Not even another victim of assault. Each woman's experience was unique. Lindsey considered herself a strong person, but since the attack, she couldn't stand to be touched.

Lindsey didn't say anything else to assure Stormy she was okay, because what else could she say? Nothing.

"Are you feeling okay today? You seem a bit paler than normal," Stormy said, but this time she didn't reach for her, thankfully.

"I'm fine. I promise," she said, a bit too loudly and with false enthusiasm. She winced at the patient look on her best friend's face.

"We should make your doctor's appointment. Last week you said your side was hurting," Stormy said, and Lindsey could see her friend's fingers twitching as if she wanted to reach out again.

"I don't want anyone looking at it anymore. Even the doctor looking at the ugly scars . . . I hate it," she said more quietly as she set down her mug on the tray and got up, pacing the room.

"I just need to do something—anything," Stormy said.

"No. Please just drop it, Stormy," Lindsey begged.

"Lins, it's just me. I've seen the scar, and it doesn't take away even an ounce of your beauty. You're the strongest woman I've ever known. Those marks just prove what a survivor you are," Stormy said, but she stayed where she was and allowed Lindsey time to try to get her breath.

"Stormy, it hurts for me to even look in a mirror," she admitted.

It wasn't easy for her to say. Really, the scaring wasn't that bad. She was a nurse; she'd seen far worse. The biggest one was about four inches long and less than a quarter inch wide. Then there were a few smaller scrapes near it, but the doctor had done a great job. The problem was that she knew they were there, and they were a reminder of what had happened. Every time she was reminded, she found panic once again choking her.

"Lins, I'm not just saying kind words to hear myself talk. You honestly are beautiful inside and out. And strong—so very strong. If the roles were reversed, I guarantee you, I wouldn't have made it out of that room alive."

Lindsey looked at her best friend and saw the truth shining from her eyes, but it didn't matter. No matter how many times she was assured the world was still spinning, it didn't help her feel okay. She was beginning to feel that nothing would ever be okay again.

"I know how much you love me, and I promise I will get back to myself," Lindsey began. "But I just need a little more time," she finished.

"I understand that. I want you to take as much time as you need. You're so important to me."

"Just as you are important to me," Lindsey told her.

"How about we get out of here for a while. We could go to the spa," Stormy suggested.

The thought of breaking up her carefully laid-out routine sent a spiral of panic right through her. Dammit! She hated weakness.

"Maybe tomorrow, Stormy. I'm going to do schoolwork today, okay?" she said, hoping her friend wouldn't argue with her.

Stormy looked as if she wanted to, but finally she let out a sigh.

"Okay, Lins. But I'm going to keep bugging you," Stormy assured her.

"I wouldn't expect anything less," Lindsey told her.

Though Stormy truly was her best friend, Lindsey found herself counting down the moments until Stormy left the small cottage. It had become her sanctuary since Stormy had brought her home.

When Stormy left, Lindsey decided to water the flowers. The sun was shining and she needed to get outdoors. She couldn't use her fear for the rest of her life. Eventually, she was going to have to really start living again.

CHAPTER THREE

Sherman sat on his nephew's back deck and enjoyed the ice tea Stormy had made for him and his friends. It sure was great to have family—and the sort of friends who you'd die for were also family in his eyes.

He looked over at Martin Whitman, who hadn't visited in such a long while. He gave him a look that made Martin chuckle before Sherman even spoke.

"It's been too long, my friend," Sherman grumbled. "I would think a retired man could get over a bit more."

Martin chuckled. "I could say the same," Martin pointed out.

"Well said," Sherman admitted. "How is the clan over there in Montana?" he asked, not able to pull off his indignation for too long.

"They couldn't be better. I've still got my youngest to marry off, but with Joseph's help, my three oldest are happy and giving me grandbabies. It took the brats long enough to do what they should have done without prodding, but I got my way," Martin said with a smug smile.

"Yeah, those kids even have the gall to say we're meddling when they obviously are happier than they've ever been," Joseph Anderson piped in, taking a long pull off his fragrant cigar.

"Ungrateful, the lot of them," Martin said.

The men sat back for a minute as they relished in their indignation.

"I think I'll go ahead and make a trip that way this summer. I've been so worried about my lot here I haven't gone far, but they're slowly but surely growing up. I'm so glad those boys of yours have begun to see the light. It's been a pleasure to keep up on their progress," Sherman told him.

"We'll go together, my friend," Joseph said. "My last few trips out there were just wonderful. I've even considered moving there. If my family weren't so settled here in Seattle, I might just do that, but I couldn't go even a week without seeing the grandkids. I'd miss them too much."

"Don't think you're going to leave the girls out of this male bonding trip. I'm joining you," Evelyn said. "I want to see Bethel and the gang. We talk on the phone, but it's not the same as visiting in person. I think my last visit out there was two years ago. My, how the time just keeps slipping away."

"It would do you some good to get away from these rowdy boys of yours. Of course, with Cooper settled down and married now, he's a whole new man," Sherman said with a smile. "Not that he's given any thanks for my help."

"Our help," Joseph said with a scowl.

"Of course, my friend," Sherman said, grinning.

"No matter how it worked out, I'm just grateful it did. No one needs to get credit," Evelyn said with a pointed look. "But with Cooper happily wed, I've been worried about my other boys."

"A little credit would be nice," Joseph said, but the group ignored him as they focused on the latter half of Evelyn's comment.

"Even though those boys of yours have given us trouble through the years, they've also grown up more than I thought possible in the past five," Sherman assured her.

"They are as stubborn as their father, aren't they?" Evelyn said with a smile of affection.

"As much as I hate to admit it, that's what makes them such fine men," Joseph assured her.

Sherman's eyes focused across the yard, and the rest of the group looked over to see what had captured his attention. Lindsey was out in front of the cottage watering the flowers just starting to come into bloom.

"That poor girl," Sherman said with sadness.

"It's been a year since the attack, but it might as well be yesterday," Evelyn said. "I'm very worried about her. Such a sweet girl. What she went through is too horrible to even fathom."

"I was at the hospital right after it happened. She was traumatized so badly," Sherman told the group. "She tried going back to her life, but the nightmares were too much. Finally, Stormy and I talked her into moving into the cottage. She's gone back to work, and she even gives that fake smile she thinks is fooling us all, but it doesn't show in her eyes."

"You and Lindsey have grown quite close," Joseph told his friend.

"I had high hopes of her and Maverick making a go of it a couple years ago. I saw some definite interest from both of them at Cooper and Stormy's wedding. But no matter how much poking and prodding I did, those two didn't fall for it. And then that tragedy happened, and I didn't want to push her anymore. But I'm worried because it seems she's given up on life. I don't want her to do that either," Sherman fretted.

"I agree with you, Sherman. She needs to move forward or she might never get back on her feet again. I know that Maverick sure asks about her a lot. I haven't ever seen him so concerned about anyone other than family," Evelyn said.

"Maybe with her needing a shoulder to lean on and Maverick feeling the need to be a hero, the two might just come together and heal one another's souls," Martin said.

"Yes, Maverick definitely loves being a hero," Sherman said with a laugh. "That boy was pretending to be a cop or a knight from the time he was just a tot."

"That shows a man's character—to be the one still helping others out when the world has turned its back on them," Martin said.

"I agree with you, my friend," Sherman told him. "Maverick is one of the good guys."

"We've done pretty dang well so far in matching couples. I thought we might have been losing our touch," Joseph said with a wrinkle between his brows. "But should we still be matchmaking with everything that's going on?"

It shocked everyone in the group to hear Joseph even ask such a thing.

"Love is the best medicine of all, and what Lindsey needs right now is a strong dose or she might be too fearful to ever face the world again," Evelyn said with a firm nod of her head.

"I couldn't have said it better myself, dear," Martin told her.

"I guess we do have an ideal track record to date. Haven't lost one yet," Joseph said, sounding more like himself.

"I'm at a loss for how to do this," Evelyn admitted.

They all sat there quietly for several minutes as they tried to put their collective brains together. Then Sherman looked at the group with a huge smile. The rest of them waited to hear what he had to say.

"The fund-raiser!" Sherman told them with excitement.

They looked at him with confusion.

"Sherry got sick and called last week to tell me she had to step down from organizing the event this year," Sherman said, barely able to contain his excitement. "Maverick's raised hundreds of millions for injured vets since he started the foundation, and this is the biggest fund-raiser of the year. The money goes to veterans suffering from PTSD. If we got Lindsey to chair the event, she would meet so many people, and she'd be alongside Maverick for the entire journey. Maybe it will help heal her and show them both they are so much better together."

"That is a great idea, Sherman," Joseph said, his voice echoing off the house as he sat up straight in his seat, practically giddy.

"I'll give Maverick a call right away."

Sherman pulled out his phone and dialed his nephew. It didn't take long for Maverick to understand what Sherman was asking him. When he hung up the phone, he turned to the group who were all eyeing him expectantly.

"It's a go," he said.

"Then it's time for a toast," Evelyn announced.

"We can now leave it in fate's hands and get to other business. When are you coming to Montana?" Martin asked.

The group leaned back as they made plans. When they all put their minds together, the world had better watch out because they were surely a force to be reckoned with. No one was able to withstand them when they were on a mission.

CHAPTER FOUR

"What call was so important you had to stop in the middle of our bout?" Cooper asked as Maverick put down his phone and grinned at his brother.

"It was Uncle Sherman. Should I have ignored the call?" Mav said with a raised eyebrow.

Cooper held up his hands in mock surrender as he grinned. "Oh, hell no. The old man would have shown up down here and taken far longer than a couple minutes of our time," Cooper said.

"Yeah, that's why I have a special ringtone for him. I know better than to ignore the old man."

"Ha. Me too," Cooper said. "What was the call about?"

"Are you just trying to get out of the fight?" Mav asked.

He was now incredibly distracted after the call with his uncle. Sometimes Uncle Sherman had the most amazing ideas ever. Mav refused to tell him that, though. The old guy's head was full enough.

"Hell no. I can kick your ass any day of the week. I am curious about the grin on your face, though," Cooper said.

Maverick danced across the ring as he gave his brother a look he knew would egg him on. Boxing wasn't his favorite sport, but sometimes a decent brawl was good for the soul. And nothing was better than taunting one of his brothers. Okay, taunting *all* of them at the same time was actually better, but Nick was on duty and Ace . . . well, he just missed Ace like hell.

"Ha. You became a new daddy, and all of a sudden you forgot how to move," Mav said with a laugh as he got a right jab into his brother's jaw.

"I can still take you to town any day of the week," Cooper assured him as he managed to get a hard hook to the left. That one actually hurt his hand.

But Maverick could tell that taunting Cooper wasn't such a great idea after all. Not when he was so distracted by that phone call and what Uncle Sherman had suggested he do for Lindsey. Nah, he couldn't be *that* distracted by the beautiful brunette, could he? Maybe he just had to pick up his speed.

"I don't think so, old-timer. Matter of fact, I can see a few gray hairs beginning to appear at your temples," Maverick said, trying to knock Cooper's concentration off balance.

It wasn't working.

Cooper managed to get a right hook followed by a quick triple jab to the left side. He was going to hate life in the morning. But he would make sure his brother was hurting too. Going on the offensive, he backed Cooper into the corner and got off a couple of good shots before Cooper came back swinging.

That's when it went downhill fast.

Cooper threw a punch to his brother's side and Maverick spun wrong, lost his footing, and slammed forward against the mat. The room went silent as a crunch louder than Cracker Jacks being eaten could be heard echoing through the gym. Cooper instantly paled as he looked at Maverick.

"Shit, Mav!" Cooper shouted as he dropped to his knees beside his brother. "Did it break?"

Breathing heavily through his nose, Mav didn't need to look down to know. He'd broken plenty of bones in his day.

"Yeah, my arm's broken," he said through gritted teeth.

"I'm sorry, brother," Cooper said.

"Not your fault, bro. I was fighting like a girl," Mav told him. Cooper smiled before he pulled out his phone and started to call 911. "I'm not riding in a damn ambulance. Help me up, and take me in," he said as he began wobbling to his feet.

Cooper dropped the phone and gave his brother a hand. He didn't argue because he would have insisted on the same thing.

Mav felt the world tilt as he, more shakily than he'd ever admit, climbed out of the ring. No way would he black out in front of his brother or the other patrons in the gym.

His arm snagged in the rope, but Cooper grabbed him before he could go down. Leaning heavily on his brother, Mav let Cooper help him into his ridiculous sports car. Normally, Mav loved the fine piece of machinery, but at the moment, he could only curse at it as he ducked his throbbing head to sit down in the passenger seat.

"Now, you gonna tell me what that call was all about that had you fighting so damn badly?" Cooper prodded, as he started the engine.

Mav swore. "I've been trying to get Lindsey to talk to me all year, been trying to get her to get out of the house and go out with me—anything but sitting there in your guest cottage."

"She's been back at work," Cooper pointed out.

"Yeah, she goes to work, school, and then back home."

Cooper frowned. "Stormy has been worried about her too," Coop said. "To tell you the truth, I'm pretty dang attached to the girl as well. I know she hasn't been doing too good, but I haven't known what to do. It's not something I'm familiar with."

"We don't like to fail. It's something in our blood," Maverick told him. They hit a bump and Maverick winced. Cooper smiled at him. A curse word was uttered in his direction, but Cooper pretended not to hear it.

"So what did Uncle Sherman say?"

They were getting closer to the hospital, and Mav was grateful. He would swear on a bible that his brother was hitting every hole and bump on the damn road just to make the trip that much more unpleasant.

"My chair dropped out for the fund-raiser. He suggested I ask Lindsey to step up," Mav said with a real smile, ignoring his pain.

Cooper was silent for a moment before he grinned back at his brother.

"Damn! That old man is good," Cooper finally said.

"Just don't tell him that," Mav said.

"I wouldn't dare," Cooper assured him.

"I've been where she's at. When I was captured . . ." Mav stopped talking. He didn't speak about those days or what had been done to him.

He'd learned quickly, though, after watching a lot of his fellow soldiers, that if he allowed himself to wallow in it, then he might sink to a place he would never come back from. He didn't want to see the same thing happen to Lindsey. He cared about this girl, though he didn't want to admit to anyone just how much.

Why she mattered to him, he wasn't exactly sure. It wasn't as if the two of them were close. Sure, they'd shared a night together—once—but he'd shared many nights with many women. Never before had he had a woman he couldn't forget.

"You are taking me to Mercy Hospital, right?" Mav said.

"Of course," Cooper told him with a wink.

"Good. There's a nurse there who I know can heal me all up."

The sad thing was that Mav knew her schedule. Whether she wanted an angel on her shoulder or not, she'd had one since the attack. But this angel wasn't willing to sit in the shadows any longer.

"Next time we're in the ring, you better bring your game," Cooper told him, changing the subject, which Mav was grateful for. He wasn't a feeling-sharing kind of guy.

"Sarge is gonna kick my ass," Maverick muttered as they pulled into the ER parking lot, and Cooper turned to look at him.

"Not worse than I already did," Cooper told him with a wink.

"Don't be getting all cocky on me, brother. I didn't have my head in the game," Maverick growled.

"Whatever. I'm going to be telling this story for years to come," Cooper assured him.

"You can start tonight 'cause it looks like I'll be out of commission for at least a few weeks. Guess who gets to be doing all my meal prepping?" Mav taunted him.

"I don't want your ugly mug at my place," Cooper said as he came around the side of the car just as a nurse came out with a wheelchair.

"Tough. You broke me, and now you get to take care of me," Mav said.

Then he turned to the pretty young blonde, who looked like she couldn't have been out of nursing school for more than a few days. "Howdy," he said, pretending to tip an imaginary hat.

Her pale cheeks blushed and she seemed to forget how to speak. Mav just winked at her as he smiled. He was used to having that effect on women. He loved women, loved them in all shapes, sizes, colors, and varieties. Women were his hobby.

"She's a little young *even* for you," Cooper said with a roll of his eyes.

"I'm just being polite," Mav told his brother before looking back at the young nurse. She *was* too young for him, but that didn't keep him from flirting. "What's your name, darling?"

She stammered something, but then they were in the ER and he was given paperwork and the pretty young nurse was hustled off somewhere else. His attending nurse ended up being old enough to be his grandma, but that didn't stop Mav from giving her his winning smile and making her wrinkled cheeks turn pink.

Yeah, he loved the ladies—ladies, plural, being the key word. Mav wasn't the type to settle down with just one fish when the sea was full of a variety and bounty of them. He was happy for his brother Cooper, and absolutely adored Stormy, his brother's wife. But matrimony wasn't for everyone—certainly not for Maverick.

He was young, able, and ready to sow a lot more oats. And if that were all true, he didn't understand what in the world he was doing pursuing Lindsey with such single-minded absorption.

"Can you get Lindsey for me? She usually attends to my wounds," he told the sweet nurse named Alice.

"She's almost off shift, but I can see if she's with a patient," Alice responded.

"I appreciate that," Mav told her with a wink that had her cheeks blushing again.

She practically ran from the room, and Mav sat back, trying to look as pathetic as humanly possible. He would milk the broken bone for all it was worth. Ten minutes passed and Mav began to get a bit nervous. He'd sent Cooper home, planning on getting a ride with Lindsey. He hoped she hadn't ditched him.

The door finally opened and Lindsey stepped through, her eyes on the chart in front of her. She shut the door before she looked up. Mav had to fight from smiling as he reminded himself he needed to appear weak and helpless.

He wasn't leaving without getting her to agree to either help him or go out with him. He could barely keep from smiling when she finally glanced up and her expressive eyes shone with shock.

Yeah, he made her nervous. But it was in a very, *very* good way.

CHAPTER FIVE

The sudden thundering of Lindsey's heart had nothing to do with fear. Well, maybe some fear, but as she looked up and spotted Maverick sitting on the exam table, his shirt off, and a sling on his arm, her throat closed and she couldn't seem to tear her gaze away.

Her first instinct was to rush up to him. Her second instinct was to run away as fast as she could. For nearly a year, she'd managed to avoid him as if he was infected. She knew he could make her feel things she felt she had no right to feel anymore. She knew he wouldn't ever give up on her.

That last part was too much for her to handle. She'd given up on herself and didn't feel anyone should believe her capable of being anything other than a blank face in a crowd. She didn't want to stand out—didn't want to face emotions.

Blending into the background just wasn't possible with Maverick around. The man drew attention to himself and anyone who happened to be within ten feet of him.

"Morning, sugar," he said when the silence between them had stretched on for far too long.

The smooth, easy cadence of his voice made her throat tighten and her heart thunder even more than it already had been. She sucked in a breath of air, which was a mistake because then his scent infused her, making the desire to approach him that much stronger.

Of all the hospitals he could have come to, why did he have to appear in her tiny one? Well, that was easy—to torture her.

"You requested me," she finally said, her eyes narrowing as she locked her emotions down tightly.

"Of course. I wanted the best," he said with a wince that immediately had her going into full-on nursing mode.

She moved forward and tried her best not to look at his magnificent chest. Why in the world was he shirtless? There wasn't a need, especially since he already had a cast on.

"It looks like you've already been taken care of," she pointed out.

"I needed a second opinion," he told her. "It really hurts."

At his last words, she looked at him with suspicion. She'd seen Maverick and his brothers brawl for fun, getting scrapes and bruises, and she'd never so much as seen him flinch. Was he snowballing her? She felt guilty at the thought. A bruise was a lot different than a broken bone.

"Um, it's pretty obvious you have a broken arm. I don't see that a second opinion matters at this point," she told him.

Then he grinned at her, that perfect, lopsided Maverick grin that made her knees shake. The man was too damn lethal to be around.

"Well, to tell you the truth, Coop had an appointment to get to and he dumped me off here. I need a ride home," he said with a pout. An actual pout!

"I'm working," she told him. "You should call up someone."

He slumped down with another wince, and she began to wonder if he really was in pain. If he was, then she was being terrible.

"The nurse who was just in here said you were just about to get off shift," he pointed out.

Damn. He was right. Her shift ended in about ten minutes. It would be better if he didn't know that.

"I hate to put you out, though. I guess I could call a cab," he said as he fumbled around with his good arm.

He moved quickly then, hopping down from the exam table, which put him directly in front of her with only about two inches separating them. Her breathing stopped, and she felt herself go a little dizzy. The effect he had on her was beyond confusing.

She tried to take a retreating step back, but his good hand shot out and steadied her. Panic filled Lindsey. She went immediately into fight or flight mode.

"It's okay, sugar," he said soothingly as his fingers loosened on her arm and he began to gently rub her bare skin.

Without trying to be too obvious about it, Lindsey stepped back, and was grateful when Maverick let her go. His touch wasn't nearly as terrifying to her as other people's were, but that thought scared her even more. She didn't want to feel comforted by Maverick. That would only lead to very bad things.

"So . . ." he said, drawing the word out. "Should I call that cab?"

His voice was so deflated Lindsey found herself saying something she would surely regret.

"I'll give you a ride home," she told him.

The instant smile that lit up his face told her in no uncertain terms that she'd been played. But what could she do about it? It wasn't as if she could take it back.

"Thanks, sug. I could be violated since the hospital has drugged me," he told her as he moved over to the chair and picked up his shirt—not bothering to put it back on, just holding it with the good hand.

"I highly doubt that," she muttered as she sent a glare his way. "Do you need help putting your shirt on?"

As much as she wanted that magnificent chest covered up, she didn't want to be the one to help him put it on. There would be far too much contact in doing so, and she had a feeling Mav would really milk the situation.

"Nah. I'm a bit warm right now anyway," he told her as he moved to the door and pulled it open. He was suddenly in a hurry to leave. "I'm sure you can clock out a few minutes early since you have a patient to deal with," he added.

"Why don't you go and wait in the lobby. I'll meet you there," she told him. In reality, she was thinking she could make a call to Stormy and see if her best friend would be willing to pick him up. She could claim an emergency at work to get out of it.

"I'd rather just stick with you," he told her, not budging from his position in the doorway.

"You can't be back in the ER," she pointed out, wanting to get out of the room, which seemed to be getting smaller and smaller by the second, but not wanting to brush by him.

"I'm a patient," he pointed out.

Blowing out a breath, she finally decided she needed out of the room. He still didn't move when she reached him, and she had no choice but to squeeze by him. At the last second, he shifted, and her entire body slid along his for a few seconds as she stepped through the doorway.

Looking up, she saw the spark in his eyes that told her he was very aware of what he was doing, and though Lindsey was about the least violent person in the universe, she had a strong urge to smack the look off his face.

She just moved forward instead, with him closely on her heels. Lindsey didn't fail to notice the look of her female peers as the two of them moved back to the nurses station. He leaned against the counter, engaging a few of the staff members in conversation as she finished up her paperwork for the day and then clocked out.

Taking longer than necessary didn't seem to bother Maverick in the least. When she was all out of procrastination excuses, she sighed as she looked back up at the man only to find his intense eyes gazing directly at her.

"I'm ready," she said before looking back down.

"Perfect. I'm starving," he said, stepping right up to her side as she made her way to the break room.

"I'm going to grab my stuff and then take you directly home," she said firmly. If he thought they were stopping for food, he was crazy.

"Oh, I'm not going home. Coop said I could crash at his house a few days. Doc said I can't drive on the pain meds."

Lindsey didn't say a word as he followed her into the break room where she grabbed her jacket and purse. Her teeth were clenched as he walked from the hospital with her, not seeming to be under the influence of pain meds at all by his confident gait.

She really didn't like the idea of him staying with Cooper. That was far too close to Lindsey's temporary home for her liking. Just knowing he was sleeping up at the main house was going to make it difficult for her to get any rest at all.

Maverick tried engaging her in small talk on the drive home, but she gave him terse answers that didn't aid in the conversation at all. Her rudeness didn't diminish his good mood in the least.

The man was unshakeable.

When she drove past the gate at Cooper's, she pulled up to the main house, but Mav just shook his head.

"Go ahead and park at the cottage. I'll walk up," he told her.

"That's okay. Why don't you get out here?" she urged.

"Nah, it's a beautiful day and it's not far at all."

He didn't budge from his seat, and Lindsey knew it was useless to continue the argument. With another long-suffering sigh, she backed out and then went around the house and down the short drive to the cottage, where she parked.

Lindsey was out of the car quickly, but still, Maverick was by her side almost instantly. She was ninety-nine percent sure the man wasn't on any pain meds. He was moving far too stealthily.

"Okay, I'll talk to you later," she told him pointedly as she began moving to her cottage, where she planned on locking the door behind her.

"I need to talk to you about something before I head up to the house," he said, striding easily alongside her.

"I'm really tired, Mav. I've had a long day," she told him.

Most people wouldn't push the issue. Mav certainly wasn't most people.

"Then we can sit," he said, grabbing her key right from her hand and moving to her front door. He had it unlocked and open before she could even blink. Then, without waiting for an invite, he stepped inside and moved to the kitchen.

Of course he knew her cottage well. It was owned by his brother, and he'd stayed in it many times.

"Good. Fresh lemonade," he said as he pulled out the pitcher from the fridge. "I need to get something in my stomach. Those meds are starting to mess with my system," he pointed out.

The nurse in Lindsey took over. Though she wanted to literally kick him in the butt all the way out her front door, she found herself pulling out sandwich fixings and setting them on the counter instead.

He poured them each a glass of lemonade, taking those and a bag of chips out to her small patio where she had a table with an umbrella set up. She was finished with the sandwiches when he got back, and he grabbed his, then waited for her to grab her own. They walked outside together and took a seat.

"I love this view," he said as he leaned back, picking up his sandwich and sighing after taking a bite.

Lindsey gazed out at the water as she slowly ate her own food, trying to maintain her irritation with this insistent man, but finding it difficult to do. He was just always so dang happy and confident that to be in a bad mood with him around was nearly impossible.

"What do we need to talk about, Mav?" she asked. The sooner he got it out of the way, the better off she would be.

"You know I run a charity for veterans with PTSD, right?" he said.

His question startled her. It hadn't been at all what she'd been expecting him to say.

"Yes," she said with hesitation. She wasn't sure where this was going.

"My chair had an emergency and had to leave."

She waited, but he was quiet.

"I don't understand where you're going with this," she said.

"I need someone to help organize the big fund-raiser coming up in a couple months. We earn most of our funding at this one event."

Lindsey looked at him in horror. He couldn't possibly be thinking of her to take over chairing the event. She knew nothing about fund-raisers. Besides, she could barely make it to work and back, let alone talk to the myriad people she would need to speak with in order to make this event happen. She'd been to one of his fund-raisers and it had been huge, with thousands of people there—very influential people—and a party that could rival a red-carpet event. There was no way she could pull that off.

"I don't have any suggestions on who to recommend to you," she finally said, carefully measuring her words.

"I already have someone in mind," he told her with a wink.

"Then why are you talking to me about it?" she said, a bit of venom in her tone.

"Come on, Lins. You know you'd be perfect. You won't be alone. I'll be there every step of the way."

She was sure that he meant those words to be reassuring, but they had the complete opposite effect. She was back into her fight or flight mode, and every instinct in her body was telling her to run as far away from this man as possible.

"Thanks for the offer, but I'll have to decline," she firmly told him.

He gave her that signature smile that made her grateful she was already sitting down. She had to get away from him, and she had to do it fast.

Maverick finished up his sandwich and then stood up.

"I'll give you time to think about it. Don't worry, though. I'll be around for a while so we can talk and talk and talk."

She now knew for sure that he was threatening her. Was he going to just keep on bugging her until she went insane? That might be his newest strategy.

"I'm working, Mav. I really don't have time to do a charity," she said, not wanting to admit to him how much panic the idea brought her.

"You're back to work part time, only two days a week right now. And I'm out of work until this arm is all better," he said.

How in the world did he know her schedule? He was much more aware of what was going on in her life than she was comfortable with him knowing.

"I'm going to get out of here. Think about it."

With that, he turned and strode off, not bothering to go back inside the cabin, just taking off down the trail that would lead him up to the main house. Lindsey wanted to chase him down until he was convinced she wasn't helping him with the dang charity, but she knew it would be a losing battle again.

The man was stronger than her. That was for dang sure. She decided her best and only option was avoidance. Even with him staying so close to her, she could avoid him. She was very good at that.

Grabbing their dishes, Lindsey took them inside, then shut and locked her back door. Next, she went and checked that the front was securely chained. She loved sitting outside in the afternoons and evenings, but not on this day.

No. She was in full-on evacuation mode right now.

Maverick was just too dangerous and smart for her to win any battle. Retreat was the only option.

CHAPTER SIX

The next day at work, Lindsey was dragging. She'd been right. Sleep hadn't come easy to her knowing how close Maverick was to her place. And then she'd woken up too many times when she had finally managed to shut her mind off long enough to catch a bit of rest.

So when she rolled into the hospital, at what felt like far too early an hour, she had hoped the other staff members wouldn't comment on the dark circles beneath her eyes. Of course, they were sort of used to those, since she'd sported them for months after the attack.

It also didn't help that life in the ER wasn't something a person could do at half-attention. ERs were full of hard-headed, controlling, stubborn egomaniacs and it took a lot of energy and patience to do her job. Maverick had once made a point about pilots having attitude because they could do something most of the world couldn't. Doctors weren't far behind them in that same way of thinking. Lindsey looked around the area that had been her home for years. There were so many stories she could tell, and some she did, leaving out patients' names of course. But some instances were just too dang absurd not to share with a best friend. Sometimes she didn't believe something had happened until she told another nonmedical friend about it.

There were the patients you knew on a first-name basis, who always seemed to have a menial problem of some sort, but in actuality were looking for drugs or for a familiar face and someone to be kind to them.

A good medical person learned the difference really quick between someone truly needing help and someone who wanted a fix.

Lindsey's favorite patients were the seniors whom she'd grown attached to because they spent more time in the ER than she did. Some of them had nobody who cared about them but the medical personnel. She'd had many honorary grandparents in her years of nursing.

At one time, Lindsey had thrived in the hospital. Now, it brought her too much fear each time the doors opened. The charge nurse had put her on day shift, knowing she would need other staff members around her. But still, the hospital wasn't the safety net it had once been.

There was a time she'd thought of no other place safer. It was where death was pushed back and lives that were tossed aside as a lost cause were miraculously saved. The hospital was comfort and love, open arms and escape.

But now, that feeling was gone. Now it was a place where attacks could turn deadly.

None of that should matter. She'd been back for months and she refused to let her fears keep kicking her back down. She refused to live her life in fear. She was a grown up, and having a career was what responsible people did. They didn't quit when the going got rough.

Making it through the hard times and coming out a better person was what defined a human being. She wouldn't be defined as a quitter, though tucking her tail and running had become a thing for her for too long. She certainly was running from Maverick—but that wasn't something she would feel guilty about.

The man was lethal, after all, and part of being a responsible person was knowing when you couldn't win a battle. Any type of skirmishes with Maverick were bound to go in his favor.

One thing she did love about being an ER nurse, though, was that she needed to be sharp, able to make decisions fast. Sometimes her decision would mean the difference between a patient living or dying. She also had to know when it was a true emergency and when it was somebody trying to take advantage of the system. She had to be confident.

There wasn't time for her to be weak or afraid.

"Spill the beans, Lins. You've been rushing from one place to the other ever since you got here, and I want to know why that hunk of a man who was here yesterday was eyeing you like you were exclusively his," Betty, the young blonde nurse said when Lindsey sat down to do some notes on her files.

Dang it. She'd been hoping the nosy nurse would be busy for a while, and she could slip in and out of the nurses' station before she got cornered into talking about something she had no idea what to say to.

"He's my best friend's brother-in-law. That's all. He broke his arm and needed a ride," she said, trying to make her voice sound bored.

"You don't think you're really going to get away with that, do you?" Betty persisted.

"Really. That's all he is." She certainly wasn't going to tell the hospital gossip that she'd slept with the man.

Maverick really was nothing to her. Yet each time she saw him, he was more appealing. It was truly a shame, actually. There were so many men out there who didn't have a thing going for them, yet God had seen fit to give this man every desirable feature anyone could ever want.

His piercing green eyes, broad shoulders, and dark hair made her want to have a redo of their one night together. That was saying something after what she'd been through. Maverick was the definition of the ultimate man-candy, plus he was absolutely noncommittal in relationships, which meant a fling with him would not lead to a lot of headaches. She wasn't interested in a fling, though. But the fact that he always seemed to be around made her wonder.

Despite her wanting her privacy, it was hard to resist him.

"Fine. You don't have to tell me anything," she said, but then her eyes lit up. "I'll stop bugging you if you agree to go out with us tonight."

"What?"

It had been so long since any of the staff had tried to get her to go out with them. She'd made excuses for so long that they'd eventually given up. It appeared that with Mav's appearance yesterday, they were starting their efforts again.

"I don't know," she said, trying to figure a way to get out of it without seeming rude about it.

"Come on, Lins. You haven't gone out with us in a long time. We all miss you," Betty persisted.

The guilt was working. She really had hibernated for long enough. Maybe if she began some of her old routines again, she would get over the one man she knew better than to get involved with.

"I guess it wouldn't hurt to go out for a little while," she conceded.

The way Betty's face lit up made Lindsey feel bad that she had sort of abandoned all her friends. They had tried for so long to be there for her, but she had been determined to get through things her own way.

That way hadn't been helping her, so maybe it really was time to try something new.

Betty got paged away and the rest of the day began to go by in a blur. As the afternoon began winding down, Lindsey even found herself looking forward to spending time with the girls.

It really did help that, as the staff found out she was going out with them, more girls joined in. It made her feel loved and comforted that no one had given up on her even if she had given up on herself.

What a fool she had been.

CHAPTER SEVEN

The music was blaring, the crowd in a near frenzy as they danced and drank and looked for a potential partner to take home for the night.

And Lindsey Helm was ready to go home—alone. Being out with the girls was nice and no one mentioned her absence or the attack or anything that would make her feel uncomfortable. However, she couldn't change her outlook.

So much had changed for her in the past year. And even if she wanted to pretend she was still the same person, she wasn't and never would be again. Maybe it also had to do with the fact that she was exhausted. A lack of sleep did mess with the brain and make it a lot harder to have a good time and truly let go.

Even though she was at the upscale club in Seattle with her coworkers, she still had a part of her that felt there was danger everywhere she looked. Lindsey knew exactly where every exit was located and she was ready to bolt at a moment's notice.

It was nice to be out with her friends, but what she really wanted was to be in her pajamas with a bowl of ice cream while watching reruns of *Buffy the Vampire Slayer*. Cheesy? Yes. Fun? Definitely. There was just something about an immortal vampire that sent good feelings to all the right places, and Angel was one hell of a dark hero.

Shaking that thought away, she pushed her way to the bathroom, stood in line for a half hour, and then tried to make her way back through the nightclub. The noise and lights were beginning to give her a headache. She'd been out with the girls for two hours already. She could possibly get away from them without hurting anyone's feelings.

She was disappointed that she didn't have to work the next day. That would have given her a valid excuse. Maybe it would be better to just suffer through it this one time. The next time she came out, it would be easier and each time after that much easier.

Sighing, she plastered a smile on her face as she got closer to her table. The girls really were being so good to her. She didn't want to ruin it.

"Are you enjoying the music, Lins?" Betty asked, her cheeks flushed from the heat and the amount of alcohol she'd consumed.

"Yes. It's great. I'm so glad you included me," Lindsey told her, hoping she sounded convincing.

"You know you're always welcome," Betty said.

The next hour went by in a blur, and then Lindsey finally saw her opportunity when one of the other nurses made her excuses to leave for the evening.

"I'd better go too," Lins said with an exaggerated yawn. "My day started too early."

There were a few protests, but no one seemed upset.

Lindsey quickly made her escape, reveling in her freedom as she neared the exit—that was, until she was grabbed from behind. Instant panic closed her throat as Lindsey's body tensed. Every nightmare she'd faced in the past year flooded her. But this time Lindsey was more prepared. She'd taken a self-defense class. She wouldn't ever be taken so easily again. Turning quickly, she raised her fists and got ready to strike.

But her muscles froze when she saw who had grabbed her. The immediate relief turned into frustration. She didn't want to be relieved. She wanted to fight.

"Maverick?"

She was shaking from the boost of adrenaline before seeing it was only Maverick. *Only Maverick.* Ha! Those words just didn't go together.

"I thought that was you, Lins," he said with his mega-wattage bright smile.

"What are you doing here?" she asked. She hated that she didn't want to rush past him, hated that she felt safer with him blocking the rest of the people from her protective bubble.

"I came down with some of the guys from the base, and I saw you walk past. You know I can't let you get away so easily."

Of course he couldn't. She didn't fully trust that it was a coincidence he was there. But she wasn't going to call him out on it because if it was just an instance of wrong place wrong time, she would be embarrassed to have assumed he was following her.

Before she could say anything, someone passed behind her and pushed her into him. His arms automatically came around her, and her body responded automatically. And it didn't respond in a negative way. She inhaled his sweet scent before letting out a sigh. She almost wished she'd feel her normal reaction of horror at being touched. Why did it have to be Maverick that made her feel safer?

"I'm on my way out," she told him, back to being in a hurry to get out of there. She was afraid she might do something stupid if she didn't leave, especially with how her head was currently buzzing from the liquor. She'd had enough of being stupid to last her a lifetime. She wasn't going to do anything with Mav again. He was forbidden. She had to remember that.

"Why don't you join me for a drink first?"

The purr in his tone, the heat in his eyes, and the flexing of his abs pressed against hers told her he was thinking about a lot more than just a drink. She wasn't a naïve woman. She knew when a member of the male population had sex on the brain. It just so happened to be on their minds quite a lot, but Maverick was looking to score, and it appeared she'd just become the center of his target.

Tempted. She was so dang tempted. It shocked her to feel such a taboo emotion when all she'd felt was fear for a year.

Somehow, even in her muddled state, she managed to pull herself away. When he released her, she was a little disappointed, but it truly was for the best. She ran through all the reasons why she shouldn't be with Maverick.

"I have a test I need to study for," she said as she took a step back and then another. He followed her. "I really do have to go." Her breathing was growing more and more shortened by the second.

When Mav set his mind to something, it was more than obvious he didn't back down. She needed to tell him that it wasn't going to happen with them. But for some reason she couldn't get the words past her closed throat, so instead of being brave she decided once again to retreat. She spun around and practically ran from the club, not stopping until she was on the sidewalk.

"It's much better out here. Not nearly as noisy or crowded."

The sound of Maverick's voice in the quiet of the evening air made her jump nearly a foot into the air.

"You didn't need to follow me out," she told him too breathily, wishing her head would quit spinning.

"I want to make sure you get home safe and sound," he told her. "After all, we're going in the same direction." There was too much excitement in his gaze at those words.

"I'm hailing a cab. You really don't need to leave so early," she said with desperation. "Go back in with your friends." She began walking away since there weren't any cabs out front. She'd go to the corner and then keep on walking if she had to. Hell, she'd walk all night if it meant getting away from the man who tempted her so much.

She really should have known better, though. He was right at her side. She would bet money he wasn't taking any of the pain meds he'd told her he was on. He didn't need them. Pain wasn't something he even thought about.

"Do you really think I would let you wander Seattle alone at nearly midnight? Not you, Lins," Maverick said before reaching out and taking her hand.

She had to control her breathing. It wasn't that he *liked* her. She was just a part of his family now—the best friend of his sister-in-law, to be more precise. Without her giving him permission to be her escort, he was doing it anyway.

She would've thought the cool air from outside would be enough to calm her nerves and ease the buzz she was feeling, but the touch of his fingers in her hand as she moved down the street hoping to find a cab—which were nonexistent at the moment—was making her feel even more drunk.

She was afraid if she didn't get away from this man really soon, she would most certainly do something she would surely regret. When she finally spotted the bright yellow cab, she rushed to the curb, Mav not letting go of her fingers as he stayed practically glued to her.

"How did you get down here?" she asked.

"My buddy picked me up," he told her as the cab pulled over.

"Shouldn't you go back in?" she said as he opened the door.

"Nope. They will figure it out."

Of course they would figure it out. They would assume he'd found a girl to hook up with. It wasn't unusual, or so she'd heard. The thought made her unusually sad. But it was just one more reason she couldn't give in to how she felt about this man.

She wasn't strong enough to have an affair with someone like Maverick Armstrong. Not anymore, she wasn't.

Her fingers were trembling as she turned to tell him good-bye. But he followed her into the cab and gave the driver the address. He started the meter and they moved out into traffic.

Lindsey was silent as she turned and caught Maverick staring at her. The heat in his gaze had her throat tightening as she tried to suck in air. When his hand moved to her neck, the fire in his eyes only intensified. And then he was rubbing her cheek, and she was trying to remember all the reasons why this was such a bad, bad idea.

Her nipples hardened and her core grew wet and hot as she continued looking at Mav. She needed to pull away from him, scoot to the far edge of the seat, and forget this entire evening, but she couldn't quite manage to do so.

"I should have done this months ago. I've given you too much time as it is." That was her only warning before he pulled her tightly against his chest and then his head descended.

His kiss was exactly like she remembered from their one magical night together. It was full of confidence and ability, and any and all protests dried up as he turned the burning inside of her into a blazing inferno.

Somewhere in the back of Lindsey's mind, she knew this needed to stop, but she couldn't quite find the strength to pull away from him. His tongue learned her mouth, and she was just as greedy to reacquaint herself with him as she reached around his neck and clung to him.

Maverick's hand slid across her hip, and then skimmed up her dress until he was squeezing her breast, making her nipples painfully erect as his palm brushed over the material. She wanted to be naked beneath him, feel his hands on bare skin. Everything else in her mind went blank except for this moment in the back of a cab with the only person who seemed to be able to reach her.

A crackling over the cab radio reminded Lindsey of exactly where she was. Mortified, she broke the connection of their kiss and pushed away from him just as they pulled up to the gate at Cooper's driveway.

"I . . . uh . . . I . . ." She was at a total loss for words.

"Lindsey . . ." He began and then stopped. Regret seemed to shine in his eyes, but she wasn't sure. He leaned over her and punched the code in for the gate to open. The cab driver said nothing as he made his way down the driveway.

Mav had him pull around to her cabin. Lindsey's cheeks were burning. How much had the driver seen of what they'd been doing in his backseat? She didn't even want to think about that.

Mav paid the driver and he turned around and left. Lindsey rushed to her front door, but her fingers were trembling too badly for her to be able to open it up. Mav took the keys from her and then the door was swinging open.

"I have to go," she said as she tried pulling away from him.

"Invite me to come in with you," he practically demanded as he tried to get close to her again.

"That's so not going to happen," she said, her head spinning as she fought with her desire for this man.

He frowned at her as he once again tried to get close. Damn, for one minute she wished she were someone else—someone who could do what she wanted and not live in fear of the consequences. She wished she could be reckless for just this one night. But she knew she couldn't.

"Good night, Maverick. Thanks for getting me home."

She didn't give him a chance to respond, just slipped inside her door and quickly shut and locked it. Lindsey could swear she heard a thump against the wood—maybe his head hitting it, or maybe his fist—but then all was silent.

She stood there a while before almost sleepwalking to her bedroom to lie down, too tired to even change. She didn't sleep well, though, not when her thoughts were filled with a sexy beast of a man who could have been there right then keeping her warm, who could make her forget her traumas of the previous year—who could make her feel whole again, if that were even possible.

It wasn't worth it. She had to convince herself it was all in her head. If she let go of the tight fist of control she had on herself, she was afraid she would break. She was afraid she would never be the same again.

Maverick would make her feel better for the night—but then he would be gone. She was afraid that if she let him open her up, and then he didn't truly like what he saw, she would see a monster in her reflection.

That couldn't happen. She wouldn't let it happen.

CHAPTER EIGHT

It was a perfect morning, the sun warm, the breeze gentle. Mav would much rather be here at his brother's place than the empty shell of a home he'd taken possession of thinking it would make him more responsible—or more of the man his father wanted him to be.

He hated it there. Hollow, it was. Empty. Lonely. He would never admit that to a single soul. He was pissed the thoughts were even going through his head. Sipping on his cup of coffee, Mav turned and then lost his air.

It took a lot for him to lose his breath, but lose it he did as he watched Lindsey's long dark hair blow freely in the breeze while she walked barefoot along the beach. Damn, she was a vision in her summer dress, looking free and innocent as she watched a flock of seagulls fly by.

If Mav were being honest with himself, he would have to admit that he'd had a crush on Lindsey from the first moment they'd met, and time hadn't seemed to dull his infatuation. If anything, time had only made it grow stronger.

Before the horrific attack she'd dealt with a year earlier, he'd chased her harder than he'd ever chased a woman, trying like hell to gain her attention. Then in a weak moment at his brother's wedding, she'd finally succumbed to him. He'd thought one night would be enough to quench his thirst.

He'd been so very, very wrong. One night had been nothing more than a tease—and he wanted the entire package now. But then the attack had happened, leaving her vulnerable—making him feel like a monster for continuing to pursue her.

And yes, he wanted her back in his bed, but he also wanted to see her happy. He'd never cared enough about a woman to feel responsible for her happiness, but it seemed that all bets were off when it came to Lindsey Helm.

She was just so vulnerable. His protective instincts had taken over. Maverick knew a thing or two about trauma. And one thing he knew for certain was that it wasn't good for a person to dwell on it. It would only fester to the point that a person might give up on living.

He'd seen it with fellow soldiers, and he'd had to deal with it after he'd been captured. That thought almost sent him through his own spiral, so he quickly shook his head and pushed it away.

The point was that he knew how important it was to heal. And if he could control his libido long enough, he might just be able to help this woman. Damn! He was sounding like a sissy even in his own head.

A smile overtook his mouth. He was sure if he helped her heal she would be back to that vibrant woman who could match him barb for barb. The fireworks would once again ignite. His smile turned up a few watts. He was back from nearly starring in a Hallmark movie, thank goodness.

"I'm beginning to think you enjoy staying here far more for the view than for my pleasant company," Cooper said with a laugh as his brother followed the direction of Mav's gaze.

He had to admit that his hulk of a brother looked pretty domesticated while cuddling his three-month-old tiny son against his chest. Both Nick and Mav were in love with the little tot. It was amazing to

Mav that he could care so much for a tiny human who did nothing but eat, spit up, and poop all the time. But love the kid, he did.

"Yeah, the view around here has certainly improved in the last couple years," Mav told Cooper as he shook off thoughts of babies and took a sip of his coffee while he watched Lindsey.

"Well, then, why in the heck haven't you done something about it?" Sherman grumbled from his spot beneath the umbrella.

"What?" Both brothers turned and looked at Sherman, who was giving Maverick a nasty look.

"If you're so dang infatuated with the girl, then stop acting like a baby and go and talk to her," Sherman said. "Or are you afraid she's too good for you?" he goaded.

"Uncle Sherman!" Maverick said, his mouth hanging open. All the boys were used to their uncle saying whatever was on his mind, but he was going over the top at the moment.

"She's not just any girl," Mav told him.

"Plus, she's broken right now. He needs to be careful," Cooper warned.

"I would never hurt Lindsey," Mav said, slightly offended.

"Of course you wouldn't hurt her," Sherman grumbled. Both boys ignored him.

"I don't think you would do it maliciously, but if anyone could hurt her, it would be you," Cooper said.

"I'm not going to hurt her. Matter of fact, I plan on helping her so this place isn't so dang depressing," Mav said.

"Now you're talking," Sherman said. "I knew you couldn't help but take care of a woman in distress."

"Help her how?" Cooper asked with suspicion.

"Not in the way you're thinking," Mav growled. Though, in reality, he wouldn't mind bedding Lindsey again—not at all. But that wasn't the objective of his mission. And he wasn't going to say anything like that in front of his uncle. He was likely to get boxed in the ears if he did.

"Just know I'm going to be keeping an eye on you," Cooper warned.

"If you're into that sort of thing," Mav said with a laugh and a wink.

"You're disgusting," Coop said with a frown as he pulled his son a bit closer as if to protect the baby's delicate ears from the crude talk.

"I'm not the one with his mind in the gutter," Mav pointed out.

Before Cooper or his uncle could say anything more, Mav set down his coffee cup and then quickly scooted away. Stepping off the back deck, he jogged down the wide expanse of lawn that led to the beachfront access.

He was officially on a mission. Not only was he going to get Lindsey to chair his fund-raiser, which would cause them to spend a hell of a lot of time together, but he was going to show her that life was too short to be wasted.

Most importantly, Mav was going to show her that she needed him right there beside her. And he wasn't going to give himself time to think about what he was doing. This girl wasn't going to get away.

No matter what it took.

CHAPTER NINE

"I give you full marks for the low back, but I have to take a few points away because of the longer hemline."

At his laughing words, Lindsey's first instinct was to run for the fence and keep on going until she was locked safely inside her cottage. Her feet twitched as she prepared to make her escape. These days, her fight or flight response was all flight and no fight.

She'd barely taken her first step when the voice registered. *Maverick*. It took all her willpower, but she stopped and turned to face him. He stood there, leaning against the fence separating Coop's property from the beach, but he didn't reach out for her, didn't try to stop her, didn't say another word after his obnoxious comment about her dress.

Instantly, Lindsey's adrenaline slowed and she felt herself relax. She hated that she felt safe with him and no one else. She hated this power he had over her. He seemed to have more power over her than she had over herself.

"You wouldn't exactly be the first person I'd call for fashion advice, Mav," she said after several moments. When she looked up into his sparkling green eyes, she felt the jolt go through her system that she now expected when meeting his gaze.

"Ah, sugar, you wound me," he told her with his standard knock-a-woman-to-her-shaky-knees smile. Between the smile, the confidence, and the damn eyes, the man was a danger to all women—young and old. So unfair in so many ways.

"Nothing could wound your inflated ego," she said, nearly feeling like smiling.

Maybe if Lindsey understood her reaction to Maverick a bit better, she wouldn't always be so thrown when in his presence. But as things stood, she just didn't get it, didn't understand how she could enjoy being around him. He was tall and broad, far too muscular for her normal tastes, let alone for how she felt after that behemoth of a man had attacked her at the hospital.

Lindsey wasn't exactly petite at five feet seven, but she'd always been more attracted to the bookish, academic type, the kind of guys who were good looking but didn't stop traffic, the kind of guys who weren't so solid you felt like you were running into a brick wall when you were pulled against them. She preferred softer men. That was her security net—had been for a long time. She liked that she intimidated men. It meant they were too afraid to hurt her.

Mav didn't fit anything she wanted. He stood six four, and had the shoulders and chest of a linebacker. His stomach was pure iron and his hips—ah, those hips were made for pumping while a woman's legs were wrapped around them. Realizing where her thoughts had just gone, Lindsey jerked her face upward, her cheeks pink as she met his eyes again.

Desire, hot and heavy, sparked in his gaze before he seemed to tamp it down, and then he winked at her and gave her a lopsided grin.

"You can look all you want, sugar," he purred.

"I wasn't looking," she said way too loudly.

He laughed—actually laughed at her, which royally ticked her off. Oh no, he didn't get to mock her without getting the sharp end of her wrath rained down upon him.

"I wasn't," she reiterated, stomping her bare foot in the sand, as if that would do any good. The action only made his grin bigger.

"It's okay, sug," he began. She was about to ream him some more when he continued. "Look all you want," he said with a shake of his head as if scolding her, making her want to pummel his arrogant ass.

Her head was spinning. Was he actually flirting? If he was, he wasn't too good at it. She looked at him for several tense moments as she waited for him to go on, but he seemed comfortable enough just standing there letting the breeze ruffle his dark hair.

Finally, she couldn't take the silence. "What is wrong with you?"

"Let's take a walk. I want to talk to you about some things."

Before she could accept or deny his invitation, he moved up next to her and slowly twined his fingers with hers, giving her time to pull away. On the one hand she wanted to move a couple of feet to the left, but on the other, there was an odd sense of security having him so close. She was torn about what to do.

"It's okay. I'm not going to do anything more than hold your hand. We're just two buddies taking a stroll down the beach," he told her as he gave her arm a gentle tug.

Lindsey looked longingly at the gate that would lead her to her friend's property and, more importantly, to the safety of the cottage— the cottage with a couple of locks on the door to keep the world out.

"Come on. You're going to hurt my feelings," he said as he tugged again.

"I . . . uh, I can't be out long," she told him, but much to her surprise she found her feet moving along as she followed him closer to the water lapping against the shore.

"I wouldn't want to keep you out too late," he said with a chuckle. It wasn't even noon yet, but she decided to let that one go.

They reached the water, and that's when she noticed his pants were already rolled up and his shoes and socks gone. He pulled her into the freezing surf, and she again tried to yank her hand away from him, but he wasn't having it. When the water was to her mid-calves, he stopped and she shivered as she stood there beside him.

"What do you want to talk to me about?" she said. He didn't appear to be in a hurry, but she figured the sooner he said whatever it was he wanted, the sooner he would let her escape. At least she hoped that was the plan.

"I want your help, and I've decided I can't take *no* for an answer."

"If it's the fund-raising, I can't do it," she told him, deciding to be firm. She wished her voice came out a little less breathy.

"You're going to help me, and in turn, I'm going to help you."

"I don't need your help with anything, Maverick," she told him, tugging on her hand again. He didn't release her. The thing was, she did need his help, but she had too much pride to ask for it. Plus, admitting she needed help would show just one more of her weaknesses, and she couldn't do that.

He didn't respond for several moments, and she began to chew on her bottom lip as she waited to see what he would say next. Lindsey felt him turn, even though she was looking out into the bay, gazing at the masts of several sailboats as they glided along the rolling water.

With his other hand, the one that had the cast all the way to the palm, he touched her chin. Her head went back, and she looked up at him, unable to pull away.

"You know I don't like to be touched," she warned. But the words didn't actually come out as much of a warning. They were more of a panting request.

"I know, sugar. But you need to be," he said, his eyes darkening again, though he made no more moves to invade her space.

"I'm not your sugar," she informed him. "And if you know, then why aren't you letting me go?"

"Because I also know that fear and pain are eating away at you, and I've decided I care too much to allow that to happen. It's my duty to not give up on you."

She was dumbfounded at his words. To her this seemed like so much more than him trying to get her back into his bed. It seemed like he meant what he was saying. And what was even more astounding than that was her response to him.

"Your duty?" she gasped. "Who in the world do you think you are? You don't know me from more than a few conversations, a one-night stand, and a few failed flirting attempts. You have no idea who I even am or what I'm thinking or feeling."

"I've been to hell, sug, and it's not a great place to be. You're hurting and there's a connection between us. You know it, I know it." Thankfully he didn't comment on the sex part of their relationship. She was weak right now, and he seemed to know it, though she didn't necessarily feel that he was taking advantage of that fact.

"That sounds like a line if ever I've heard one," she said.

"No lines. I've decided we're better off together right now. I need help, you have time, and this will be good for you and me both. I've been told I'm a bit arrogant. You can help me out with that since you seem to have no trouble holding back what you really think about me," he said with a smirk. "And this fund-raiser is truly for a good cause. I know you will love being a part of it."

She looked into those green eyes and found herself almost getting lost in them. If she didn't know any better, she just might think there was a touch of vulnerability there. But that couldn't possibly be the case. Not with a man like Maverick, who held the world in the palm of his hand.

"Even if I were foolish enough to accept this . . . kind . . . offer, what in the world do you think I need? And how do you plan on giving it to me?"

When his lips turned up in a wicked smile, Lindsey thought it might have been a good idea to rephrase those last sentences. But if he made some crude remark, she would at least be able to put him back in the sty where he belonged.

"I'm far too much of a gentleman to give in to that question," he said with a laugh and a wink. "No plans. We will just plan the fundraiser, make it better than ever, and see where it leads us. You got out the other night and the world didn't end. Let's take it a day at a time."

What she should do was tell him *thanks but no thanks*, and then let him watch her backside as she disappeared. But dang it all to heck, she was intrigued by the idea. No pressure. He promised no pressure. But could he actually keep that promise? It seemed that there was always pressure building within her whenever he was around.

Oh, this was already messy and complicated. She was a fool to think spending more time with the man wouldn't make that worse. But for some reason she wasn't telling him no.

"I don't know. You have to give me time to think about it."

"I can give you time to think, but not too much. I don't want you talking yourself out of this," he said.

"I haven't talked myself into it, so how could I talk myself out of it?" she pointed out.

At her words he laughed and tugged her against him. Her stomach stirred and she wanted to pull away—but at the same time she found she was exactly where she wanted to be.

Complicated. This just proved how complicated the situation was.

"And when we're all done with planning," he said as his lips widened in the biggest grin she'd ever seen, "we can celebrate."

Lindsey had no doubt what kind of celebrating he had in mind. She wanted to tell him he really did need an adjustment in his arrogance if he thought he was getting her back in bed again, but the lashing she wanted to give him seemed to get lodged in her throat.

"Want to clarify that?" she asked with narrow eyes.

His fingers rubbed along her lower back as he held her tightly to him. "I won't lie to you, Lindsey. I want you night and day." The intensity in his gaze had her heart thundering. "But don't worry. I won't act on it until you're the one dragging me into the bedroom."

It took her several seconds to process his last words, and once she had, the thumping of her heart increased, but this time it was because of irritation. She decided emphatically that Maverick Armstrong really did need to be taken down off his high horse. If anyone could reach him all the way up there, that might just be possible to do.

She shot him a look that should have killed him on the spot, and this time when she yanked to free herself, he actually released her. The momentum almost sent her on her butt into the freezing sea water that had already numbed her feet.

"Do you honestly think I have so little pride that I would need to force you into my bed?" she cried in outrage.

"That just goes with the territory, sugar. I'm impossible to resist. But that's not the point of this mission. That's just a pleasurable detour."

"You pompous, assuming ass. I wouldn't sleep with you again if you were the last man on the planet," she scolded.

So quickly, she didn't even have time to blink, he was right up on her again, his hand behind her head. Her breath rushed out and her body shook, but this time it wasn't from fear. This time it was from something she didn't even want to begin to analyze.

"I never said anything about sleeping, sugar," he said.

Then he leaned down and brushed his lips across hers. It all happened too quickly for her to have much of a reaction, but just as quickly as he'd grabbed her, he let her go again and took several steps back.

"See, sugar, you can feel so much more than fear. You can feel anger and desire," he said with his smile back in place.

"Are you playing games with me?" she gasped.

"Nope. I just like that I can inspire so much passion in you," he told her.

"That's not passion, you ass. That's fury," she snapped.

"Fury and passion go hand in hand. Not everything is about sex," he said. She took a menacing step toward him and he backed up real quick. It made her feel powerful. That was something she hadn't felt in a very long time.

"I think I better get out of here while I still only have one broken arm. I'll pick you up tomorrow," he told her with another laugh.

With that, he turned and walked away, soon disappearing. Lindsey watched him until he was gone, and only then realized her fingers were pressing against her lips where his had barely brushed against them.

He'd made her run through a gamut of emotions in the past half hour, and she wasn't sure exactly what any of that meant. But she knew one thing for sure. She wasn't going to help him with the fund-raiser. No way, no how. She standing firm, battening down the hatches, and locking the doors and windows.

Maverick Armstrong was dangerous, probably the most dangerous man she'd ever met. And if Lindsey wanted to keep what was left of her sanity in place, then she had best stay away from him.

That decided, she slowly made her way back to Stormy's yard, peeking around before slipping through the fence and then rushing to the guest cottage. Maybe it was time to move.

That thought sent fear through her. No. It wasn't time to leave yet. She just had to be more aware when Maverick was around, that was all. If she avoided him, she'd be just fine.

If only she believed that were actually possible.

CHAPTER TEN

The floor was getting worn out as Lindsey paced back and forth across the living room. She wasn't waiting on Maverick. No way, no how. Again, she turned and looked at the clock: 10:00 a.m.

What did the time matter? For one thing, she had vehemently decided she wasn't going with the man. For another, he hadn't exactly set a time that he was planning on showing up, so it did her absolutely no good to sit there and gaze at the clock.

"Argh!"

The low grumble escaped her mouth as she turned again only to be stopped in her tracks.

"Miss me?"

There he was, leaning against the wall next to her open door. Had she left it unlocked? No way. She couldn't have done that. She hadn't forgotten to secure the doors once since the attack. Was this man seriously messing with her head so much that she couldn't even remember to lock the doors anymore?

"No, I didn't miss you in the least," she said through clenched teeth. "Ever heard of knocking?"

"The door was open and you seemed to be in a world of your own, so I thought I would wait until you worked through whatever it is that has you pacing the floors," he told her with that damn grin of his that made her legs shaky.

"How long have you been standing there?" She would have thought she'd notice the intrusion. That she hadn't felt anything amiss worried her on a whole new level.

"Not long. Just enough to see you wearing holes in the floor," he told her as he pushed off from the wall.

"Well, you can turn around and leave now. I'm not going anywhere with you," she said decidedly.

"We both know you're frustrated because you want to go out and *that*, more than anything else, is what's worrying you. And since you're all dressed and ready to go, we don't want to waste the day," he said, coming closer.

She backed away from him until her butt hit the back of the couch, trapping her as he boxed her in.

"I do not," she whispered.

Those damn fingers lifted and he brushed her loose hair back behind her ear as he held her captive with his gaze.

"Listen, sugar, I've gotten wounds before. I've seen things most people can't even imagine actually exist. I've watched helplessly as fallen soldiers haven't been able to pick up the pieces of their sanity. I'm not willing to do that with you. What you went through was tragic. But I'm going to give you a reason to keep on living, to keep on loving life, and to forget about the bastard that tried to take all of that away from you."

No passion, no cockiness, no alpha male rested in those piercing eyes as he spoke to her this time. Only compassion. She wasn't sure what scared her more.

"I . . . I'm not afraid," she said, knowing the crack in her voice belied the words.

"You're strong, sug. Trust me, I know this, but it's okay to show a few cracks when we've been hit," he said, his hand now resting on her shoulder. "We all have a few open wounds."

"Quit calling me sugar," she said, trying to clear her head.

"But you are so damn sweet," he told her. *There* was the cockiness she'd been looking for.

That was so much easier to face than the kind, gentle person he turned into sometimes. The jokester, alpha macho man she could resist—mostly; the gentle giant she wanted to fall against.

No. She refused to rely on anyone.

"You ready to go?"

"I told you, I'm not going anywhere."

"Look, I'll back off on the fund-raiser for the day. I want to take you somewhere special to me. Only if you agree afterward will we talk about the project."

She tried to find a flaw with his reasoning but couldn't. She sort of wanted to go out with him. Why else would she have gotten up and dressed, taking extra care with her hair and makeup?

He saw her hesitation and pounced.

"Lins, I don't take no for an answer. Just give me a chance, and you'll see I'm a great guy."

There was the gentle giant again. Still, she hesitated. He sighed as he gave her a look.

"Okay, sug, I'm not looking for a marriage. There are reasons for that, but it's the last thing I want. However, I can't keep thoughts of you away, and I want to see where this is going," he admitted.

"I don't even know who I am right now, so I don't want some fairy-tale ending, either," she whispered.

"Then let's just be friends, and I'll give you a great day."

He was so smooth, and he was telling her upfront that this wouldn't last. That's what she wanted, she assured herself. She hadn't decided to go with him, yet she found herself nodding her head. What the heck? That hadn't been what she'd intended to do.

"You need to tie your hair up and put on some tennis shoes," he said with a wicked smile that had her worried all over again. The gentle giant was gone again.

"Fine. If I agree to this . . . outing, will you leave me alone?"

"Nope. I didn't say I would back off, I just said I'd give you a break," he said.

"What if I can't stand being around you?" she challenged.

He leaned forward, his body heat scorching her. Her breathing shortened and she had to fight not to reach around and tug him closer.

"Sugar, we both know that's not the case. We're going to be lucky if we both don't spontaneously combust while spending time together. But don't worry, I won't take you until you're ready . . . and begging me to."

Gulping, Lindsey stood there without moving a muscle. She had the strong urge to pull him the last inch needed for his body to brush against hers. Dang it! Why him?

When Stormy touched her she flinched. And Lindsey skirted Cooper like he was a demon trying to suck out her soul. So why was it that, of all people, Maverick was the one she didn't fear? It wasn't as if they had an actual connection. So why, in her darkest hour, did it seem he was the only person she could stand to be so close to?

"It's chemistry and trust," he whispered as he leaned forward and brushed his lips against her cheek.

"What is?" she gasped as her stomach trembled.

"What you're feeling."

Could the man also read minds? Did she have to veil her thoughts? She squinted at him as he pulled back.

"Your brown eyes are like an open book, sugar. I can read the conflict in them, the confusion. I can see you don't understand what draws you to me. I'm just a very likeable guy," he told her.

The shining smile he gave her stabilized the turbulence she was feeling.

"You are so full of yourself, Mav."

"That I am, sug. That I am," he said, but blessedly he moved backward. "Finish getting ready. We're going to be late."

Pulling herself away from the couch, Lindsey decided it would be easier not to fight the man. Hopefully the outing would be such a disaster he'd give up on this mission of his and let her go.

Why that thought brought instant sadness to her, she would never know. But somehow she found herself going to the closet and grabbing a light jacket and changing into tennis shoes.

Let the adventure begin.

CHAPTER ELEVEN

Though her nerves were stretched a little bit thin, at least the panic was at bay as Lindsey climbed into Maverick's large Ford F350. It was a good thing he had running boards on the dang truck, otherwise she would have had to take a running jump—and still most likely would have come up short.

"I don't think your truck is quite big enough," she commented when he was sitting in the driver's seat.

"I like big things," he told her with a wink.

"Are you making up for something?" she muttered.

Instead of scowling at her as she'd expected, his eyes twinkled as he hit her with that killer smile before turning the key and having the engine roar to life.

"Sugar, you have a firsthand account that there's nothing small about me. Just in case you've forgotten, all you gotta do is ask to have another peek," he said as he threw the truck into drive and began pulling down Cooper's long driveway.

Much to her irritation, Lindsey's cheeks flamed as she folded her arms and wisely decided to stare ahead of her. She hadn't bothered asking where they were going. She knew she was at the mercy of Maverick.

There was a real sort of freedom in letting go, in letting the man take over for a few minutes, or more likely a few hours. For some reason she knew he wasn't going to lead her into danger. He wasn't even going to lead her into something she couldn't handle.

When they pulled up to a large building and stopped, Lindsey was confused. She looked around but couldn't exactly figure out what they were doing. Where was he bringing her?

She was . . . disappointed. She really shouldn't have had any expectations about the day, and she didn't—not really. She hadn't allowed herself to even think about it. But she hadn't expected him to bring her to the city.

"Ready?"

Lindsey hadn't even seen Mav get out of the truck, but there he was with an eager smile holding open her door.

"For what?" she asked as she allowed him to assist her out of the monstrous truck.

"For our first official date," he said as he closed the door and took her hand.

She tried tugging away from him, but it was useless. She gave up.

"This isn't a date," she informed him. "It's an outing."

If she could possibly sound any more proper she didn't know how. Mav wasn't bothered by her coldness though. He just threw back his head and chuckled before tugging her along.

Lindsey was even more confused when they came up to a building with a large sign on it saying "Animania." It had different animal paws adorning its windows. Mav walked up to the door with her trailing behind.

"Do we have a pit stop?" she asked as he pulled her into the large lobby filled with people, furniture, animal toys, and laughter.

"Nope," he said, excitement practically beaming off him.

Before she could say anything, a perky, petite blonde came rushing forward and threw her arms around Mav before standing back.

"You're late. I think Benji is about to gnaw his way out of the cage," she said before turning her full attention to Lindsey. "You must be Lindsey, it's great to meet you. Mav said he was bringing you in today. I'm Cindy. Your companion is going to be Princess."

"My companion?" Lindsey asked.

"Yep. Princess has been sad this week so she will really love a little extra-special attention," Cindy said as she began moving toward a door.

Apparently they were following the girl, because Mav tugged on Lindsey's hand and they went through the door and down a hall, then out another door that led them to a breezeway.

"What is this place?" Lindsey asked as they kept moving. It was huge.

"This is Animania, the best animal shelter in all of Washington. Mav here is the founder, and he comes in at least once a week if not more when time allows."

"You own this place?" Lindsey didn't know why she was so surprised. He seemed to be a sucker for lost causes.

"No. It's a nonprofit. I just started it," he said as he looked away, seeming uncomfortable.

"I . . . uh . . . wow," she whispered, a little too awed by him at the moment to form words.

"It's not a big deal, sug. I love animals and too many people don't. So if they have to be boarded up, I figured they deserved a nice vacation home," he said, getting his groove back as he winked.

"What are we doing here?" she asked. She'd long since stopped trying to pull her hand away.

"We're taking a couple of the dogs out on a walk to the park. We have lots of volunteers who walk the dogs, but the more hands the better."

They entered another large area where a huge field was fenced and several animals were running around. There were also clean, roomy areas where several animals were resting.

In the middle of the structure, they came up to a cage where two dogs were eagerly gazing out. One had his tail wagging a mile a minute, and the other was peeking up before looking back down again, its tail twitching a little bit as Mav bent down and spoke.

"Hey Benji, it looks like you have a new pretty companion," Mav said in a silly voice.

Benji looked to be a cross between a poodle and a lab and maybe even a boxer. Lindsey didn't know much about animals, but he wasn't the prettiest animal she'd ever seen. He appeared to be about forty pounds, ten pounds of which had to be fur. Princess was smaller, probably only about fifteen pounds, and looked like maybe a cross between a Chihuahua and a beagle. She was cute with her silver fur and shy eyes. Could dogs have shy eyes?

Lindsey found herself sitting down on the floor as the door to the enclosure was opened. Suddenly her throat was tight as Princess slowly moved toward her, frightened. Lindsey instantly wanted to protect this puppy.

She hadn't ever been much of an animal lover. It wasn't that she didn't like them, just that she was slightly afraid of dogs—especially big dogs. But Princess seemed so vulnerable that she wasn't at all afraid of the little girl.

"Hi, Princess. Want to walk with me today?" She didn't even think twice about speaking so seriously to a dog.

The little girl's ears perked up, and though she moved tentatively, she came up to Lindsey and sniffed her hand. When Lindsey moved her fingers, Princess took a step back and flinched, and tears immediately popped into Lindsey's eyes. Someone had hurt Princess. It was more than obvious, and everything inside her ached to protect this puppy from ever being abused again.

Lindsey understood the puppy's fear because of what she herself had gone through, but she didn't want to focus on that. She just wanted to take care of this hurt animal in front of her.

"What happened to her?" she asked in a choked voice as she continued holding out her hand. Princess walked back up, taking her time. This time Lins didn't move her fingers but stayed still.

"She was rescued from a breeding camp where they'd kept her in a tiny cage producing puppies. Obviously, she wasn't shown a lot of affection, and one of the people in the house, who is currently in jail, liked to kick the dogs for fun." The barely contained rage in Mav's voice was mirrored in the horror that Lindsey felt at such monstrous behavior.

"How could someone hurt her? She's so small, so afraid," Lins said with a choked voice.

"Because there are monsters out there who get off on inflicting pain on people and animals."

As he said this, he gave her a look of understanding. Had he brought her here knowing she would make comparisons with her own abused soul? She had a feeling he had. But she wasn't upset with him. She was actually starting to understand that there was a lot more depth to Maverick than he wanted the world to know about.

"Thanks for bringing me here, Mav," she said as Princess climbed into her lap.

Slowly Lindsey began petting her. The dog was shaking, but she wasn't pulling away. Lins wanted to pull her tight to her chest and reassure her that everything would be okay now, but she knew better than anyone that it wasn't always okay.

"Thanks for coming with me," he said as he reached over and chucked her chin, then stood up. "Ready to take these guys on a walk."

"It looks like they have a giant playground here," she pointed out. They'd passed a huge grassy field coming into this part of the shelter.

"Yes, but they like getting out of here too. It's good for them to experience lots of new smells. I chose this location to build because a couple blocks down the road is a great animal park, and they get to meet new friends."

He helped her stand, though Lindsey didn't want to let go of Princess, who looked up at her with those shy eyes once she was on her feet.

The aide snapped the leash in place and handed it to Lindsey, then said good-bye and trotted off as a coworker called her to come and help.

Benji was raring to go, so they began the journey out the back of the shelter. Though Princess wasn't in a huge hurry, she was staying pretty close to Lindsey's feet as they began making their way through the streets.

"He's pretty full of energy, isn't he?" she said with a laugh as Benji tugged on his leash when a cat ran in front of him across the sidewalk. He barked a few times before he lost interest.

"Yeah, he's been with us a few months. I'm pretty attached to him," Mav told her.

"Have you thought about adopting him?"

"Every single day. But I'm gone a lot, and sort of live out of a bag. It wouldn't be fair to him, or any animal. I've been thinking more and more about changing my life. If he's still with us . . ." He trailed off.

"Changing your life how?"

"I'm just gone far too much to have an animal I'm responsible for. It might be time to change things." He didn't elaborate.

They reached the park. There was a fenced section where smaller animals were playing without leashes on. There were even a few play structures that the dogs were climbing. It was the funniest thing Lins had ever seen.

"Is this all for the animals?" she asked as they walked inside, Mav latching the gate behind them. He led her to a bench and then undid Benji, who raced off to play with the other dogs.

"Yep. It's all for them," he told her.

She undid Princess's leash, but the dog just looked up at Lindsey with those beautiful, sad eyes. So instead of making her run off, Lindsey picked her up and cradled her in her lap while she leaned back and talked to Mav.

"She's not getting exercise sitting in your lap," he said with a laugh.

He moved slowly as he brought up his hand and let Princess sniff it before he scratched her behind her ears.

"She needs snuggle time more than running," Lins told him, feeling over-protective of the animal she most likely would never see again. That thought sent a pang of sadness through her.

"She still needs a home," Mav said.

The instant desire to take her was overwhelming. But before Lins could even entertain that idea, she tamped it back down.

"I can't take her. I don't even have my own place right now."

"Coop and Stormy wouldn't care at all if you had Princess living there with you," he told her. "And I know for a fact that neither of them are in a hurry for you to leave," Mav said.

Princess was obviously getting comfortable because she fell asleep in Lindsey's lap, practically purring as she relaxed.

"I can't hide there forever," she said with a sigh.

Instantly, Lindsey wanted to kick herself. She hadn't wanted to admit that hiding was exactly what she was doing, especially not to Maverick, who seemed to be far too intuitive as it was.

"You won't feel like hiding at all by the time you realize how great life can be," he told her. "That is, how great it is to have such an amazing friend like me," he added with a wink.

She was grateful he didn't harp on her admission that she was hiding. She much preferred that he joke with her. She would rather deal with his slightly obnoxious flirting than talk about real feelings and emotions.

"Now, come on. Let's throw some balls." She gave him an odd look and he laughed. "Not my balls, sugar. I'm sort of attached to those."

Lindsey hated the instant blush suffusing her cheeks, but when he took her elbow, she gently set Princess on the ground and then let him pull her along. She was thrilled when Princess trotted after them.

Mav called Benji over and then pulled out a couple of small tennis balls from his pocket. They went to the side and threw them. Benji was great at chasing them down and bringing them back for another throw. Princess looked at her like she was crazy when she told her to go get one.

Lindsey laughed and sat down on the ground. Mav handed her a small rope and she brushed it on the ground in front of Princess. After a little while, the dog let out a quiet little growl and then attacked the rope. But even her bites were gentle as she tugged on it, making Lindsey laugh.

They stayed a couple of hours and still, when Mav told her it was time to go back, Lindsey wanted to refuse. She wasn't ready to let Princess go yet, especially since she was starting to look a little less sad.

When they walked into the shelter, this time with Lindsey carrying Princess since she was worn out from all their playing, Lindsey wanted to just turn around and run out the front door with the puppy safely in her arms. But it was selfish of her to keep the dog. She wasn't prepared enough to do so.

Still, as they walked out, the little dog's sad eyes trailing after them, Lindsey couldn't help the tears that popped into her own eyes.

"She's yours if you want her," Mav said as he stopped with her leaning against the truck.

"I . . . I can't," she said, feeling like crying her eyes out. He didn't push her any further, just helped her inside the truck.

They drove for several moments without either of them speaking.

"Thank you for the day, Mav. It was a lot . . . better than I expected," she told him.

"You didn't think it was going to be something lame like dinner and a movie, did you?" he asked with his token twinkle.

"Well . . . uh . . . sort of," she admitted.

"Ah, sugar, you'll soon know that I'm anything but predictable."

When Maverick dropped her back off at the cottage with no more fanfare and Lindsey walked inside, she wondered why she was disappointed. It wasn't until later that she realized that she was upset that he hadn't even attempted to kiss her.

It had been a date after all. Even if she had told him it *wasn't* a date. It had been a date. And to tell the truth, it was the best date she could ever remember having been on.

But she didn't want Mav to kiss her again. She didn't want any man to kiss her. It was ridiculous to even think such a thought.

But as the rest of the day passed and she went to bed, all thoughts were on Maverick, and Lindsey knew she was in trouble. This man was getting beneath her skin. If she wasn't careful, he was going to burrow too far to be removed.

CHAPTER TWELVE

It seemed that every time Maverick turned around, something else was changing in his life. He didn't even fully understand it. Yes, he was the one at the controls, but it was almost as if he wasn't the one making the decisions.

Earlier in the day, he'd found himself at his animal shelter. When it had come time for him to return Benji and Princess back to their kennels, instead he had told the staff he was taking them home.

What was he doing? He'd explained all the reasons he couldn't own an animal, much less two of them. Then, later in that same day as he'd sat in the cold confines of his family home—the home he'd been living in for the past few years when he was actually home—he'd looked around at the cathedral ceilings, antiques, untouchable furniture, empty rooms. Suddenly, he'd found himself searching his computer for new places to live.

So that brought him to the end of another hectic day.

He sat on the back deck of a for-sale house as he looked out over the water as the sun began going down. Princess was curled up in his lap, keeping him warm as she snoozed away, her sweet snores almost comforting. She calmed him in a way that was more appealing than just about anything else in his life.

As if she knew he was thinking about her, she looked up with her sad eyes, begging him not to leave her. Benji barked from about twenty feet away as he ran after a squirrel that quickly climbed a tree before turning around and yakking at the dog, protesting at the intruder for being on its property.

"What do you think, Mr. Armstrong?"

For a moment, Mav had forgotten the woman was even there. The water was lulling him into peaceful oblivion as the breeze blew through the many trees scattered on the property.

"I'll take it. Tell escrow I want to close by next Friday. I'll pay full asking price." What was he doing? He didn't want a new house—not really—so why was he telling this woman he was buying it?

"I'm not sure we can close that soon," she stuttered. He'd obviously flustered her.

"I'm not financing. It will be paid for out of pocket. We *can* close that quickly," he informed her. Money talked.

"Oh, well, I didn't . . . uh . . . didn't realize. Of course. I'll call the seller's Realtor right away."

The woman went inside as he leaned back in the lawn chair. The owners had moved out of the country and the home came furnished. It was one of the biggest perks about the house. Sure, he'd have to get rid of some of the stuff, and certainly he was bringing his own bed over, but other than that, he didn't have to do a hell of a lot to move in.

He didn't want his family furniture because his nephew couldn't climb all over it without the threat of getting injured. He wanted a home, not a mausoleum. Mav wasn't even sure if he knew who he was anymore. So much was changing.

Mav was even finding himself thinking about a future, about having a wife and kids of his own. That thought sent a shudder through him. No. There was no way that was going to happen. This was just a temporary lapse in his sanity.

He'd vowed not to marry—not ever—after that reading of his father's will. No one would dictate his life, especially not his deceased father. Yes, he'd loved the man, but that didn't mean he was the man's puppet. Of course, at the moment, he was being daddy's good little boy.

And Mav couldn't forget the fact that he loved women . . . multiple women. He didn't want to settle down with just one. He was simply trying to help out Lins, that was all. Once she was back to herself and well on the road to happiness, he'd have no problem stepping back and letting her live her life the way she'd been doing before the attack.

With that all settled in his mind, he felt much better. He even managed to smile as Princess wiggled to get down off his lap and tentatively stepped off the cement patio and out into the grass to see what Benji was up to.

The two of them jumped at the tree as a second squirrel came out to investigate what the barking was all about. Both squirrels continued yelling at the dogs. It was highly entertaining.

"I spoke to the other Realtor. Let's draw up the papers for a formal offer and we should have an answer by this evening if not by tomorrow for sure," the Realtor said, shattering his peacefulness.

Still, Mav signed what he needed to, a small piece of himself hating to leave the place he was already considering his home. Lindsey was really messing with his head. He could already see that.

But when there was a mission to accomplish, an Air Force pilot didn't give up just because he got scared. Hell, for that matter, Mav wouldn't admit he was scared even if he did happen to feel that unfamiliar emotion.

Getting the dogs and himself in his truck, he decided it was a good time for a beer and some brotherly talking. Calling Cooper, he headed in that direction. There wasn't any part of him that was hoping to run into Lindsey.

This wasn't one of their nights together, so he wasn't seeking her out. He felt much better telling himself that. Now, he just needed to believe it.

CHAPTER THIRTEEN

Lindsey was startled out of the story she was reading when she heard a dog barking at her front door. What in the world? Shaking her head, she tried to find her place on the page when the bark sounded again.

That couldn't be right. She must be imagining things. Maybe it was because she hadn't stopped thinking about Princess since the day before when she'd left her at the shelter. It was unbelievable how much she missed the little mutt.

Never before had Lindsey owned a dog, so why would she miss one she'd only spent a few hours with? It didn't make sense, and Lindsey was tired of things not making sense. She wanted her life back, and imaginary dog noises weren't helping to make her feel any saner.

Still, she found herself setting the book down, getting up, and going to the front door. That's when she heard scratching. Her heart racing, she cracked the door open, leaving the chain in place.

When a set of chocolate eyes gazed at her through the opening, her heart hammered as she held in a sob. It was Princess. She'd know those sad eyes anywhere. But how had she gotten there?

Shutting the door, she heard a whimper. But she moved fast undoing the chain and opened the door again. The little dog rushed inside and scratched at her leg, demanding to know where Lindsey had been.

"How did you get here, Princess?" she asked as she dropped to the floor and the little furball climbed into her lap and stretched out, gently licking Lindsey's chin.

A few minutes passed and Benji ran in through the open door and barked up at her as if to say *hi*. Not far behind them was Maverick.

"Sorry about that. I didn't mean to bug you tonight. We're having a barbecue at my brother's and Princess must have smelled you or something because she was playing in the yard and then all of a sudden she just took off," he said as he leaned against the wall.

"Do you practice that pose?" she asked before she was able to stop herself.

His brows furrowed as he looked at her. "What?"

"You love to lean on things in just that way with your arms crossed and your lips tilted up just the slightest bit, and your eyes . . . your eyes all glinty and stuff," she rushed out.

That glint she'd been talking about took on a whole new sparkle as his lips turned up into a mega-wattage smile that had her breathing shallowly in an instant.

"You sure notice a lot about me for a woman who isn't interested," he practically purred.

"I'm not interested, I'm just . . . well, I'm just . . . uh . . . observant," she spluttered.

"You can observe me anytime you want to, sugar," he told her.

"I see you have two extras over for dinner," she said, deciding she would never win with him in a verbal exchange, especially one that included flirty little sentences.

"Yeah, I seem to have gained some pets," he said with that beautiful grin.

"You're keeping Princess." Her heart almost sank as she clutched the dog tighter. If he kept her that meant she was gone—unavailable. And for some reason that was something she couldn't even think about without getting upset.

"Nope, she's not mine," he said.

Now Lindsey was confused. The dog was clearly there, curled up in her lap, enjoying the attention she was currently getting.

"Oh, you're taking them back tonight?" That option didn't seem appealing either.

"Try again."

"Do you love to play games?" she asked, exasperated.

"Well, as a matter of fact, I do," he said, his eyes darkening as he gazed down at her. She had no doubt the games he was thinking of were most certainly triple X.

"Go away, Mav. I'm busy," she said on a frustrated sigh.

"Stormy told me if I was coming all the way down here to save her the trip and drag your butt back to the house. Her words, not mine," he said with a laugh. "She wants you to join us for dinner," he added.

"I don't want to eat with you," she told him, sounding like a petulant child.

"Tough. She told me to get you there by any means necessary. Oh, please, *please* resist," he said with a waggle of his brows.

Dang. She was actually tempted to resist just to see what he would do. That was another sobering thought around this man. She never thought she would be comfortable flirting again, let alone with an alpha man with way too much sexuality for a woman to deal with oozing from his pores.

"Fine. I'll come, but not because I'm afraid of you or anything, but because I was planning on going to see Stormy and the baby anyway," she said as she cradled Princess close to her chest and stood up. The dog barely moved.

"So really, what are you doing with the dogs?" she asked as they began walking the long expanse of lawn up to the main house.

She let Princess down, who sniffed at the grass, staying close to Lindsey's side.

"She's yours."

Lindsey waited, but he didn't add to that. "I told you I can't take a dog right now," she reminded him.

"Doesn't look like you have much of a choice. She's bonded to you. We don't really pick dogs. They pick us. Haven't you ever noticed that no matter how many people in a house, a dog will bond to one particular person the most? Well, that's what we look for at the shelter, for that bond. I haven't seen a bond as quick or as strong as the one between you and Princess."

As if she knew they were talking about her, Princess barked up at them before running in a circle around their feet. Then she finally ventured a little farther away as they neared the house. But Lindsey noticed that the little dog turned and sought her out every few seconds.

"I hadn't really thought about that before," she said.

"You should. I love animals. I try not to get too attached because then I don't want to let any of them go, but they all deserve good homes. Sometimes you just can't help but bond. The animal chooses you, and then you would be cruel not to want its love."

"Are you saying I'm terrible if I don't take this dog?" she gasped.

"Nope. Not at all. I'm just saying that she will spend her nights crying in her kennel if you don't." He didn't even pause as he said this.

"That's awful, Maverick Armstrong!"

"I know," he said with a smile. "Is it working?"

"The guilt? Yes!" she hissed.

"Good. You two were meant to be together. And don't worry, I brought some toys, a dog bed, and food."

And that was the end of that. She knew it was stupid to take on the responsibility of an animal at this point in her life, but like he'd said, the dog had chosen her and she didn't want to let her go now.

Besides that, it was actually pretty empowering that, for the first time in over a year, Lindsey was the one doing the rescuing instead of being rescued. There was this precious little dog who had been neglected and abused who loved and trusted Lindsey. She couldn't turn her back on the animal.

It looked like she was becoming a pet owner. And it was the happiest she'd felt in a very long time.

CHAPTER FOURTEEN

"Oh my goodness, Lins, I'd have never taken you for a dog person, but I absolutely already love Princess even after just visiting with her for a few minutes," Stormy said as Lindsey and Maverick climbed up on her deck.

"I'm sorry I didn't talk to you about it first, Stormy. I wasn't planning on getting a dog at all. It's just that Mav took me there to walk them and then . . . wait." She stopped and looked at her best friend. "How did you know I decided to keep her?"

Stormy just smiled. "Mav told me the two of you had bonded and needed each other."

"Mav doesn't make decisions for me," Lindsey said as she glared first at Stormy and then at Mav.

"Of course not, sugar," Mav said, infuriating her all the more.

"You're impossible," she snapped. He had made the decision for her the moment he'd brought the dog to her.

"I've been told that a lot," he said as he grabbed a beer and sat down in a lounge chair, kicking back.

In her past life, as she saw it, she would have never let him get away with behavior like that. It made her feel a whole lot better about the situation because she did want the dog even if she hadn't known how badly she did until Princess had shown up at her front door.

It didn't take long for Benji to wear himself out. Then he came flying up on the deck and jumped on the end of the lounge chair, quickly curling up and falling asleep at Mav's feet as if the two of them had always been together.

It was really difficult to stay irritated with a man when he had such a shaggy mutt by his side, or in this case, at his feet. The picture was too dang adorable.

She decided to ignore Mav and his overbearing ways as Cooper joined his brother and the two started talking airplanes. It seemed easier that way. She focused on Stormy instead.

"Where's baby Aaron?" Lindsey asked.

"The little tiger is all worn out. I fed him and he crashed hard," Stormy said.

"Oh." Lindsey was disappointed. Holding the baby always soothed her nerves, and with Maverick around, her nerves were at an all-time high.

The four of them had a nice barbecue, then sat by the fire for what must have been hours before Lindsey found herself all alone with Maverick. Cooper and Stormy had disappeared on her.

Traitors!

"Sit with me."

It wasn't a question, it was a command, and though she wanted to resist him, she couldn't seem to do it. Lindsey found herself pulled into his arms as the fire crackled in front of them.

"Why do you like to push me so much?" she finally asked him. Her guard seemed to be dropping.

"Honestly, I can't explain it," Mav said as he poked the fire with a stick.

"I don't want to do the fund-raiser," she said.

He was quiet for several moments. "If you truly don't want to do it, then I will stop bugging you, but I think you'd do great," he said. He wasn't looking directly at her, which made it somehow easier to communicate.

"Why do you think I could do it? I haven't ever done something like that before," she pointed out.

"Because you know what it's like to go through a traumatic experience, which means you can empathize with the cause," he said.

She thought about his words for a moment, and it made her flash back to that awful night in the hospital. She'd spoken to counselors and they all told her she was suffering from PTSD. She didn't necessarily believe that.

"It's not the same," she said.

"What's not the same?" He turned to look at her then, and she was captured by his expression. There was just so much understanding in his eyes. It was almost too much.

"The soldiers go through so much more than what I went through," she told him.

"Don't do that, Lins. Don't downplay your own pain," he told her.

"I just don't see how I can help anyone when I can't even help myself," she admitted in a rare moment of vulnerability.

He paused as he looked at her, as if he could see straight into her soul. It was very unnerving. She wanted to take back the words. But he wasn't going to give her a chance to do that.

"You know you can talk to me, Lindsey. It really does help."

"I can't . . . can't talk about it," she told him. Even thinking about it hurt. She didn't want to pull away from him, but she didn't want to talk about the attack either.

"I'm not going to make you talk. I just want to let you know that I'm here for you if you need me. I had a bad experience while in the military, and I went through some serious crap after until I finally trusted someone with my story. Letting it out helped me more than anything else did."

Lindsey pulled back so she could get a good look at his expression. He'd told her he understood what she was going through, but she hadn't realized he'd been speaking from personal experience.

She tried remembering what he'd said to her before, but she couldn't.

"Can you tell me about it?" she asked, expecting rejection.

"It's not pretty, sug. But if you want to know, I will tell you," he said as he gently ran his fingers through her hair.

"I really think I would like to know."

"Let's get a bit more comfortable."

He arranged the cushions against a log, then leaned back into it and pulled her into his arms. His hands were wrapped around her middle as he rested his chin against her shoulder, turning to press a light kiss on her neck. She was surprised that she wasn't pulling away from him, but right now she felt safer where she was than any other place.

She waited, knowing he needed to take time if he was about to speak of something traumatic. Everyone needed time when they were opening up.

If it were daylight with the sun shining down on her, she might think twice about where she was. But it was dark, and she was comfortable, with the buzz of alcohol zinging through her system. She didn't want to move.

The dogs were curled up beside them. The moon was a dim glow in the sky, the stars were twinkling down on them, and the warm fire in front of them crackled, making her feel like they were the only two people in the universe.

So she silently waited. She realized she could wait there all night. If she could freeze this moment, she would. Maverick had broken through her carefully constructed barrier, and she knew that there was no going back. She wasn't sure she wanted to go forward, either, but maybe the two of them could stay right where they were—frozen in this particular moment.

Of course that was impossible, but at the moment nothing seemed unreasonable. Nothing seemed real. She was safe. It was all that mattered.

CHAPTER FIFTEEN

Maverick wasn't sure if he should share this story with Lindsey. He wanted to help her, but so much of his story was dark and disturbing. He didn't want to make her more afraid than she already was and he worried that his darkness would be too much, that it would make her shy even farther away from him.

But he'd already told her he would. He couldn't back out now or she might lose some of the trust in him that he'd managed to earn. Plus, he felt strongly about her, and he wanted to open up with her. He wanted her to know him better. And like it or not, this was a huge part of who he was. Maybe if he shared, then she would be more willing to do the same.

Only two people knew the extent of what had happened to him—Cooper and Nick. He would have gladly shared with Ace as well, but his lost brother wasn't around. Maverick wouldn't give up on him, though—wouldn't give up on him coming home someday.

Taking a deep breath, he began his story.

"It was a surface-to-air missile that came up and knocked my F-18 out of the sky. My radar officer and I both ejected, but when we hit the ground, they were waiting. They shot Ken in the head right in front of me and laughed. It made their day to hurt wounded soldiers. They considered us the ultimate enemy and they took power in the fact that they thought they could do anything they wanted to us."

"Oh my gosh, Maverick, you don't have to tell me this," Lindsey said in horror.

"It's okay. I've come to terms with what happened. If this helps you even the tiniest bit, it's worth telling you the story of my capture," he said as he ran a hand down her arm. "I want to be there for you in every way I can."

She kept quiet and listened.

"They tied me up, and beat me so badly that the first night I couldn't see out of my right eye. I figured my days of flying were over—if I even made it out alive."

Lindsey clung tighter to him and it made the story so much easier to tell with her there with him. Maybe she was healing him in a way he hadn't realized he'd needed healing. He was supposed to be there for her, but she was growing on him in a way that should be a lot more terrifying than it was.

"The next few days were hell. I heard soldiers screaming in pain, and once in a while I heard the gurgling of men's dying breaths filled with blood. Those sounds will never leave me."

"No, I guess they wouldn't," she said so quietly he barely heard the words.

The fire continued crackling. They were in a cocoon the rest of the world wasn't allowed to enter. He wouldn't mind keeping it that way forever. It would just be the two of them.

"After a few days, I was sure I was going to die. My only regret was that I hadn't been able to save the other men in the prison. I focused on their pain instead of my own. There were a few female soldiers there, and I can't even explain the torture they were subjected to. There are rules to war, and these people weren't following them."

He wouldn't speak of all that had happened in that prison. It was too much for civilians to handle. Hell, it was too much for many of the military crew to handle. That's why a lot of the soldiers still weren't doing okay, even after years of being back home. That's why he'd had to start his organization to help as many as he could. Too many were forgotten about.

"How many people were there?" she asked.

"I don't know how many when I first got there. By the time we were found by a special ops team and rescued, there were ten of us left—nine soldiers and a journalist who ended up succumbing to his injuries before leaving the camp."

"Do you keep in contact with them?"

"The four of us who are left do. Two died later from complications, and the others . . ."

He stopped speaking because this part of the story might not have been the best idea for him to share.

"They took their own lives, didn't they?" she asked.

"Yeah, it happens too often after people return from war—especially after being captured and tortured." Anger filled Maverick even thinking about the loss of good men and women. More should be done to protect those who serve—who keep the country safe for everyone.

"I'm so sorry, Mav. I know I can't, but I want to take away some of the pain."

"I deal with it. Sometimes I still have nightmares. The voices of the men and women screaming—strong soldiers who were weeping like babies . . ." He trailed off, took a breath, and continued. "Certain days make it all come back to the front, such as Veterans Day, Independence Day."

"But you stayed in the military after it happened?"

He couldn't explain why he felt so determined to stay in the military. A lot of soldiers couldn't go back—and they weren't expected to. They had done more than enough for the people of the United States.

But after his recovery, there had never been any question that he'd return to duty.

"Most men and women I've talked to feel the same. We love what we do, we love making the country a safer place for everyone. I just think of all the lives that are saved because of what we do. I wouldn't change that. Does my job come with more risks than a desk job? Well, yeah. But it's war. And war sucks."

"Would you go back to overseas?" He could hear the fear in her voice and it hurt his heart.

"When I first got back, I would have said yes, for sure. It wasn't a matter of would I or wouldn't I. It was a matter of what was right and what's wrong. I would have done anything that needed to be done."

"Is that different now?"

She seemed to be holding her breath as she asked this question. He realized it was important. So he really thought about his answer. He flexed the arm still in a cast from his recent injury.

"I'm thinking of leaving the Air Force. I spend more and more time with my organization, and I realize it's my true calling now. I don't like to quit anything, but I'm not as young as I used to be, and my priorities have changed."

"What does that mean?" she asked him.

Again he had to think. What did that mean? He wasn't exactly sure. He just knew that his love of flying was still strong, but maybe it wasn't the strongest thing anymore. He was different now.

Seeming to know he was struggling, she asked another question. "Did you take time off when you returned?"

"I had no choice. I had a broken bone and was malnourished. But I was ready to get back to work. I haven't gone back to Iraq since that capture. It was five years ago. But I still fly my jet, and now I work with newbies. Before I joined the Air Force, I was a punk, doing nothing to make a better world for anybody but myself. Even when I joined, I still had attitude."

"What changed?" Her hand rubbing along his leg was both a comfort and a distraction. This woman did something to him—took away pain he didn't even know he still carried. She made him feel whole again. And he didn't fail to notice that she was touching him without prompting. Already they had come so far together. She wanted to heal.

"For one thing, attitude doesn't do you a bit of good during boot camp. Sure, it might piss you off enough to get through the workouts and the sergeants screaming in your face, but it will only get more work added on for you and the rest of the men, which in turn pisses them off. What really changed it for me, though, was respect. I had respect for my commander and he had faith in me. He saw something in me that I hadn't seen before. It made me believe in myself. And when I found out I could fly F-18s if I worked real hard, that changed it all. I had a goal to work for, and I didn't stop until I reached that goal."

She chuckled. The sound was the most beautiful music he'd heard in a long time. He knew it wasn't something she shared too often anymore. It made him close his arms a little bit tighter around her.

"I bet you still haven't stopped," she told him.

"I haven't even thought about slowing down until recently," he said against her ear, enjoying it when a shiver traveled through her.

"It seems that you have a lot of extreme circumstances in life that make you take new routes," she said. "What changed for you this time?"

"Some things are best left secret," he said as he kissed the smooth column of her neck.

Then he went silent as he held her, letting his story sink in. He just wanted to enjoy this moment, holding her in his arms without her fighting him. She relaxed even more against him and Mav knew his life was changing.

He couldn't help but think of his father, of what the old man had wanted for his sons. Money wasn't an issue for any of the boys—hadn't been an issue even before the reading of the will. That hadn't been what his father was trying to get them to understand.

He now realized that his father had wanted to save them all. He'd wanted them to be better people. For a long time, Mav had thought joining the military had been what made him a better person. Now, he realized that, with his resources, his mission had changed. He could help so many more people by being on the ground than being in the air.

His new attitude had a lot to do with the woman in his arms. If he could feel so strongly about her—about helping this one person—then couldn't the two of them together do the same for so many others?

"Please help me with this fund-raiser," he said. "I can keep pushing you, and keep forcing myself in, but I want you to want to do it. I want you to be a part of it willingly, and I want to show you a side of me that I don't show anyone."

He knew he was giving too much of himself up, but he couldn't seem to stop. Mav found his breath stuck in his throat as he waited for her answer. This was a defining moment between the two of them.

He felt her begin to pull away from him and he wanted to clasp his arms even more tightly around her, but then he would be taking away her free will and he'd just vowed not to do that.

This was her decision and he would respect her for it—no matter the cost to himself.

CHAPTER SIXTEEN

Hearing Maverick tell her about his time of being captured tore Lindsey apart inside. As she moved away from him, she knew she didn't want to feel this bond with him, but she did. She felt a connection to him unlike anything she'd felt with another person.

She also knew what he was asking her. She knew this fund-raiser had so much more to do with them than it did a single project. Was she willing to take a trip down this road she wasn't sure of?

Lindsey found that she wanted to. But at the moment, she felt safe and cozy, having relaxed for the first time in months. She had to wonder, would she still feel the same about wanting to chair the fund-raiser when she was lying alone in her bed later that night? That was the real question.

It was time to call it a night. She'd sat forward, but her body was cold where she'd been leaning on him, and it felt unnerving, like she should simply lie back and resume her position. She knew, though, that she needed to give it some thought without Maverick being around.

She answered his question, finally. "I don't know. I'm not saying no. I just need to think about it," she told him.

"I can respect that," he said, shocking her. He didn't usually take no for an answer, and uncertainty on her part would be considered a no for Mav.

Standing, she tried sneaking away while he put out the fire. But she should have known it wouldn't be that easy. With a very tired Princess at her heels, she didn't even get ten feet away before Mav was magically at her side.

"You're calling it a night early," he said, the dim lighting along the path to the guest cottage far too intimate after what the two of them had just shared.

"It's not early," she told him with a smile.

"It's only . . ." He looked down at his watch. "Oh, I didn't realize it was nearly midnight. Thank you for staying with me. Thank you for letting me share. I liked it."

"Thank you, Mav. I know that must not have been easy for you to do."

"It was easier than I thought," he told her. There was something in his tone she didn't recognize and it scared her.

But wasn't this fear so much better than the terror she'd suffered for so long? Even though letting a man into your heart without knowing where it would lead was dangerous, it was a risk she should be willing to take. The consequences weren't life or death. Still, she hesitated.

"I don't need to be escorted back to the cottage."

"I can't let a beautiful woman go home alone," he told her before reaching for her hand. She didn't even bother tugging against his hold this time. He was back to his usual self, his voice full of confidence. The meeker Mav hadn't lasted long. She realized she enjoyed both sides of this man.

They were silent the rest of the way to her place, which didn't take long at all. She stood in front of the door, feeling that first-date sort of awkwardness she'd hoped to never feel again. Of course, she reminded herself, it wasn't a date.

This was simply her returning home after eating with her friends. Not that Mav was her friend . . . not exactly. But it almost felt like a date, especially the part where he'd held her so tenderly by the fire and shared so much of himself.

"I have a meeting tomorrow with some big clients for the fund-raiser. Will you come with me?"

"Mav . . ." She sighed. He'd promised to give her time.

"I'm not asking you to commit. I'm just showing you some of what we do and that will help you make an informed decision," he said, sounding far too innocent.

She sighed again. The man was infuriating.

"I don't think it's a good idea to go with you," she said with a frown before she smiled. "Last time we went out together, I ended up with a dog," she pointed out. "If we go somewhere again, I might find myself with a monkey."

That made him laugh, and the rich sound of his natural joy was enough to warm her to the bones and shake off the rest of her melancholy.

"I promise not to get you attached to any monkeys," he said as he crossed his fingers over his heart.

"Where would we be going then?" she asked.

"I can't tell you. That would ruin the surprise," he said as he took a step nearer to her. She leaned back against the door. It wasn't locked. All she had to do was turn the knob and step inside. But the command wasn't connecting with her hand.

"I'm not big on surprises," she pointed out.

"That's because you haven't been surprised by me enough," he said with a waggle of his brows.

"Hmm." The buzzing sound on her lips made them tingle as she found her eyes straying up to his. Dang, she wouldn't mind a kiss good-night. That thought annoyed her. She didn't *want* to want his kisses.

Princess whined at her feet, which snapped Lindsey out of her reverie. She really did need to go inside. Just looking at her sweet new pet made her realize that Mav wasn't completely off in the things he was doing for her.

"Even though you strong-armed me, I have to thank you for Princess. I sort of already love her."

"She chose you," he said, leaning just a bit closer. Now he was less than six inches away and she could feel the heat pouring off him. This man's body temperature only ran on hot.

"Just don't be giving me anything else," she warned.

"I can't promise that. I think I like seeing your face light up when you get a gift," he countered.

"Well . . . refrain," she squeaked. If only she sounded more convincing.

He didn't say anything else, just closed the remaining distance between them so his body was brushing hers. She couldn't breathe as she looked into his dark eyes and waited to see what he was going to do.

Slowly and without pause, he leaned down until his lips were whispering against hers. He brushed them across once . . . twice . . . three times, a light contact of his lips on hers, just enough to make her want to cry out in frustration.

Then he leaned in closer, his hard chest now pressing lightly against hers as his hand came up and cupped the back of her neck. She should be screaming and running, but she was feeling anything but fear. This man . . . oh, what this man did to her.

She finally stopped thinking when he pressed his lips firmly against hers and embraced her, his tongue running along the seam of her mouth. She gasped and that was all he needed to slip inside and claim her.

The heat was almost too much to bear. She couldn't help her pleasurable moan from escaping, which made him press even harder against her.

His hand was in her hair as he explored her mouth. She couldn't get enough of his taste. She was ready to lose herself in this man she professed to not even like most of the time.

Just as his hand traveled down the side of her body, a sharp bark broke her out of the spell she was under. Mav pulled back, fire burning in his eyes.

"Sorry about that, sug. I was only going to give you a little goodnight kiss. You make me lose control," he said. He was trying to joke, but for once, his voice was as breathless as hers.

"Um . . . well, I gotta go," she stuttered as she reached behind her and found the doorknob. She twisted it and then almost fell backward into the cottage.

Mav's hand shot out and steadied her. That small touch almost sent her over the edge into the abyss.

"I've got it. Thanks," she told him as Princess wound her way between them and darted into the house. The dog was making sure Lindsey didn't leave her again.

His eyes burned and it looked as if he wanted to say something more, but he stopped and turned, took a few steps, then turned back around.

"Tomorrow. Six. Wear something comfortable—pants, tennis shoes."

With that, he turned and began jogging back up the path to his brother's house. Feeling almost like she was in a dream, Lindsey shut the door, then found Princess looking up at her with those sad eyes.

"Yeah, Princess, we both have problems, don't we?" Lindsey said.

When she walked into the kitchen, she found the dog bowls with water and food all set up. That must have been what Mav was doing when he disappeared for a little bit earlier in the evening. She couldn't help but be touched.

When she climbed into bed a bit later, though, Princess barked at her from the floor. Lindsey smiled. The dog wanted nothing to do with the beautiful purple bed set up in the corner of the room.

To tell the truth, Lindsey wanted her with her as well. She picked up the dog, who insisted on getting beneath the covers. Even though she was confused about Maverick, she fell asleep without worries for the first time since the attack. There was definite comfort in having Princess with her, snuggled up at her side.

That night she didn't have nightmares for the first time in a year.

CHAPTER SEVENTEEN

Maverick was a few minutes early, and Stormy was by his side at the door, insisting on babysitting Princess. She'd been at the house most of that day and Princess liked Stormy and little Aaron. Princess had snuggled up next to the baby and the two of them had napped together. The only thing keeping Lindsey's jealousy at bay was that when Princess got tired it was Lindsey's lap she came to curl up in.

With reluctance, she agreed to go with Maverick and felt guilty when Princess whimpered as the two of them walked away.

"What if she panics while I'm gone?" Lindsey asked as they climbed into his truck.

"She's in good hands. And I know Stormy has already gotten her treats for when she comes up to the main house," Mav said with a laugh.

"But what if she doesn't want to leave there with me when I come to pick her up?"

"She's already attached to you. She'll go anywhere you do," he said before turning to her. "But you know you don't have to be in a hurry to leave, right? Cooper and Stormy really do love you and want you to stay. I'll tell you that over and over again until you believe it."

"I don't want to be a burden to them," Lindsey insisted.

"It would be so much more of a burden to them if you left before you were ready," he said, and there was so much truth shining from his eyes it was impossible for her not to believe him.

"Thanks, Mav. That does make me feel better," she told him.

They chatted as they left the harbor and got on the freeway. He still wasn't telling her where they were going, but when he pulled up to a nearly empty parking lot at Safeco Field, she wondered what he had up his sleeves.

"Engine trouble?" she asked.

"Nope. We're gonna play some baseball. Hope you have your swinging arm ready."

She waited for the punch line but one didn't come.

"I thought we had a meeting about the fund-raiser," she pointed out.

"We do. We're meeting with the manager of the team, who is a huge supporter of the organization, and then we're playing with the team."

"But I really don't get it," she said, confused.

"Part of fund-raising is friendships. People want to support organizations for causes they empathize with, but they also need to like the people they work with. However, most of what I do is about making people feel relaxed and appreciated. We all help each other out."

"I really don't understand this. I'm so not the girl to chair your event. All I see is that this is a pro-ball field. We can't just go in there and play," she told him.

He laughed before he leapt out of the truck and came around to open her door. "We're not sneaking in. We're having a meeting and then playing with the team."

He was so matter-of-fact she almost felt silly questioning him.

"Normal people don't get to go and play with a major league baseball team," she said, hoping to knock some sense into the man.

"Whoever said I was normal?" he asked as he reached up and grabbed her by the waist with his good arm, pulling her down from the truck. He gripped her hand and began tugging her toward a side door.

"We can't do this. I'm not good enough to do this," she said, digging her feet in, which at least stopped him.

"We're just going to have a little fun," he said with his "trust me" smile.

"Falling on my face in front of the Seattle Mariners is not my idea of a little fun," she said.

"How am I going to show off in front of you, sugar, if I can't even get you on the field?" he said with a laugh.

"Do you play?" *Was there anything he didn't do* would be the more accurate question.

"A little," he said with a shrug.

"What's a little?" she asked with narrowed eyes.

"I played in high school, and Duke offered me a full baseball scholarship, but I was a moron back then and didn't take it."

"Duke? Like *the* Duke?" she said in shock.

"Yep, one and the same. My life ended up taking a different path. I'm grateful I joined the Air Force, even more grateful I fly F-18s, but I sure wish I would've played ball. I have some great friends here, though, and come play with them once in a while to get the bug out."

"Wow, just . . . wow." She didn't want to be in awe of this man, but it was getting more and more difficult not to be.

She was deathly silent, though, as they made their way inside the stadium. He took her down tunnels she'd never even dreamed of walking through before, and then he pushed his way through a door that she knew instantly was the locker room. That smell was something they couldn't disguise no matter how fancy a place was.

"Cover up, boys, I brought a lady," was the only warning Mav gave before he turned a corner.

Lindsey was both fascinated and embarrassed as she entered the sacred locker room of athletes she'd admired for years. Baseball was her favorite sport, and to be in the locker room of the Mariners was about as cool as it got. She went to as many games as her schedule and budget would allow.

"Dang, Mav, how did you get such a hottie to go out with you?" one of the guys asked as he sat shirtless on the bench tying his cleats.

"I've got charm," Mav said with a grin. "Aren't you girls ready yet? We're running late. I figured you'd be on the field by now."

"Half the team's out there. A few had to drag their butts in. We had a long week on the road."

"Sounds good. We're meeting with John and then we'll be out to kick some butt. Where's Lindsey's stuff?"

"John put it over there," the man said and pointed, and much to Lindsey's delight, Mav took her over to a pile where a jersey and hat were sitting.

She had to fight tears as Mav handed them to her. It was authentic gear from the team.

"These are mine?" she asked, feeling foolish as she fought not to cry.

"Yep. You're part of the team tonight," he told her.

Without a second thought, she threw her arms around his neck and hung on tight. This was truly the greatest present anyone had ever given her.

"Thank you so much. I don't know how I could possibly ever pay you back for this," she said as she stepped back.

There was something burning in his eyes that she couldn't quite read so she turned and looked away. She didn't want to feel confused, and whatever that look was, it was certainly making her head spin.

"No prob. I needed you to see how fun this can be," he said with a chuckle as he caressed her cheek.

"This is bribery, you know," she said, feeling as if she were going to burst.

"Then my plans are working. I know your weaknesses now," he told her with a wink.

She really was caving far too easily. But she couldn't find it within herself to care. She threw the jersey on over her shirt and then got her hair tucked up under the hat before sending a beaming smile to Mav. She didn't even care if she fell on her face. It would be worth it. Just getting to go out on the field would be the greatest night of her life.

"Maverick, you're just in time."

Lindsey turned to see a man dressed in a suit walking up to them.

"Good to see you, John. Let's get business out of the way so we can go hit some balls," Mav said as he walked up and shook the man's hand. "This is Lindsey. I'm trying to talk her into chairing the event. Bringing her here has given me some good points," he added with a laugh.

"It's a pleasure to meet you, Lindsey. Let's step into my office."

They followed John through some more tunnels and then sat with him for a half hour speaking about numbers and projects. What shocked Lindsey was that she was able to keep up with the conversation. What shocked her even more was that she found herself jumping in and coming up with her own ideas.

By the end of the conversation, as Mav led her back through the tunnels, she was ready to commit. The cause truly was something she felt she could promote. But fund-raising was pushed out of her mind as they made it back to the locker room.

"Now that work is out of the way, are you ready to play?" Mav asked.

"More than ready," she told him.

He took her hand again, but this time he didn't have to drag her. She practically dragged him as they made their way out onto the field where the players were already hitting and throwing balls. She stood there on the edge and watched the magic for a few minutes before the rest of the team joined them. Then they split up.

"All right, Lins, you're up at bat first," Mav said before he trotted off to first base.

Her heart was racing as she selected a bat and slowly approached home plate. She prayed she didn't completely fail. That would really suck in front of her heroes.

"Ready?" Jonathan Arturo Aro called and her heart beat a bit faster. The very talented Mariners pitcher was talking to her.

"I think so," she said in a choked voice.

He gave her a grin that nearly made her faint, and then he leaned back.

The first ball whipped by so fast she didn't even see it, just heard the sound of it hitting the mitt behind her. In astonishment she turned around and looked at the catcher who was grinning ear to ear.

"Doesn't that hurt?" she gasped.

He smiled even bigger as he stood up and threw the ball back, not quite as fast, but pretty dang quickly, in her opinion, before winking at her through the mask he was wearing.

"Nah. He wasn't even putting any real heat in it," Steve Clevenger replied.

"Dang. If that wasn't putting heat into it, I don't want to see what he can really do," she mumbled.

"Okay, quit showing off now, Jon," Mav yelled from first base.

"Ah, I was going easy on her, Mav," Jon yelled back.

"She's already taken, so give up the showboating," Mav called back.

Lindsey's head whipped back and forth at the exchange. Then Jon laughed and got back into position, so she returned to a batting stance and waited. The next ball went much slower, and she was satisfied when the bat connected and the ball went soaring through the air.

Dropping the bat, she ran as hard as she could while Mav stood on the base, waiting to tag her out. When she landed before the ball, she knew the players were letting her get away with it, but she didn't care. This was way too much fun and she didn't want to be sent to the dugout.

"You didn't tell me you were a baseball superstar," Mav said as she edged off the base a couple of feet and waited to hit second.

"We all have secrets," she said, moving another couple of inches toward second.

Then so fast she almost missed it, Jon turned and threw the ball to Mav, making her drop down and slide back to the base before he tagged her out. Her forward motion was too fast, though, and she connected with Mav's legs.

The ball went flying and Mav teetered in the air before toppling over, landing right on top of her. The breath rushed from her lungs and then the field faded away as their eyes connected.

"If you wanted me on top of you, all you had to do was ask," he murmured before closing the gap between them and taking her lips hard and fast.

Lindsey was completely enchanted by him, forgetting all about the game—until she heard the catcalls from the other players.

Mortified by what she was doing, Lindsey pushed against Mav's chest, and with obvious reluctance, he pulled back, his eyes heated and confused.

"Do you two want some privacy?" Jon called out through laughter.

Mav got his wits back and scrambled to his feet to help her up. The scarlet hue on her cheeks was enough to guide a sleigh as the game resumed, along with a bunch of snickers from the guys.

Though there was a lot more flirting going on the rest of the evening, Lindsey took it in stride. This team was a group of really great guys with pretty dang big hearts.

When it was all over she was disappointed to leave. But she didn't walk away empty-handed. The team signed her jersey, insisting she leave it on while they did it, making her giggle and causing Mav to scowl. They gave her some baseballs and other gear and told her she'd better come back and visit them again.

She'd thought dog walking had been the best day ever, but playing baseball at Safeco Field would be unbeatable. She felt almost in another world as she rode back to her cottage with Maverick.

She even allowed Mav to hold her hand as he walked her to her door, not once trying to pull it away. She wasn't sure how the evening was going to end—or how she wanted it to end. He'd already kissed her a few times now. And she was sort of hoping for another kiss as they reached her door.

But then the door swung open.

"Did you two have a good evening?"

Sherman was standing there, holding Princess in his arms as he grinned at both of them ear to ear.

"It was amazing. We played baseball with the Mariners," she told him, feeling all the excitement all over again.

"There's nothing quite like being on a major league field, is there?" Sherman asked her as Princess wiggled in his arms to be let down.

"Have you done that before?" she asked, taking Princess in her arms. Lindsey was immediately attacked with kisses as Princess squirmed her greetings.

"What are you doing here, Uncle Sherm?" Maverick asked as he followed Lindsey into the house.

"I showed up to visit with Cooper, and when the kids got tired I told them I'd watch Princess until you two got home."

"That was thoughtful." Though Mav said the words, Lindsey was picking up on some weird vibes between uncle and nephew. She wasn't quite sure what that was all about.

"I'm a helpful guy," Sherman said with a wink.

"I'm sure you two have a lot to talk about this evening. I'll leave you youngsters alone. I did leave out a bottle of wine for an after-date drink, though," he said with a sly smile as he gathered up his coat.

"It wasn't a date. We were speaking to the manager about the fund-raiser," Lindsey was quick to point out.

Mav grumbled something that made Sherman smile, but didn't correct her, thankfully.

"How did the meeting go?" Sherman asked.

"Perfectly," Mav said, almost sounding impatient, which confused Lindsey. She didn't want Sherman to feel unwelcome.

"You don't have to rush off. I'm on sort of an adrenaline high right now from the game and stuff," Lindsey said, trying to fix the situation. "Would you like a glass of wine?"

"Thanks for the offer, but I have to drive home. Even half a glass is too much for me these days when I have to get behind the wheel," he told her. Then he leaned in and kissed her cheek before she could even think about stopping him.

Lindsey automatically took a step closer to Maverick without thinking about it. And just like that, Sherman disappeared out the door.

"My uncle is quite meddlesome," Maverick said with a laugh as he took a step away from her.

She didn't like the instant feeling of emptiness when he wasn't close. That didn't bode well for her sanity.

"I'm going to take off too. I'd feel better if I see that Sherman gets home safe and sound. He might not want to admit it, but his eyes aren't the best these days," Maverick told her.

"You're not staying at Coop's tonight?" she asked, surprised by the disappointment. When had she gone from not wanting him so close to almost needing him nearby?

"Not tonight. I miss my bed," he said. Then there was a look in his eyes like he wanted to say something more, but he began making his way toward the door and she brushed it aside. She must be imagining things.

"Thank you again for taking me out to the field, Mav," she said shyly, setting Princess down and following him to the door. He faced her on the porch and gave her a sizzling look before smiling.

"It was my pleasure," he said, and then he took off at a brisk pace back to his truck. She watched him pull from the driveway before she went back inside and sat down, Princess immediately jumping into her lap to curl up.

Sitting there for a while, she petted her dog, finding the peace she'd been without for a while. Between Maverick and the dog, she really did feel like she was letting go of the fears that had held her in their grasp for too long.

Later that night when she curled up in bed with Princess snuggled to her side again, she realized Mav was right about it all. These excursions were helping her in a way nothing else had been able to.

She was beginning to become more herself. And now that she was finding her happiness again, she wasn't so sure she was willing to let it go.

CHAPTER EIGHTEEN

As good as Lindsey was at pacing, she considering applying to have it recognized as an Olympic sport. She certainly would win gold if it were. Chewing on a nail on one hand, she looked down at her other, which was gripping her phone.

To call or not to call, that was the question. She hadn't heard from Maverick in a few days. Now that really wasn't much time at all, but she hadn't really thanked him properly either after her incredible night of baseball.

The man had taken her out twice on dates—yes, she was admitting they were dates. He could say it was about the fund-raising, but really, they'd spent a total of a half hour talking to one donor and they'd spent hours having fun. He might be sneaky on how he did things, but really, he was smarter than she would have ever given him credit for. Her time with him at these events had been fun. He was thoughtful and considerate, and she had to admit, she had an incredible time when she was with Maverick.

So how did one thank a person for going above and beyond to make your day absolutely unbelievable? The only thing she could think of was baking. She was a great baker. She couldn't cook super well, but she could bake as well as Betty Crocker.

Was Betty Crocker an actual person? Or was she a brand? Maybe she'd have to look that up sometime. Ugh! Shaking her head, she continued walking a circle around the path surrounding the guest cottage.

Her nails were down to nothing, and her phone was hot from being squeezed so tightly in her other hand. This was so stupid. He'd said he wanted her to chair his event and she'd agreed. That meant he obviously planned on seeing her again.

So it wasn't a big deal for her to call him up and invite him over for dessert. It didn't mean anything, really. It was just a thank you from her to him for believing in her when a lot of people would have given up.

She stopped walking and plopped down on the patio chair as Princess sniffed the bushes looking for a place to go potty. The dog had been following her the entire time she'd been pacing and was probably exhausted. At least Princess was getting exercise.

Lindsey looked at the phone as if it were her mortal enemy and then decided a text message was just as good as a phone call. And that way if he couldn't come, she wouldn't have to hear his voice. He'd just say "Thanks but no thanks." Easy peasy.

Now the key was to not sound too dang needy. That she could do. It was simple. She was just going to give out a quick invite. Still, she retyped it a dozen times before she finally decided the message was good enough.

I'm baking today. If you aren't busy, or if you have a sweet tooth, I'll have extra. No big deal.

Before she could change her mind, she hit Send. Then, of course, she began second-guessing herself. What if that did sound sort of needy? She was getting ready to send another message that said she might not bake after all when her phone chimed. Her fingers trembling, she opened the message.

I was wondering when I was going to get to taste some of your sugar. I'll be there at six.

She reread the message a dozen times, her cheeks heating, her stomach shaking. She was sure he wasn't meaning *her* sugar. Mav was just a flirt. He couldn't help how things sounded, especially through a text.

Six is fine. I'm not good at real cooking, so I just have dessert.

She wanted to make sure he wasn't expecting a full-blown meal. Then he'd be disappointed. Oh, this was such a bad idea. She knew it was a bad idea, so why had she started this?

Tapping her toe, she waited for his reply. She didn't have to wait too long, thankfully, or she might have begun pulling her hair out a few strands at a time.

Let's go ahead and make this a work night. I'll bring the food and we'll make dinner together . . . and then have plenty of time for dessert . . .

His choice of wording made her clench her knees together.

Was she going to allow something to happen between the two of them? Did she even want another man to ever touch her again after what had been done to her? A week ago, she would have emphatically said no. She'd been terrified of even the softest of touches.

But in only a few days' time, Maverick had managed to get beneath her skin and had made her begin to think about things she didn't want to think about. She didn't cringe when he touched her, didn't hate it when he looked at her.

"What are you doing?"

So lost in her thoughts about Maverick, Lindsey hadn't heard Stormy walking up. The greeting made her jump before she spun around and smiled.

"I was just strolling, taking Princess for a walk." For some reason she guiltily stuffed her phone back into her pocket.

"Okay, Lins, something is up and I want to know what it is," Stormy demanded as she followed Lindsey into the house.

"Nothing is up," Lindsey said as she moved over to the cupboards to see what she had and what she might need. What dessert was she going to make? How badly did she want to impress this man?

"I feel like you're shutting me out more and more each and every day," Stormy said, her voice sad.

That stopped Lindsey in her tracks. She didn't want to hurt her best friend. She turned and faced her, not quite ready to approach and wrap her arms around her, but still needing to comfort her.

"I . . . uh . . . I just invited Maverick over. He's been really great to me and I wanted to do something for him," Lindsey said in a rush of words.

Stormy's eyes widened, and then she smiled.

"You weren't going to tell me that!" she exclaimed.

"I don't know," Lindsey said as she shifted from foot to foot.

"You don't think I'd be upset about it, do you?"

"Well . . ." Lindsey stalled.

"I think it's great that you two can barely keep your eyes off each other," Stormy exclaimed.

"We can keep our eyes off each other," Lindsey insisted.

"Mmm-hmm," Stormy said before chuckling.

"We can," Lindsey insisted, feeling like a broken record.

"Well, I will make sure that Coop and I keep ourselves locked tightly inside the house tonight so there aren't any interruptions. I'm going to take Princess too," Stormy said as she sat down. Princess immediately went over and snuggled by her side.

"You don't need to take Princess," Lindsey said in almost a panic.

"You just ring me when the date is over, and I'll bring her right back."

"She doesn't have to leave," Lins said again.

"I want you to have a distraction-free night. What time is the date?" Stormy said, ignoring her protests.

"It's at six, and it's not a date. I'm just making him dessert as a thank you."

"Sure, sure, not a date. Okay, I'll pick up Princess in a couple hours."

"Wait!" Lindsey said, stopping Stormy from leaving. Her friend looked at her patiently.

"I know Mav is your brother-in-law, and I don't want to make things awkward for you. I just . . ." She stopped talking, feeling her cheeks heat.

Stormy's eyes widened as her mouth hung open. She pulled herself together quickly, though.

"You don't actually think I would be upset about the two of you becoming an item, do you?" she asked.

"Well . . . it could be awkward," Lindsey said.

"Oh, Lins, not at all. I love Mav, and you know how much I love you. Why would I be upset about you two dating?" Stormy asked.

"Because when things go sour . . ." Lindsey stopped speaking.

"When?" Stormy said with a confused look. "Why do you assume it will go bad?" She sat back as if she were going to get comfortable.

"Come on, Storm, there's no way this will be fairy-tale perfect," Lindsey said. "I'm a realist."

"You're protecting yourself," Stormy corrected. "And that's okay. But don't dwell on what could happen. Live in the moment. Enjoy yourself and know that you have my full support no matter what happens."

"What if it gets bitter?" Lindsey said, choking out the words.

"Then we cross that road when it happens," Stormy said reasonably.

"I can't lose you, Stormy—not ever," Lindsey said, tears threatening.

Stormy crossed the room and stood in front of Lindsey, not reaching out to her, but letting her know she was right there.

"Nothing in this world would ever make you lose me. Just like I know that you will always be there for me. We are so much more than friends. We're sisters by choice. And I have no problem causing physical harm to my dear brother-in-law if he hurts you."

She said this so seriously that Lindsey couldn't help but smile.

"I promise you, I won't ever ask you to maim Maverick, no matter what," Lindsey said.

"You wouldn't have to ask. That's just what best friends do for each other," Stormy said.

Before Lindsey realized what she was doing, she leaned forward and tugged Stormy close, giving her the first hug in a year. Stormy was shocked for a moment and then she wrapped her arms around her friend and clung on tight.

When they let go, Stormy had tears coming down her cheeks.

"I love you, Lins, more than almost anyone in this world."

"I love you too, Storm."

"I'm running away now so I can soak up this moment."

Before Lindsey could say anything more, Stormy rushed out, sniffling as she practically ran up the trail to the main house. Lindsey looked at Princess, who gazed at her a moment before shutting her eyes again and continuing her nap.

It was a pretty perfect day—even with all these emotions coursing through her. She felt happiness she hadn't thought she would ever feel again. Her life was getting back on the right path.

Maverick being in her life was the best thing that had ever happened to her. That was a sobering thought, but not enough that she wanted to stop the ride she was on.

CHAPTER NINETEEN

Files tucked beneath his arm, flowers in his hand, a grocery sack in the other, Maverick walked quickly up to Lindsey's door, feeling awkward with the damn cast. The sweat on his palm was simply because it was hot outside. It had nothing to do with nerves.

Maverick didn't get nervous before dates—umm, meetings—even impromptu ones when the girl invited him to come over. He was too far above something so silly as that. Still, he stopped in front of her door, set down the items he was carrying, and wiped his sweaty palms against his jeans.

It would be good to get into some air conditioning, that was for sure. Picking up the items, he rang the bell, then impatiently waited for her to open the door.

When she did, his palms became sweaty all over again. Beautiful was too tame a word to describe her with her hair pulled up in a hazardous bun, an apron draped across her body trying to disguise her beautiful lush breasts and full hips, and a genuine smile upon her lips along with a sprinkling of flour.

Even with only a smidgeon of makeup on her naturally beautiful, somewhat olive complexion, she was stunning. She really had no clue how appealing she was. Maybe that was just one more thing he appreciated about her.

As much as he was fighting against his father's last wishes, this girl made him think he might just want to cave in to the terms of his father's will. It was something he would have to tell her about so she would never think he wanted her for money. She wouldn't think that. He had enough of his own already. Hell, he'd sign away every penny to his organization. Maybe she didn't have to know.

No! He wasn't considering marriage. That was foolish. He just wanted to be with her. It didn't have to be forever. Damn, his mind was a mess.

"You're a little early," she said with a shy smile, snapping him out of his wayward thoughts.

"I didn't want the food to go bad," he lamely replied as he took a step forward, instantly wanting to lay his head against her shoulder and inhale her intoxicating floral scent. It was a subtle mixture that drove him crazy anytime he was around the woman.

"Let me take that from you." She reached out for the bag.

"You take these. I'll deal with the groceries," he offered as he handed her the flowers.

She inhaled their scent and that simple gesture stirred images of her trailing her nose down his body doing the same to him. Dang! It was hot outside, and the house felt like a furnace had exploded.

"What are we eating?" she asked as she trailed after him into the small kitchen. She found a vase and took her time arranging the flowers until she had them just right.

"Salmon and rice," he said. His voice must have been tight, because she looked up a bit startled, but Mav knew she had feelings for him. He could see it in her eyes, feel it in her body. He wanted to scrap dinner and go right to dessert, and the sweetness he wanted to devour had nothing to do with whatever she'd been working on this afternoon.

"That sounds great," she said before moving away from the flowers and pulling something out of the oven when the timer went off.

"Something smells delicious," he said as he peeked at the cake she was taking out.

"It's just a cake with chocolate and strawberries," she said nervously.

"Mmm, aphrodisiacs," he told her with a laugh.

"They are not!" Her eyes went wide as she gazed at him in surprise.

"Are you nervous around me, sugar?"

He backed her into the counter as he brought himself a little bit closer, inhaling her sweet perfume mixed with the scent of the sweet dessert in the air. He needed just one little taste. Barely brushing his body against hers, he leaned in and gently sucked the skin of her neck.

"No," she panted. "Okay, a little."

The sigh escaping after her words made his thickness even harder. There wasn't a time he ever recalled wanting a woman as much as he wanted this one—especially without taking what he wanted. Hell, nope, not even then. This desire was unquenchable, he feared.

"Shouldn't we . . . um . . . cook?" she asked breathily.

"Definitely. I'm already hot," he told her. But he backed off, almost satisfied with the glow in her eyes. He could tell how much she desired him.

They worked side by side, cooking the salmon and rice, and chopping a salad. He felt high every time she laughed. During all the prep, he continuously brushed against her, making sure she was more and more comfortable with his touch.

There was a radiant glow about her cheeks the entire evening, and the one thing Maverick knew beyond a shadow of a doubt was that he had to have a taste of her. He had to show her how great and unselfish lovemaking could be.

He just prayed he had the restraint to keep himself together while giving her this gift.

The two finished dinner, and then it was time for dessert. His favorite part of the day. Undoing the top two buttons of his shirt, he followed her back into the kitchen while she pulled out a couple of pots and several ingredients, including chocolate and strawberries.

That had him instantly hard again. But tonight wasn't about him finding satisfaction. It was about helping Lindsey feel good about herself and helping her to feel safe, especially in her own home.

"This is a chocolate strawberry layer cake," she told him as she took the cake portion and began frosting it. She set it in the freezer to rapidly cool.

"Looks good," he said, trying to calm himself as he swiped a taste from the bowl she'd mixed the frosting in.

"Um . . . yeah." Her gaze was centered on his lips as he sucked the frosting off, and the look in her eyes made his body pulse painfully.

She went back to the stove and began mixing more ingredients until she had a creamy chocolate mixture. Then she pulled the cake from the freezer, set it on the counter, and placed strawberries on top. When she grabbed the chocolate sauce and drizzled it over the top, he thought he just might have a high-school moment and embarrass himself right there in front of her.

Maverick couldn't remember the last time his body had ached so much from wanting a woman. It was just about killing him. But when a dribble of chocolate splattered the counter and she wiped it up with her finger and then sucked on it, he knew it was over.

Taking the pan from her hands, he carefully set it aside, ignoring the slight tremble in his own fingers as he backed her against the kitchen island.

"I need to put the cake in the fridge to cool," she huskily told him.

"You know that's not the dessert I want, sugar," he said as he pressed against her, making sure she had no doubt how turned on he was.

"Oh," she replied barely above a whisper. "It's really good."

Her gaze was looking right at his lips again and when her tongue came out and ran across her bottom lip, he knew he had to taste her. But he couldn't lose control. This night was about her—and her alone.

"Let me show you exactly how I like my dessert," he said before dipping his finger in the melted chocolate and swiping it across her lips. She stuck out her tongue to lap it off, but he shook his head. "Allow me."

Though he wanted to ravish her, he slowly leaned forward and ran his tongue along the outline of her mouth, lapping up the chocolate that was bitter compared to her sweetness.

She shuddered in his arms and he had to remind himself not to lose control. With just a touch of the chocolate left, he clasped his lips onto hers and dove inside her mouth, exploring, savoring, enjoying every moment they were connected.

The sigh escaping her sweet lips fed his soul, and he wrapped his arms around her so he could lift her to the counter, his chest pressing against hers, his hips pushing inward. He rested his hardness against her hot core.

Too many clothes were between them.

But that was good. If he lost control, she might never trust him or any other man again. He couldn't do that to her—wouldn't—even if it nearly killed him.

"I'm going to show you what trust is all about, Lins. I'm going to give you pleasure without taking any for myself," he whispered as he moved his lips along her jaw and brushed them across her ear.

"Wh . . . what do you mean?" she panted.

"Your voice undoes me, sugar. I want you so bad," he sighed before sucking on her neck and inhaling her sweet, sweet scent. He paused for a moment as he pulled strength from deep inside. "I'm going to please you, sug, and then I'm going to leave so you can think about it over and over again, and you can want me. When you're ready, we can both be pleased, but for now, all of this is for you."

She said nothing, but her breathing deepened as he continued sucking on her neck. He took his time, not wanting to startle her as he took off her apron and tossed it aside. He slowly undid the buttons on her blouse. Moving back to her lips, he drank from them as the last buttons were freed.

Her skin was as silky smooth as he remembered it. He ran his fingers up her quivering stomach and over the lace of her bra before reaching her shoulders and pushing the shirt down off her back.

"Mav, I want you . . ." The tremble in her voice told him she was nervous. He needed her not to be.

"I won't hurt you, sug. I promise I won't hurt you," he whispered before gently kissing her. He took her shirt off her arms and pushed it away. "Remember how good it is between us. Remember that I only want to bring you pleasure."

His hands moved up and down her back as he hungrily sipped from her lips, relearning every secret hideaway of her mouth. Only when she was squirming against him again did he undo the clasp of her bra and pull it away, sending it flying off onto the kitchen floor.

She groaned into his mouth when he brought one hand around and cupped her tender breast, the nipple hard and responsive as his palm ran across it.

"Oh, Mav, don't stop . . ." The trembling hunger in her voice pushed him, made him want to strip them both down and finish what he'd started. He had to remember this was about her, no matter how difficult that was going to be.

Breaking his lips away from hers, he slowly leaned down and kissed a path to the breast he was holding. Beautiful, so absolutely beautiful. He cupped the other one and then took a moment to savor the beauty of her full breasts spilling from his fingers as her hard cherry nipples begged for him to taste them.

Leaning forward, he did exactly that, taking one perfect bud into his mouth and sucking it deep, making her buck against him as a cry of pleasure escaped her. Her fingers wound through his hair and he felt the gentlest of tugs as she held him against her.

He took his time moving from one luscious nipple to the next until she was more than ready for him to make her come. Kissing his way back up her body, he looked into her half-closed eyelids and ran his fingers across her cheek.

"Trust me not to hurt you, Lins. Tonight is only pleasure," he said before kissing the corner of her mouth.

She might have nodded, but he wasn't sure she was even fully aware in her excitement. He knew how pleased she was feeling. But he wanted—needed her to know that this was only about her.

Lifting her up, he carried her into the bedroom and gently laid her on the bed, the spill of her hair on the pillow too gorgeous not to take in for a few breathtaking moments. Then he joined her and began undoing the clasp of her pants. That's when she stiffened.

"The lights!" she cried out.

"I want to see you, sugar," he said as he undid the zipper.

"No! Please, turn out the lights. I have scars . . ." She trailed off and he knew this was a battle for another time.

"Sugar, everything about you is beautiful, absolutely stunning. But I can look at you later. For now, I'll just memorize your body with my fingers," he said.

Not wanting to take too much time, he jumped up and shut off the lights, then quickly rejoined her on the bed.

She sighed as he pulled her into his arms and kissed her again while his fingers pinched and teased her nipples. When she was wiggling beneath him, panting, he moved down the bed and finished removing her pants and panties in one quick motion.

How he wanted to see her, but it wasn't about him, it was about her.

Kissing the smooth skin of her stomach, he took his time, making his way to the sweet center of her. Spreading her thighs, he rested between them before he finally found her core.

Her sweet scent caused his head to spin as he laid a gentle kiss against her smooth folds. Her body jerked off the bed as his tongue ran up and down, lapping her juices and sucking on her tender bud.

"Mmm, you are perfection," he growled, barely able to maintain his control.

Spreading her wide open, he devoured her. The cries escaping her as she thrashed against the bed only made him go faster as he pushed his tongue deeper inside her. When he fastened onto her swollen flesh and thrust two fingers inside her, she cried out as she began shaking and clenching at the same time.

He slowed his tongue as he lapped at her until the final throes of pleasure faded and she sank onto the bed, breathing heavily. Only then did he crawl back up her body and pull her against him, rubbing the back of her head while she shook in his arms.

"Maverick . . ."

"Shh. It's okay, sug." He kissed her forehead and held her. His body was on fire, but he didn't care. All he cared about at this moment was *her* happiness, *her* trust, and *her* pleasure.

"But . . . don't you want to . . . you know?" The frightened timbre in her voice told him he was doing the right thing by waiting.

"More than you can imagine, sugar. I hurt," he said as he gently took her hand and placed it over his pants where his pulsing erection was practically ripping the material open.

"You can," she whispered as she squeezed him the tiniest bit. He might just do it right in his pants if she moved her fingers the slightest bit more.

He took her hand away. "No. I made a promise to you tonight. I wanted to give this to you."

"But it's wrong," she said.

He pulled back and twisted over so he could turn on her bedside lamp. She screeched a bit and grabbed the blanket, pulling it over her. He didn't try to stop her, but he wanted her to see his face as he spoke.

"It is never okay for a person to owe sex to another. People make love because they need each other, they can't breathe without the other person—without being buried deep inside them. You don't owe me sex, just like I wouldn't owe you if I didn't want to give it. I wanted to give you, and *only* you, pleasure tonight. And knowing that I did is better than any orgasm."

Her eyes widened as she looked at him, but he saw the appreciation in her eyes. Though he was certainly going to pay for his altruism, it was well worth it to see trust coming back to her.

He kissed her and then stood.

"What about dessert?" she asked as he moved toward the door.

She sat up with the blanket clutched tightly to her. He looked at her as if he could see through the thing. He almost could. He licked his lips as he smiled at her.

"Oh, baby, I had dessert." Her cheeks flushed.

"Can . . . can you hold me?"

The trust and vulnerability in her eyes shook him to the core. Without hesitation, he moved back to her and climbed on top of the covers. He felt a strange stinging sensation against his own eyes when she curled against him, her delicate fingers resting on top of the blankets where his heart thundered.

"Thank you, Mav," she told him, her voice growing sleepy as she snuggled safely against his side.

"Anytime, sug," he whispered as his fingers wound in her silky hair.

Lying there caressing her, Mav focused on her breathing. He didn't move so much as a muscle over the next hour as she drifted off to sleep. He didn't want to move, didn't want this moment to end, but his body was still pulsing and she hadn't invited him to stay the night.

If he fell asleep and she woke next to him, he might betray that fragile thread of trust he'd built within her. He wasn't willing to bet their relationship on it.

When he was sure he wouldn't disturb her, he untangled himself from her arms and stood up, gazing down at her delicate face as she frowned in her sleep, her hand reaching out toward him—or at least that's what he chose to believe she was doing.

She needed him, especially when she let down her guard. They needed each other. He couldn't stay any longer or he might not find the will to leave.

With hesitation, he walked from the room and straight out her front door, making sure it was securely locked behind him. He had his shirt and pants off by the time he reached the beach. He left them on the sand and didn't stop running until he was diving into the freezing cold water. It took a good ten minutes in the Pacific before his hardness began going away. Mav had a feeling it wasn't going to end even after he took her again.

He was that infatuated with the woman.

The obsession with her would pass when their time together ended, he assured himself as he climbed from the water, his skin covered in goose bumps. But as he walked past her place to his truck, just the thought of her lying naked in her bed had him sweating and hard all over again.

This might not pass so easily after all. She might just be the one woman in the world he refused to ever let go.

CHAPTER TWENTY

Lindsey woke up with Princess's cold nose in her face telling her it was time to get up and take her outside. She'd woken up to find her bed empty and then she'd wanted Princess—needed the dog. Even after the incredible pleasure Mav had shown her, she still hadn't been able to sleep without either him or the puppy there.

She'd grown attached to her dog in only a few days' time, so much so that she couldn't even sleep without her now. As soon as she'd called the house, Stormy had walked outside with Princess, who'd run straight to Lindsey.

Lindsey had brought her inside and the two had fallen into a dead sleep. Now it was time to get up. After taking Princess out and feeding her, Lindsey showered and got dressed, all the while waiting for embarrassment to hit, or fear.

She'd nearly made love to Maverick the night before. A few weeks ago she had thought she would never let a man touch her again. Then she was crying out in pleasure as Mav had worshiped her with his tongue and hands.

But as she made breakfast, feeling ravenously hungry, the guilt and fear never came. All she felt was sweet satisfaction. Was it because she had nothing to fear with Maverick? Was it because she was selfish? He'd walked away, getting nothing from the experience, while she'd had the best sexual encounter of her life, or one of the best. Her time with him at Stormy's wedding had been just as earth shattering.

It was all so confusing.

When his call came during the middle of her musings, a grin spread across her lips as she looked at the caller ID. There was no hesitation in answering.

"Good morning, sug. How did you sleep?"

The soft growl of his voice was a perfect way to start her day, but Lindsey didn't want to get too attached to it. She knew this was temporary. What she hoped was that the reprieve she was feeling while she was with him would last long after he was gone.

"I slept pretty dang well, actually. You?" she replied.

"My dreams were filled with you so I would say that's a good night."

"You flirt more than any other man I've ever known," she said with a chuckle.

He growled into the phone, which seemed strange.

"Don't even think of what other men have done with you while we're talking," he told her, a teasing edge to his tone. The tiny hint of seriousness scared her. She had to be imagining that, or wanting it to be the case.

A jealous man was a man who wanted a woman all to himself. Maverick obviously wasn't a one-woman kind of man. But it sure would be amazing if he were hers, even if only for a few weeks. She wouldn't ask him if he was, though. That would break this spell they were under.

"What are your plans today?" he asked when she was quiet for several seconds. His voice was immediately back to relaxed.

"I'm not sure yet. My mom has left five messages in two days, so I'm thinking I should probably call her back," she told him.

"Yes, family is very important," he said with a sigh.

"What's the sigh all about?"

"I just heard some stuff about my brother the other night, and it's been bothering me. I miss the little punk," he told her.

"I don't know a whole lot about Ace, just the few things Stormy has told me."

"Yeah, I've been trying to talk to him for a while now. He's not even in the country at the moment. I know if he would just sit down with all of us, he would see that things aren't as bad as he's made them out to be," Mav said with a deep sigh.

"Aren't you some fancy military guy? Can't you hunt him down?"

He laughed that beautiful sound she enjoyed so much. "The government tends to frown upon its soldiers using special ops equipment for personal business."

"Oh, I didn't think of that," she said, a bit embarrassed.

"It's okay, I *have* done that actually, and my guys have helped me from time to time," he admitted.

"Will you get into trouble?" She leaned back, her legs curled beneath her as she enjoyed the sound of his voice while she sipped coffee on the front porch.

"Family is worth getting into trouble over. I'd do anything if it meant bringing Ace home," he said.

"Now I *have* to call my mom. Here I have all this family wanting nothing more than to spend a few hours with me and I've been avoiding them, and you are out doing all you can to find a lost brother."

"I think spending the day with your family sounds like an excellent idea. But make sure you think of me no matter what you do. I'll miss you today."

Oh, the sound of him saying that sent shivers down her spine.

"It's going to hurt your reputation of being a maverick if you're too sweet," she said with a laugh.

He was quiet for a moment. Only the sound of his breathing could be heard through the phone line. She wondered if she'd offended him with her little joke.

"We all have to grow up some time," he told her. She couldn't tell from his voice what he was thinking or feeling.

"I used to always want to grow up, and then I hit twenty-one and I was afraid of getting too old. Now, I would do anything just to feel, I don't know, normal," she told him.

"I don't think it's a matter of feeling good or bad, happy or sad, young or old. I think it's about living in the moment. It's too incomprehensible for any of us to think what might be ten years down the road. Time is fleeting. If we live in fear or always do what the world expects of us instead of what we expect of ourselves, then one day we will wake up completely unhappy and alone, no matter how many people are around us."

His words struck something deep within her that she didn't want to focus on too much. He was right, though. If she even attempted to look too long into the future, her head would spin, and thinking about the past was unacceptable right now. She was far happier living in the moment—especially when Maverick lived with her in the now.

"Thanks for calling me, Mav," she said, feeling a little mushy.

"Always a pleasure, sug," he sighed, making her belly quiver.

As she hung up the phone she knew she was in pretty dang deep. But she'd been living in fear for a while now, and she refused to continue to do so. For now, at least, she felt happier being with Maverick.

If it all ended up crashing around her, then she would deal with that later. For now, she had something to do that was far scarier than unpredictable men—she had to call her mother.

Deciding she needed another cup of coffee first, she got nice and comfortable before dialing her up. This was going to be a long conversation.

CHAPTER
TWENTY-ONE

Fund-raising events weren't easy. Not easy at all. It really didn't help trying to organize something when Lindsey was doing it with a man she couldn't stop thinking about in all the wrong ways.

Well, she wouldn't necessarily say the wrong ways, but in inappropriate ways when they were trying to put on an event to help people. How could she go from being afraid of people touching her to not wanting to keep her hands off one certain man?

Confusion. She was filled with utter confusion.

And now she was with Maverick—finally alone again and she couldn't get her mind out of the gutter. She wanted more of what they'd done a few nights ago. It had been only three days since he'd made her come undone.

And now, being in his truck with him was absolute torture. Lindsey had always noticed his scent before. It was musky and raw and all man. It made her stomach do strange little flips. But after their night together, all her senses seemed to be heightened. She wanted him morning, noon, and night, and the feeling wasn't going away any time soon.

She hadn't been feeling sorry for herself the last few days. Yes, she was still sleeping with a light on, and yes, she was still making sure her door and windows were locked before going to sleep. But she wasn't afraid all the time. She'd even gone to lunch with Stormy the day before. And she wasn't flinching when she needed to shake someone's hand. She was realizing that she was in control of her emotions. She was realizing that what had happened to her was a freak thing. The world wasn't out to get her.

Maybe it truly was just being with Maverick that made her feel safer. If that was the case, she was going to be in for a world of trouble when he was no longer around. That was something she couldn't think about right now.

"We're here."

She looked through the window at the crowded parking lot. She'd been so lost in thought, she hadn't even realized the truck had stopped.

"Where's here?" she asked.

"Evergreen Speedway."

"I haven't been here before."

"Then this will truly be a pleasure. We're going to watch a race. Nothing will get your heart pounding like a good car race," he assured her.

"Sounds interesting."

She waited for him to come and open her door, and then they walked into the stands. "That's why we met with your friend Bob today?" she questioned.

"Yes, he's a big sponsor. Several of the racers do a lot for the organization."

"I can see why you like fund-raising. There are a lot of perks," she told him.

"I don't do it for the perks," he said, his face serious. "But I do love to enjoy life. I don't see a reason not to. I make sure I live each day to the fullest. I try to show that to the people the organization helps, no matter what events I attend. I bring a lot of returning soldiers to these events too."

"You are just a sucker for us broken people, aren't you?" she said, trying to make a joke, but it fell flat.

"You're anything but broken, sug. I'm bringing you out to places I love because I want to spend time with you," he emphasized.

"I want to spend time with you too." It was the first time she'd admitted it. His eyes lit up, and she was glad she'd told him.

"You know, you could get just about anything you wanted out of me," he told her. He was smiling, but the serious light she saw in his eyes scared her a little. She wanted to feel empowered again, but not at his expense.

"How about we don't try to take anything from the other?" she said with a laugh she hoped eased the more serious tone of their conversation.

He was quiet for a minute and then the sparkle returned to his eyes.

"Deal," he said before they started walking again. She was grateful when he began speaking on lighter topics. "I like to watch the races on the big screen, but really there's nothing more exciting than sitting in the grandstand and getting a taste of all the excitement."

They got inside and took their seats, and Maverick quickly flagged down the vendor for hot dogs and beer.

"I have to admit, I've never watched a single race," she told him.

"You've missed out then. I love being the one to pop . . ." He stopped and gave her a wolfish grin. "I mean, I'm glad you're here for the first time with me. You might just become an addict after this."

Though she didn't even know why, her cheeks flushed as she looked at him. Finally, she focused instead on the track, where last-minute preparations were being taken care of before the race started.

"Who are we rooting for?" she asked, wondering how it would be possible to pick out certain cars in the huge lineup.

"Well, there are some great drivers out there for sure. I'm a fan of the Rodney Childers team, and they've been doing great, finishing first and second in the last several races. But I do sponsor a car. I'm not going to tell you which one yet, just to see if you become a fan anyway," he said with a laugh.

"That's not fair. What if I hate your car and boo it?" she said as she took a bite of her juicy hot dog.

"Then I will have to find a suitable punishment for you," he told her with a gleam in his eyes.

The hot dog was forgotten when he captured her in his gaze. He might have been talking about punishment, but his expression promised satisfaction. She might just have to boo for every single car out there on the track.

When the race started, though, it was difficult to talk. Restarts happened, and Maverick tried explaining to her about repositioning and how the game could change easily since there were so many laps taken.

When Jeff Gordon and David Ragan easily maneuvered themselves around other cars toward the front of the pack, the entire stand was on its feet, including Lindsey, who didn't even know any of the players.

"People sure seem to get excited when that number twenty-four car passes," Lindsey said.

"Yep, that's Jeff Gordon. He's a legend. He's won so many awards, it would take an hour to name them, but he's going to be broadcasting now. The fans hate to lose him on the track, so they are showing their love."

"I guess it's sort of dangerous, not something people would do forever," she said as the race finished and the fans went crazy.

She didn't even know who'd won. But the stands had certainly been filled to capacity and the crowd was energetic. Even with the cars no longer speeding past them in unbelievable maneuvers, Lindsey was fascinated by it all.

"Want to meet the winner?" Mav asked, pulling her out of her daze.

"Can we do that?" she asked, then shook her head. "Never mind. Of course *you* can," she added with a laugh.

"Yeah, I sponsor number nineteen," he said with a chuckle. She hadn't booed that car once, thankfully. Though that meant she wouldn't be getting her punishment. Darn.

"I'd be surprised if that *hadn't* been your car," she told him with a grin.

Trophies were given and pictures taken, and then it was time for the winner—number nineteen—to take his victory lap.

"Ready, Mav?" the man asked.

"Yep, I've got her helmet," he said with a grin.

When Lindsey realized what they were saying, her face went a little green as she looked back and forth between the grinning men.

"You think I'm getting into that thing?" she gasped.

"You haven't lived 'til you've gone two hundred miles per hour," Jet said with a laugh.

"How old are you?" she exclaimed. "You don't even look old enough to have a driver's license, let alone to be traveling at such high speeds." That made the guy throw back his head with laughter.

"I'm twenty-five, Lindsey, but if it makes you feel any better, my dad had a mini-track for me and my first racecar when I was five years old. Granted, the thing only went five miles per hour at the time, but she could corner like nobody's business," Jet said with a chuckle.

"Okay, but if something happens to me, then I'm haunting you both," she warned.

But when she was strapped into the car, securely in place with the motor revving, she felt a rush of adrenaline flow through her.

"You ready?" he asked, his grin almost as mesmerizing as Maverick's.

"I guess it's now or never," she said with a nervous giggle.

And then they were off. The tires squealed as the engine purred. They were flying around the track. But he didn't stop at just one lap.

He took her around several more times before skidding to a stop where Maverick was waiting for them, a big grin on his face.

What she didn't realize until the helmet was off and Maverick was scooping her up into his arms was that she was grinning madly too.

"That was the biggest thrill I think I've ever had," she said, completely out of breath.

"I knew you'd love it," he said before leaning down and kissing her.

"Hey. I'm the one who gave the thrill. Don't I get a little kiss too?" Jet said, interrupting them.

Without even thinking about it, Lindsey let go of Maverick and gave Jet a hug, then kissed him on the cheek.

"Thanks, darling. It was fun," Jet said before he was bombarded by media people.

Once he turned away, her smile fell as her eyes rounded in shock at what she'd done. She'd initiated touch with a stranger—and not just any stranger—a man.

She looked at Maverick, who looked very proud—and slightly jealous.

"Am I going to have to kick his ass?" Mav asked with a crooked grin.

"I . . . I can't believe I did that," she gasped.

He wrapped his arm around her and began walking her out to the parking lot.

"It's the adrenaline. I still get it when I fly. There's a thrill that's indescribable when you are speeding like that," he told her.

"But . . ." She stopped. She didn't know what to say or how to explain it.

"You're learning to touch again. You're learning it doesn't hurt, but that it's actually necessary," he said before leaning down and kissing her on the cheek.

He was right. Everything he was doing for her was helping. She hated how absolutely right he was. The man was a freaking magician.

"Thank you for another remarkable day, Mav. Truly, it was indescribable," she said.

"It was my utmost pleasure," he told her as they reached his truck.

When a wicked smile appeared on her lips, she could see she had begun making *him* nervous. She spoke.

"Okay, now I'm going to ask you to do something *truly* dangerous," she said.

"Is there something more dangerous than driving or flying fast?" he asked with a laugh.

"My parents are having dinner tomorrow. Want to accompany me?"

Her stomach was tied in knots as she waited. It was so intimate to ask him to her parents'. She kind of wanted to take it back now that it was on the table. But she didn't know how she would manage to do that.

He grinned as he looked at her. "I'd love to. And trust me, that's not dangerous at all."

"Believe me, after an evening with my family, you might be rethinking that," she said with a laugh.

She laughed even more when he got just a touch of worry in his eyes. Oh yeah, meeting her family was going to be quite the entertainment. Especially since she'd never brought a man home before.

Maybe she hadn't really thought this out after all. Her family was going to be giving both of them the third degree all night.

CHAPTER
TWENTY-TWO

It was so odd to be at work and have her mind other places. For years, Lindsey would look forward to her shifts at the hospital, and now what she looked forward to was spending time with Maverick.

Yes, she knew that work was never going to be the same again after the attack, but she should still get satisfaction out of her job. She wanted to get that feeling back. She'd spent too many years in school to ever let one event, no matter how awful, stop her from doing what she'd wanted to do from the very first time she'd slapped a bandage on one of her brothers and declared him healed.

But she had only a couple of more semesters of school left and then she would be a nurse practitioner. Maybe she just needed a new scene. It had been her stubbornness that had brought her back to the hospital where she'd been attacked. She wasn't letting those men beat her.

She'd proven she could come back. She didn't need to keep tormenting herself. It was hard working at this hospital, and even harder when it was slow. But she wouldn't dare voice that thought aloud, because she would be tempting fate, and in a hospital, you never wished for more activity. When you did that, emergency calls tended to pile up, and that wasn't fun either.

Lindsey was startled out of her thoughts by the radio.

EMS please respond to 45893 Main Ave. Seventy-year-old female, cut on hand.

Betty turned to Lindsey and smiled before she laughed. Lindsey let out a long-suffering sigh. They all knew that address well. They also knew Lucy must be sitting at home feeling lonely.

"I guarantee you she scratched herself so she could get the ambulance there," Betty said with a laugh.

"Yep. None of us are going to take that bet," Lindsey told her as the new nurse on staff began walking up to them.

"Oh, I bet I can get Suzanne to take the bet," Betty said wickedly.

"That so wouldn't be fair," Lindsey said with a scowl. "Quit hazing the new girl."

Betty grumbled, but she did it in good humor.

Dr. Beel walked up as they were talking and heard who was coming in. He scowled.

"She had better have a finger hanging on by the skin," he grumbled. He wasn't feeling too good and obviously wanted to go lie down. He knew Lucy came in for attention, and not the medical sort.

"I think she has a crush on you," Lindsey told him with a smile.

He grumbled before moving toward the ER.

It took only about ten minutes before the ambulance was pulling into the bay. Lindsey waited by the back door, a shiver rushing through her when it opened and the cold wind blew in.

Her favorite medics strolled inside with Lucy on the gurney, a grin on her face as she chatted with the young guys. They didn't seem put out in the least. They got a kick out of the woman they called *their favorite patient.*

Of course she was their favorite. She'd been in the hospital more times than most of the nursing staff. She had come in for everything: complaints of chest pain (which ended up being her skin rubbed a bit too raw from a too-tight bra), a broken leg, arm, and hand, which had all been fully intact. She'd come in for burns that had really been scratches, and for fevers when her temperature was normal.

The first half-dozen calls, the paramedics had tried to assure her she was fine, telling her she didn't need to come in. But she would always tell them it was an emergency, that she would die if they left her.

They couldn't refuse to transport her. Lindsey wondered when her insurance was going to cancel her. They'd even given her a psych evaluation, but she'd loved that. There was nothing physically or mentally wrong with Lucy. She was just lonely.

"Hello, Lindsey dear. I'm so glad you're here. How are you doing?" Lucy said with a smile more vibrant than most seventy-year-old women had.

"I'm fine, Lucy. The question is, how are you feeling?" Lindsey asked as the paramedics got her moved from the stretcher to a bed.

The team hooked her up to a cardiac monitor, checked her blood pressure, which was fine, and all her vitals. She was healthier than most twenty-year-olds.

"I got this cut on my hand, and I don't want it to get infected," she said, trying to make her voice sound feebler. It wasn't fooling any of them.

Dr. Beel examined Lucy, asked her the standard questions, and put notations in her ever-expanding file. When he tried to find out what had happened with her bandaged hand, she refused to let them look at it. He blew out a frustrated breath and gave her his sternest look.

"I need to know what's going on, Lucy, or we can't help you," he told her.

She nervously shifted on the bed as she gripped her fingers together. She looked at each staff member before looking back down at her hands.

"Well . . ." She paused as her eyes filled with tears. Lindsey pulled out a tissue and handed it to her. "I . . . um . . ."

"Come on, Lucy. Spit it out."

Dr. Beel normally had more patience. It looked as if that weren't the case on this shift. There was nothing crankier than a sick doctor with a patient wasting his time.

"I just wanted to be with my family today," she said as a tear dripped down her cheek.

"Where's your family?" Lindsey asked, feeling terrible for the woman.

"Well, I think of you guys as my family," she said. Then the tears dried up, and Lindsey knew the woman was putting on the show of her life.

"What is it really?" Dr. Beel snapped, clearly not falling for her tricks.

"Well, I'm ticked off, that's what it is," she said, her expression turning sour. "I applied for a loan today and was denied. Who in the heck denies someone like me a loan when I want it?"

Lindsey and the rest of the staff were silent as they processed what Lucy had just said. It made no sense.

"What are you trying to buy?" Lindsey finally asked.

"A zoo," she said with the utmost seriousness.

Dr. Beel threw his hands into the air and stomped from the room. He'd had enough. He wasn't even going to pretend to try to humor the patient. Lindsey was bored enough that this was the most entertained she'd been all day.

"A zoo?" she questioned Lucy.

"Yes, there's a zoo in South Carolina where they are going to kill all the animals because they said it's not getting enough people. I want to buy the zoo and move there so I can take care of those poor defenseless creatures."

Lindsey had no idea what to say.

Suddenly, Dr. Beel popped back into the room, pulling his wallet out of his back pocket, and taking out a hundred-dollar bill. He set it into Lucy's wrinkled fingers and actually grinned.

"I think that's a fantastic idea, Lucy. I'm starting a collection for you right now."

Lindsey stared at him in confusion, and then at the rest of the staff members as they all reached into their pockets and pulled out cash.

"Let's buy this woman a zoo that moves her far away."

When Lindsey realized what was going on, she was horrified. Lucy had no idea that they were all mocking her, or celebrating the possibility of her leaving.

"Horrible," Lindsey choked out. "You are all horrible."

She turned and walked from the room. She prayed that she would never get so cynical in her job that she would mock a little old woman. Sure, that woman was a lot slyer than the average person, but it all boiled down to the fact that she was lonely and wanted to come to a place that made her feel safe.

Lindsey could empathize with that. She went in and checked on Lucy several times during the rest of her shift. She was now complaining of heart pains so the staff couldn't make her leave.

Good. They could deal with that after their awful behavior.

Maybe she related so well to Lucy because she was afraid she would end up like her—alone and in need of companionship. Maybe it was because she generally liked the woman.

Whatever it was, she decided she wasn't going to keep pushing people away. She wanted friends and family surrounding her when she was seventy. She did not want to be alone at all. Lindsey was grateful she was going home for a visit.

Suddenly she missed her mom and dad something fierce. She even missed her very over-protective brothers. Lindsey just hoped Maverick wasn't scared off by the lot of them.

CHAPTER TWENTY-THREE

Maverick's nerves were slightly wound up as they turned off the road and shot down the long, tree-lined driveway. He'd never actually met a girl's parents before. Of course, he wasn't *meeting* them, meeting them. He was just going to dinner with a friend.

As he had that thought, his mind immediately went to Lindsey's bedroom a few nights ago and how she'd moaned as his mouth was devouring her. Yeah. She was a bit more than a friend.

Even if she were more right now, though, it wasn't something that either of them wanted to last past a few weeks, a month tops. He had to get back to work soon—his arm was already much better. And Lins, well, she was doing great and soon wouldn't even need him. He'd already seen an amazing transformation in her.

She'd been afraid for a long time but that was because no one had shown her she had nothing to truly fear. There were bad people in the world, but if a person chose to live his or her life in fear, then those monsters were the ones who won.

He had seen too many bad men during his time in the Air Force. He didn't want to give them any more victories than they already had. And Lindsey was too good a woman to let anyone hold her down.

"We're here. Are you ready?" she asked as he pulled up to the huge ranch-style home and parked his truck.

"As ready as I'll ever be," he said with a grin.

He was Air Force. He didn't fear anything, except maybe parents—okay, okay, and rats. They were creepy little beady-eyed things. No one knew that, though, not even his brothers. Luckily he lived in a place where you didn't see too many rats unless you went to a pet store. Anyone who chose to own one as a so-called pet had to have a screw loose.

"No one is ever ready for the chaos of my family."

She opened the door, and he put his arm out to stop her. "What are you doing?" Looking confused, she waited. "A gentleman always gets the door for a lady," he finished.

The confusion went away. In its place, a beaming smile took away any shadows of fear about the upcoming visit. He wanted to haul her over the center console and kiss her breathless. Knowing she had five brothers who were probably waiting on the other side of that door stopped him—but just barely.

"You make me want to do dangerous things, sugar," he whispered as he leaned across the console and gave her a quick kiss, unable to help himself.

She blushed before looking down. "I don't know what you mean," she mumbled.

He chuckled as he jumped down from the truck and ran over to her side, wrapping his hands around her waist and pulling her from her seat, the two of them partially blocked from the house by his open truck door.

"You know exactly what I mean," he corrected her. Then he leaned in and gave her a far-too-short kiss. Her taste lingered on his lips as he pulled back, and the glow in her cheeks had him wanting to haul her off to bed.

"I better get you inside before I do something foolish and end up getting myself shot," he said before taking her hand and moving away from the truck.

The second they hit the bottom step of her parents' massive porch, the front door opened, confirming his suspicions that they had an audience. Seven people piled out of the house. Lins hadn't told him how large her brothers were. It wasn't that Maverick was afraid. Hell, he was about the same size as them. But he sure as hell was outnumbered at the moment.

"You're late," one of the men said with a scowl aimed at Maverick.

Mav didn't break the eye contact, but he nodded at the man. The message was well received. The guy was telling him he'd better not be screwing with his sister. Mav could respect that.

"We are not, grumpy," Lindsey said.

But it was odd because as they drew closer to her family, Lindsey scooted just a tad bit tighter to his side. What was going on with that? She wasn't afraid of them, was she?

Maverick checked out the group with a bit of a wary eye. She'd never said anything about abuse. Matter of fact, when she spoke of them, she only said good things. Sure, she said they were overwhelming, but she said it with love.

"I'm so glad you're here, baby girl. It's been a while," the woman who was obviously her mother said. She stepped closer, and Lindsey's hand tightened in his for a moment before she released him and moved over to her mother, giving the woman a hug.

Mav saw the surprised elation in the other woman's eyes, and it nearly broke his heart. How long had it been since Lindsey had allowed her family to show her affection? He didn't want to think about it.

She kissed her father on the cheek, and then she moved right back over to Mav's side, her hand finding his. He squeezed her fingers, but he didn't fail to notice the suspicious look her brothers were sending his way.

"Thank you for having me over for dinner, Mrs. Helm. I truly appreciate it," Mav said to break the tension.

"I'm glad you're here, Maverick. Lindsey told me all about you the other day on the phone and of the fun adventures the two of you are having. I will have to correct you, though, because I don't like being called Mrs. Helm. You just call me Ma or Leila. Your choice. All the kids' friends have always called me Ma 'cause I think I fed an army while they were growing up."

Maverick instantly liked the woman. His manners wouldn't allow him to call her by her first name, though, and he was a bit too uncomfortable to call her Ma, so he just tilted his imaginary hat at her and didn't call her anything.

"I'm Darren, this clan's dad. It's a pleasure to have you over, son. This here is Brett, Kellan, Dante, Erik, and Seth in order of ages," the man said as he pointed to each of the boys, all of whom were looking at Maverick with suspicion despite Lindsey remaining plastered to his side.

"Why don't we go inside and get something to drink?" Leila said. Maverick was grateful for the invitation. Standing on the large porch being eyeballed wasn't exactly the most comfortable thing, though he was sure it wasn't going to get much better inside.

Then again, it was rare for Mav to ever meet someone he couldn't get along with. Lindsey's family was just being protective of her. As soon as they figured out he meant her no harm, they'd be his new best friends, he was sure.

"Want a beer or something harder?" her father asked as they made their way into a large family room with ample seating and a burning fireplace.

"A beer would be great," Mav told him. "I rarely break into the whiskey."

"I like a good bourbon myself, but I usually only have one on Friday nights these days. The wife doesn't like too much drinking."

"No I don't," she said with a smile. She sat down next to her husband after getting him and Mav a beer.

"I do have some excellent cigars if you're up for one after dinner," Darren said. Mav wasn't sure if this was a test or not. "A man who didn't appreciate a good cigar just wasn't trustworthy" was something his own father used to say.

"That sounds like a pretty dang good dessert to me, sir," Mav told him.

And just like that, most of the tension left the room. Lindsey stayed by his side for the first half hour, but eventually she got up and went somewhere with her mother. He was left alone with all the guys. He was sure they'd been waiting for just this moment.

Though Lindsey was back to showing physical affection with her mother, and a little bit with her father, he'd noticed she hadn't touched her brothers. Maybe it was just harder with guys. Why she was so much more open with him, he didn't understand.

It wasn't something he was going to question, though. He wanted her to feel comfortable with him. He wanted her to feel a lot with him, if he were honest.

"I've noticed Lindsey seems to be clinging an awful lot to you," her father said, pulling Maverick from his thoughts. The words weren't exactly spoken with malice, but there was a trace of suspicion in the protective father's voice.

"I care about Lindsey. I think she understands that . . ." He stopped. He wasn't sure what to say to her family about their touching—innocent and not so innocent.

"I'm glad to see she's trusting someone. I sure as hell hope you don't hurt her." Now *there* was the threat he'd been waiting for.

"She's not a plaything," her oldest brother, Brett said, but he'd toned down the alpha-male routine.

"I know that. I respect her. I've been through some of my own stuff during the war and I just want to . . . to help her," Mav told them as sincerely as he could.

"From what I've seen in the past hour, it appears you're doing just that. That makes you a pretty hell of a guy in my book," Darren said.

With the approval of their father, the five brothers relaxed. The final bit of tension that had been left in the room evaporated, thankfully.

"Dinner is ready," Leila called.

Maverick walked into the massive dining room with Darren and Lindsey's brothers. He took a seat next to Lindsey and the sweet smile she sent him made his heart race.

"What do you do for a living, Maverick?" Leila asked.

"I fly F-18s for the Air Force," he told her.

"Dang! That is cool," Lindsey's youngest brother Seth said from the other side of the table.

"I thought so, too, which was why I decided to make the military a career instead of a hobby," Maverick told him.

"I bet you've been to some great places," her next to oldest brother, Kellan, said as he wolfed down enough food for three.

"Yeah, I've been on tour twice. I pretty much stay at home base now teaching the new recruits. I'm lucky that I'm based near my family. I was away for several years when I first joined," Maverick told them. "I might be retiring soon."

"You're pretty young to retire," Brett told him. They had to be close to the same age.

"I've made some smart decisions in life. It might just be time to focus on other things."

Lindsey squeezed his hand. He watched her brothers look at each other. It was obvious they were trying to analyze him. Maverick wasn't going to bring up his wealth. It was no one's business, but he also could understand how her family wouldn't want her with a man not willing to take care of her.

"If you do stay in, do you plan on moving bases?" her dad asked. That was a loaded question if ever he'd heard one. Lindsey's father was fishing on how serious their relationship was and if Maverick was planning on taking her away.

"It's highly unlikely, sir," Maverick told him.

What he should probably say was there was a good chance he'd be shipped off at any minute. That way her family would discourage her from dating him and there wouldn't be a messy breakup at the end. He couldn't make himself say it, though. He couldn't say anything that would jeopardize his time with Lindsey.

The inquisition slowed down after that, and the rest of the evening was actually enjoyable. They finished the delicious home-cooked meal, laughed, had another drink with their cigars, and then reluctantly pulled themselves away.

They were both quiet as they made their way back to Lindsey's cottage. Maverick was worried about what their future together held, and he was sure Lindsey was thinking about her evening at home with her family. They were a bit overwhelming. But they were obviously loving as well.

Mav didn't want to hurt Lindsey, didn't want to hurt her family. He'd best figure out what in the hell he was doing and figure it out soon. If this was nothing more than a fling to him, then it would be best for him to walk away. But even having that thought nearly ripped him in two. He didn't know what to think or what to feel, so he sat there silently, focused instead on driving.

CHAPTER
TWENTY-FOUR

Rain started pouring down as Maverick and Lindsey drove on the freeway away from her parents' home. She hated to see the evening end, but she didn't hate being alone with Maverick again. She didn't even need conversation to feel comfortable with him. She just needed to be in his presence. She enjoyed their drive together as she sat back and listened to the sound of water splashing off the windows of Mav's truck.

"Want dessert?" he asked, and she immediately perked up.

"I wouldn't mind ice cream." She considered ice cream to be a meal, not a dessert. So many people didn't take ice cream seriously enough.

"My philosophy has always been that no matter how full a person is, there's always room for ice cream because it just melts anyway and slides around all the other food," Mav told her. Such insightfulness made her think he must be her soul mate.

"I would have to agree with that," she told him. "Of course, when you add the peanuts, hot fudge, and cherries, it becomes a little less liquefied."

"Nah. As long as it's touching the ice cream, it's all good."

They pulled up to a Dairy Queen. She got the Peanut Buster Parfait, while he got a chocolate-dipped cone so he could still drive.

Then he surprised her. Instead of turning toward her cottage, he drove up the mountain and pulled off to park. The rain had tapered off, so they had a view of the city with all its lights sparkling below them.

"I've never been up here before," she told him, enjoying the warmth of the truck and the coolness of her sweet treat.

"Over the years, I've come up here a lot with my brothers to go hiking and skiing. I like this spot because of the view."

"You've lived here your whole life then?"

"Yep. We took vacations pretty often, and I've been all over the world, but this has always been home," he told her. "Has it been for you?"

"Yeah. I grew up in that same house we had dinner in with my parents tonight. But after my oldest brother went into business and made a lot of money, he had the place remodeled to make it a lot bigger. My mother told him she didn't need all that space with the kids almost grown, but he told her she would have grandbabies someday and might want the extra rooms. Once he said that, she told him to make it even bigger. She wanted a house full of screaming kids on Christmas morning," Lindsey shared.

"My mom would probably like the same. Our home was strict, so there wasn't much screaming, but my brothers and I got into some loud fights once in a while. We'd get in trouble pretty quickly, though, so we learned to keep it outside as much as possible. Ace was the worst at that. He had a quick temper. I guess we all did, but he was the youngest so he'd get the blame most of the time," Mav told her.

"You sure miss him a lot, don't you?" she said as she finished her dessert and turned to look at him.

"Every single day. I know he'll come back, I just don't know if I'll recognize the man he's turned into."

Maverick said this with so much sadness she couldn't help but reach across the seat and pat his hand.

"I'm sure he's turning into a great man, Maverick. I've always heard that it takes guys a whole lot longer to mature than it does women. So by the time he comes home, he should be just as perfect as you are," she said before she could take the words back.

"You think I'm perfect, huh?" he said as he tugged on her hand.

She was both grateful for and a bit irritated by the divider between them. At the moment she was embarrassed, but oh how she wouldn't mind being in his arms.

"You're close to perfect. I'm sure there are a lot of flaws you've kept hidden from me, though," she told him with a nervous laugh.

"You can't take back something like that once you've already said it," he told her.

"Well, tell me more about yourself, and I'll be the judge on whether you fit the 'perfect' profile or not."

"I'm an open book. What do you want to know?"

So much! But a lot of the things she wanted to ask him were personal questions about his past relationships, and she wasn't going to go there. It wasn't her business how many women he'd dated, or if he was dating anyone else besides her right now.

Not once had he tried to deceive her or tell her that they were in a relationship. She just wasn't that dating-a-new-guy-every-week kind of girl. Before the attack, she had been busy a lot and didn't go out with too many men, but when she did, she normally was in a committed relationship. Having an undefined relationship status was all very new to her.

"Are you where you want to be in life?" she finally asked, knowing she had to say something.

"What do you mean?" he responded.

"I know you love your career, but back when you were in high school and pictured where you would be right now, is this even close to where you imagined yourself?"

His head tilted as if he were really thinking about the question.

"No. I was too selfish back then to picture anything beyond the moment. We had money, so I never thought twice about needing to make any of my own. I was arrogant, self-centered, and didn't really care about the next day, let alone ten or twenty years down the road."

That hadn't been at all what she was expecting.

"What about you, sug? Are you where you wanted to be?"

"Yes." She didn't even have to hesitate. "I wanted to be a nurse from the time I was very young. Then after doing it for a while, I wanted the challenge of being a nurse practitioner. Any one of my brothers would have paid for med school if I had wanted to be a doctor, but I love being a nurse. Don't get me wrong, I have total respect for doctors, but I wanted to be able to really spend time with patients in a way I'd never be able to as a doctor," she added.

"Yeah, I understand loving a tough job. Even if I sort of fell into the military, it's something that shaped me."

"How long will you be in?"

"Don't know," he said. Maybe he really was planning on leaving. Before she could ask, he continued. "My turn again to ask something about you." He paused as he looked at her in a way that had her a bit worried. Then he smiled. "Don't worry. I'm not going to delve too deeply."

"The grin doesn't inspire confidence," she told him.

"I thought my grin was my best feature," he countered.

"Oh no. Your eyes are your best feature, especially the way they sparkle with a touch of humor and a whole lot of heat," she said. Then she clamped her mouth closed.

Why was it that she often spouted exactly what was on her mind? It wasn't an endearing quality in her humble opinion.

"Heat, huh?" he said as his brows rose and he wiggled them.

"I just meant . . . um . . . that they are bright," she said, hating that her cheeks gave her away every time she was mortified.

"This is a good time for me to ask about your most embarrassing moment," he said with a laugh.

"Oh, that's so easy. Just about any time I'm with you and I open my mouth without letting my brain catch up," she said with a laugh.

"You can open your mouth around me anytime without letting your brain stop you," he told her as he tugged again on her hand. "I really need a new truck," he grumbled when she didn't fall into his lap.

"Saved by the console," she told him, though the atmosphere in the truck was a heck of a lot hotter now, with or without the heater running.

His eyes—those eyes she'd been talking about—took on a whole new level of heat as he gazed over at her. Just when she thought he was going to lean across the divider and kiss her, he smiled that beautiful smile that took her breath away.

"Saved for now," he said. "We'd better get back."

If his voice hadn't sounded so disappointed, she might have been worried. But they continued chatting as they came down the mountain and headed for home.

She learned about every pet he'd ever owned, his dream vacation spot, and the stupidest pranks he and his brothers had pulled. By the time they arrived at her cottage, her side hurt from laughing so much.

Again, though, he walked her to her door, and then barely brushed her lips before disappearing into the night. She was beginning to want to punch the man as much as she wanted to kiss him.

The anticipation of waiting for him to take her into his arms again was killing her. If he didn't do something about it soon, then . . . well, pretty much then nothing. She just wasn't brave enough to initiate. Not yet, at least.

CHAPTER TWENTY-FIVE

Another meeting down. The fund-raiser was shaping up nicely. Lindsey was also noticing that Maverick used the meetings as an excuse to then take her to outrageous places afterward. Their current spot was a place she never would have come to on her own.

The noise in the bar they were at was nearly deafening, but the sweet taste of Lindsey's drink was beginning to drown it out. It wasn't quite a dive bar, but close enough. She both liked it and was a little horrified.

Never would she have found herself alone in a place like this, but she knew she was safe with Maverick by her side. No one would dare approach her while the six-feet-plus giant of a man was near. He was just too dang intimidating for anyone to even think about coming too close.

Lindsey wondered why *she* wasn't afraid of him. He could easily subdue her. Maybe she felt secure because she knew there was no way he would do that. He wasn't that type of man.

"Are you ready for the real fun now?" Mav asked.

"What do you mean?"

"You didn't really think I brought you to this bar for drinks and fried food, did you?" he asked with a wicked smile that had her lifting her glass and taking another big chug. She had a feeling she was going to need the liquid courage.

Before she could ask him to explain, a man stood up on the stage and the crowd cheered. She looked at the man and then back at Maverick with suspicion.

"Are you all ready to karaoke?" the man called out. Lindsey's face drained of color.

"You can't possibly think I'm getting up on that stage and singing, can you?" she gasped.

His eyes were glowing.

"Trust me, it's a healing experience. When you learn not to care about what other people think and just live for the moment and for your own happiness, your worries will fade away. These are strangers, people you most likely will never see again, and they are all here to have a great time," he said as he tugged on her hand.

"No way, Mav. There's no way I'm going up there. Not even with the buzz I have," she threatened.

"Too late," he told her.

"We're going to start the evening off with a special duo. We've got Maverick and Sugar about to sing for you all," the man on stage called out, and the crowd cheered again.

"Sugar? You told him my name was Sugar?" she snapped as he pulled her closer to the stage.

"Every star needs a stage name," he said as they reached the steps.

"You don't have a stage name," she pointed out. He laughed.

"Baby, I'm already a star," he told her.

Lindsey was horrified. Within seconds, she found herself on the stage with at least fifty people staring up at her. A mic was placed in her hand.

"I have never sung karaoke before. I don't know how," she exclaimed.

"Don't worry, I picked the best song. You just follow the prompter," he said.

She wasn't going to do this. He couldn't make her, she decided. But then the crowd was staring at her, and the music began playing, and Lindsey knew she was going to make a fool out of herself either way. There were only two choices. She could either sing the song, which would be terrible with her tone-deaf vocals, or she could run off the stage in humiliation.

Her only solace was the fact that the patrons were most likely three sheets to the wind already. In their drunken bliss, they wouldn't pay her any attention. Plus, she was standing beside Maverick. Who in the world would look at her when he was there with a mic in his hand?

And then the words started, and he began to sing. She was rooted to the spot. Of course, the man had an incredible voice to go along with everything else that was absolutely perfect about him. But not only was it his voice, it was the lyrics.

She was a huge Johnny Cash fan, and he'd picked a fun song to sing. Lindsey actually found herself smiling as he sang the first verse of "Jackson."

"*. . . goin' to Jackson . . . I'm gonna mess around . . .*"

Without even thinking about the crowd below them in the crowded bar, Lindsey lifted the mic and began singing with a grin on her face.

"*. . . make a big fool of yourself . . .*"

The smile Maverick sent her way made her cheeks glow for a whole new reason. The song was flirty and fun and both of them got into it. She even found herself dancing with him as he talked of going to Jackson and messing around, and she countered.

"*. . . people gonna stoop and bow . . .*"

"*. . . hah!*" That was her favorite part of the song. She even chucked him beneath the chin and was rewarded by his brilliant smile.

The crowd went crazy and sang along with them to the old classic by the man in black. As the song wound down, Lindsey couldn't keep the grin from her lips.

There she was, on the stage with Maverick, grateful he had pushed her into doing something she hadn't wanted to do. He leaned down and kissed her briefly, which had the bar patrons cheering again, reminding her of where they were.

"That was a great song to start our night off. Next up is . . ."

The host continued speaking as Maverick led her offstage and back to their table in the corner of the bar. She sat, picked up her glass, and looked across at him.

"What are you doing to me, Maverick Armstrong?" she asked, not sure if she were asking this of herself or of him. She took a sip.

"I'm teaching you to enjoy the small stuff," he answered, drinking his beer.

"And what happens when it's finished?" She hadn't meant to ask that question. She knew what happened when she did. She wanted to take it back immediately, but his eyes fired up as her smile faded.

"Who says it's ending?" he said as he reached across their small table and grabbed her hand.

"Well, unless we're heading down to Jackson . . ." She tried to make it a joke, but for some reason the thought of him fading from her life was making her throat close.

"Are you proposing to me, Ms. Helm?" he asked, the sparkle back in his eyes, but something else was there too that both scared and excited her.

"No!" she said as she tugged against him.

"Hmm? I know I'm irresistible."

Her cheeks heated and she was grateful for the dim lighting surrounding them.

"Yes, you are pretty suave," she said, downing the rest of her drink. The waitress came up and asked them if they needed anything else.

Lindsey held her fingers up indicating she wanted two more. She had a feeling she was going to need them.

"It's a pilot thing," he told her when the waitress left.

"What's a pilot thing?" she asked.

"The attitude. Being able to do something most people can't makes you pretty dang confident," he told her with another wink.

"Hmm. I think it's a Maverick thing," she countered.

"Want to get out of here?" The hunger in his eyes was unmistakable. And her body responded to it instantly.

"I just ordered more drinks," she panted.

He leaned over to the table nearby, slapped a couple of hundred-dollar bills down, told them to enjoy the drinks, and then stood up and pulled her with him.

"The table next to us says thank you."

And with that, they were moving rapidly toward the parking lot.

Anticipation burned in Lindsey's stomach as he practically tossed her in the truck and ran around to the driver's side. Maybe tonight was going to be more than just foreplay.

CHAPTER
TWENTY-SIX

Maverick was punishing her. She was sure of it. That's why he'd gotten her body all revved up two nights ago and then had left her burning after a few hot kisses. He'd jumped into his truck and gone home. She'd wanted to make love to him, wanted to quench the fire he'd stoked.

But he said it wasn't time yet.

And just like that, he'd left her standing there, royally ticked off. Then to make matters worse, he hadn't called her the next day. If this was part of his mission, he was failing completely, because she didn't feel better. She felt frustrated.

"I have a good mind not to see that man ever again," she said through clenched teeth as Stormy sat on her couch nursing Aaron.

"You're awfully wound up over a guy you don't care about," Stormy pointed out.

"He's just so frustrating. He takes me on all these adventures, makes me laugh, really makes me burn, and then he just walks away like he's not affected in the least."

"Don't let him walk away," Stormy pointed out.

"He's just a tad bit bigger than me, Storm. It's not like I can stop him," Lindsey told her.

"Make him *unable* to walk away," Stormy told her.

Lindsey stopped and looked at her friend. "What do you mean?"

"Seduce him." Her friend said it so simply, as if that were the easiest thing in the world to accomplish.

"How am I supposed to do that? I haven't *ever* chased after a guy," Lindsey told her.

"I'm not exactly the best teacher on the subject," Stormy said with a laugh. "However, you have sex appeal oozing off you in giant waves. You've always been beautiful and confident. If you put your mind to it, you'll have Maverick lapping at your feet like a starving puppy."

"Hmm. Mav on his knees *is* sort of an appealing idea," Lindsey said with a chuckle.

"Yeah, the boy is pretty dang delicious. Not quite as delicious as his brother, but I can see his appeal," Stormy said.

"I love how much you adore your husband," Lindsey told her. "I thought he was a hopeless case when I first met him, but I see that he would also do anything and everything for you. It's pretty spectacular."

"He's my soul mate," Stormy said simply, as if that was a common thing.

"You do realize that epic romances like yours and Cooper's aren't usual, don't you?" Lindsey told her friend.

"That's why it's that much more special. I know what we have is rare, and I plan on never letting it go. It's not always easy. People can forget how it felt in the beginning. Time can wear on a relationship. We can take advantage of each other if we aren't careful. But I won't allow that to happen because I love Cooper with all my heart and soul and I won't ever let him go."

"I don't want that, Stormy. I don't want to feel like I can't live without another person," Lindsey told her as she sat down, suddenly feeling drained of energy.

"Oh, sweetie, you won't have a choice," Stormy said with a sigh. "When you find your soul mate, there's no choice other than to be with them, because you can't breathe right without them at your side. Yes, it's rare. Most people settle for what they think they want instead of for what makes them happy. But when it hits you, there's no place far enough you'll be able to run. You will find each other no matter what."

"That doesn't sound pleasant at all," Lindsey told her.

"The pain you go through to find each other isn't pleasant. But at the end of the road, when you're in each other's arms, it's absolute bliss."

"I think I want my old friend back, the one who likes to bitch with me about men," Lindsey said, only half kidding.

"She's long gone, darling. This is the new me, and I'm here to stay," Stormy said with a laugh.

"Well, I'm more focused right now on satisfaction, so I think I'll take your advice and attempt to seduce Maverick."

"Maybe because he's the one," Stormy said with a knowing smile that Lindsey wanted to smack away.

"There's no chance he's the one. I'm not interested in *the* one. I'm interested in the one *right now*. Forever isn't going to happen for me," Lindsey insisted.

"If that's what makes you feel better for now," Stormy said.

When her friend left, she was grumpy. She didn't want to think about soul mates and forever-type romances. There were far too many that never worked out. That's what would most likely happen to her. She didn't want to feel like she couldn't make it through another day unless a man was by her side.

So she put her plans into motion. She might not be willing to play with her heart, but she was more than willing to see if her body was still working correctly. And she knew just the man to play with to find out.

CHAPTER TWENTY-SEVEN

Something was different in her eyes. Maverick knew from the moment he walked into the house. He could see it, feel it in the air. He'd been honorable the past couple of weeks. He'd put her needs above his own.

He'd been aching with a desire that couldn't be quenched the entire time.

"This is my night to cater to you," she said with a gleam in her eyes.

He coughed as he tried to tell himself not to read too much into her words. "Huh?" He was losing control fast, and the look in her eyes was making his head spin.

"I'm in charge for the evening." He would let her be in charge any damn time she wanted if she kept looking at him like that.

"What's the plan?" he practically panted.

"You'll see. I'm going to freshen up."

And just like that she disappeared into her bedroom, leaving the door cracked open. He knew the bathroom was in there, and when he heard running water, he practically drooled.

Maverick knew this cottage inside and out. He'd stayed in it several times over the past few years. Just knowing she was sleeping in the same bed he'd slept in countless times was messing with his head enough. But imagining what she was doing in the bathroom right now was making him feel faint.

Moving over to the fridge, he pulled it open and spotted a six-pack of beer. He needed one, or maybe the entire thing, if he planned on making it through the night with this sexy woman. Undoing three buttons on his shirt, he was still sweating as he pictured her in the bathroom . . .

Was she in there changing into something . . . silky, soft, and easily removable? Was she putting on more of her intoxicating perfume or touching up her pink lips? Was she preparing herself so he could then unwrap the gift she was presenting him?

Or was he fantasizing way too much?

Yes, there had been a look in her eyes, but that didn't mean she was ready for them to have sex. He'd promised her he wouldn't do that until she was asking him. He was seriously considering taking back that promise because right now he couldn't think of anything other than sinking deep within her silky pink folds.

Her bedroom door was cracked open, and he wanted to walk through it, and straight into the bathroom. He didn't know how he was finding the restraint not to do exactly that. But then she called him.

His body froze at the soft purr of her tone. He didn't have to be called twice. Almost as if he were being pulled by strings, he began moving. He entered her dark bedroom and saw the bathroom door open.

There was a soft glow emanating from the bathroom, the flicker of light casting shadows on the wall. He moved to the door. Then his heart might have stopped beating for a few seconds.

There she was, sunk deep in the bathtub, only bubbles covering her in the dim lighting. A bottle of wine rested in a bucket on the side of the tub and two glasses sat within reach. His head began buzzing at the absolute beauty of her. She was perfection and he her willing slave.

His mouth dropped to the floor with the look she was giving him. Her eyes told him she wanted him. Damn, he didn't know if he could actually make her utter the words. Without even thinking about it, his fingers lifted as he began undoing the rest of the buttons on his shirt, then quickly tossed it away. Pride filled him at the appreciative gasp from her ripened lips.

Peeling the rest of his clothes off, he stood there, not even trying to hide the fullness of his arousal that was reaching for her. She stared at him and he moved with purpose to the tub.

Lindsey shifted over as he stepped inside and sank down so he was facing her.

"I have to say I'm enjoying your plans a hell of a lot more than going out to play baseball or watch a race," he told her, surprised at how thick his voice was.

"You told me to tell you when I wanted to have . . . to, you know . . . to have sex," she said, the last word barely a whisper.

"I want you so badly, Lindsey. So while this is killing me to say, I want to make sure you're ready," he groaned as he leaned back, feeling her legs rubbing alongside his beneath the layers of bubbles.

"I'm sure—that is, if you want to."

And right there he saw her insecurity and all of his hesitation vanished.

There was no more wavering as he reached across the tub and lifted her up. A squeak escaped her moist lips as she landed in his lap. He wrapped both arms around her, letting her feel the power of his desire pushing against her skin.

He was careful not to sink inside her, although that's all he wanted to do. He wasn't going to take her like that, though. No, he would get her nice and hot first.

"I'm . . . uh . . . I'm on birth control. I have been for a long time because of my periods," she said as she nervously shifted on his lap.

"That's a definite plus," he groaned before needing to feast on her mouth.

The talking stopped as he pressed his lips to hers and ravaged her mouth like he'd been wanting to do from the moment she'd opened the front door. There was a new franticness to his touch, knowing he was going to get to slide inside her.

It took everything in him not to do it right away. The sudsy water, the candlelight, and her moans were all too much for his senses to bear. He had to have this woman—and soon.

Trailing his lips down her neck, he nibbled and tasted where her pulse was pounding before going lower and lavishing attention on her breasts, which were floating just above the water line. They had been beautiful before, but with water and bubbles glistening on them, they were marvelous and tasted so ripe.

She ran her hands through his hair and tugged before trailing her nails across his shoulders and part way down his back. Each touch from her heightened his pleasure as he continued to devour her body.

Reaching between them, he glided his finger across her opening and rubbed against her nob, making her groan as she leaned against his neck and bit down. The pain was pleasure and torment at the same time. He returned the favor by making her groan again as he sank a finger inside her. She squirmed on top of him, and he was the one groaning next.

"I need you, Lins," he said as he shifted, feeling the head of his arousal slip an inch inside her delicate folds. He was trying to hold back. He knew he should take her to the bed, but he didn't think he could wait even that long.

"I need you too," she told him and then she shifted, pushing down on him, and connecting their bodies together. His heart thundered at the pure ecstasy on her face, at the joy and beauty radiating from her eyes.

He kissed her again as he gripped her hips and began moving her up and down on top of him. She was so tight, so achingly tight as he moved within her hot folds.

"Oh, Mav, I . . . I . . ." She threw back her head and cried out, and then gripped his thickness as she shook on top of him. Maverick followed right behind her, shooting his pleasure deep inside her heat.

They both panted hard as they came down off the amazing high, and then he pulled back, looking into her mesmerizing brown eyes. Her skin was flushed and he needed more. Now maybe they could take their time and truly enjoy each other's bodies.

Still holding her on his lap, he stood up, water and bubbles dripping off them. He grabbed a rag and cleaned them both before pulling her from the tub and drying them off. She tried shielding herself this time, but he didn't allow it.

She had trusted him to make love to her, and now she was going to trust him to admire her beauty. Lifting her into his arms, he carried her to the bed and laid her down. She reached for the blankets.

"Don't," he said. Her eyes widened, but she left the blankets alone and looked at him with both fear and trust.

"You are so beautiful, Lins. Everything about you is beautiful. Don't hide from me, please."

He crawled over her body and kissed his way down her stomach, running his lips across the scar she was so ashamed of. At the same time, he slipped his finger inside her and began building up her pleasure again, so she would never think of the scar as ugly, only think of her body as passionate and desirable.

Soon she was moaning beneath him. He had never lost his erection. He wanted to be buried inside her for the rest of the night. But he also wanted to taste her.

Moving down her hips, he kissed her thighs, then moved up to her sweet center and devoured her until she was crying out in pleasure.

Her taste on his tongue, he kissed his way back up her body because he needed to sink inside her again.

Pushing her thighs wide apart, he looked into her eyes as he slammed inside with one deep thrust, making her back arch off the bed to meet him. He moved in and out of her slick folds, her tightness gripping him, making them one flesh as they moved in sync.

When Maverick came again, she was right there with him, their cries echoing off the walls. But still it wasn't enough. He was starving for her. He couldn't stop. Looking deep in her eyes, he kept thrusting in and out of her body, and she wiggled beneath him as her shocked eyes connected with his.

He knew this was an experience neither of them had ever had before. He kissed her lips, her neck, and the sweet buds of her breasts, all without stopping. He thrust deep in and out of her tight body.

When he came again, he shook within her arms before he collapsed, both of them panting from the pleasure and exhaustion of endless lovemaking.

Knowing he was crushing her, he finally gained enough energy to turn over, but he couldn't stand not to have her in his arms, and he quickly pulled her close, their sweat-slickened bodies sliding against each other.

They lay in silence. He tried to figure out what exactly had just happened between them. Never had he experienced lovemaking like that. Never had he not wanted to stop. Normally, he came, the woman came, and he was done. It was pleasurable but it wasn't all-consuming.

When he heard the steady breathing of Lindsey in his ear and felt her chest brushing his in sleep he knew he should get up and leave, but he couldn't release her, couldn't let her go. He was sure the sensation would pass, but at this moment, he wasn't going anywhere. Grabbing the blanket, he covered them both and slowly began to drift off.

His last thought, though, was that his brother was going to most likely murder him. Both Benji and Princess were at Coop's house. It was going to be obvious Maverick had stayed the night with Lindsey. There might just be the demand for a shotgun wedding since his brother and sister-in-law were so protective of Lins. That thought should terrify him to his very bones.

It didn't.

CHAPTER TWENTY-EIGHT

"Mmm."

Sensations rushed through Lindsey as she slowly began to wake. So good. Something was so good.

"I need you."

And then Maverick was buried deep inside her and her body responded quickly as she grabbed him. They'd made love so many times the night before. She could feel aches in muscles she hadn't ever used.

No, she wasn't exactly a virgin, but she'd also never had a night like the one she'd just experienced with Maverick. That hadn't been sex. That had been a marathon, and she'd come so many times she'd lost count.

It didn't take long for them both to cry out in pleasure again.

"Good morning, sugar."

"Morning," she mumbled, feeling a bit shy as he held her tight. He'd stayed the entire night with her. She didn't know what to think about that. They weren't a couple. They hadn't agreed to be anything, really.

"Are you having regrets?" he asked.

"No!" she nearly shouted, then lowered her voice. "No. Not at all. That was . . . I can't even describe what that was," she told him with a laugh.

"That was heaven," he said. Their bodies were pressed against each other, their hands still caressing skin, neither wanting to break the connection. "It was certainly something that doesn't happen very often, that's for sure."

"Really? You aren't just saying that?" she asked, hating the insecurity she was feeling.

His eyes were bright as he forced her to look at him. "I promise you, I've never had an experience like last night—not ever. It was even better than the first time we were together because now we know each other. It's not just a one-night stand."

She was suddenly soaring. It had been as great for him as it had been for her. And then, even though she was completely satisfied, she found herself pressing up close to him, wanting to feel him inside her again even though she ached and would most likely have a hard time walking.

His thickness began growing against her leg.

"You are the devil, woman," he said with a laugh before he kissed her long and hard. "And I'm insisting on feeding you before I take you again."

She would have felt rejected if it weren't for the evidence that he was indeed in pain as he crawled out of the bed. His incredibly thick, hard manhood was standing at attention, and she couldn't help but lick her lips as she gazed at it.

"If you do that again, I'm going to forget about being honorable," he warned.

Her eyes snapped up to his, and then she couldn't keep the goofy grin off her face. This man—this incredible, sexy, funny, sweet man desired *her*. She didn't feel quite so broken anymore.

He'd even looked at her scars, and he still wasn't turned off. She wanted to test her power. She let the sheet drop down, showing her breasts, her nipples already hard and aching.

His eyes dilated as he gazed down at them. Then, with a growl, he dove back onto the bed, his body atop the blanket as he latched his lips onto her nipple and sucked hard. She was instantly soaked, wanting him.

He pulled the cover aside and slipped a finger into her, feeling that she was wet and ready for him. Always. She had a feeling that any time she was around this man she would be wet and ready.

And though she did hurt, when he slid back inside her again, she sighed with pleasure. The pain was worth it because unfathomable pleasure was her reward.

This time when they finished, he jumped from the bed, pulling her with him. He took her to the bathroom, where they shared a long, hot shower. The feel of his soapy hands lathering her entire body had her ready to make love again, and he didn't disappoint her. With her hands braced against the cool tiles, he easily slid in and out of her soaked folds until she was falling down the wall.

When they dressed and moved out to the kitchen, she was walking a bit stiffly. Wow, a sex marathon was such a better workout than doing cardio in a gym. Lifting weights had never reached the muscles that were sore right now.

"Sit at the island. I'm going to show off my amazing cooking abilities," he told her.

She gladly did what he asked, though sitting wasn't comfortable at all, especially on a hard stool. She went and got a pillow and sat on that. He laughed knowingly.

They were halfway finished making breakfast when there was scratching at her front door. Maverick went over and opened it. Benji and Princess ran in, giving them both an evil eye.

"Oh, Princess, I'm so sorry," she cried, shifting her pillow to the floor so she could sit down and give her baby love. She'd been so enthralled with Maverick the night before, she'd forgotten about her dog. What kind of horrible person was she?

"They were both with Coop and Stormy," Maverick said as if he could hear her thoughts once again.

Lindsey's cheeks instantly heated. "Oh. That means they're both going to know you stayed over," she said, her eyes widening.

"Yeah, I would say that cat's out of the bag," came Stormy's voice from the doorway where she was standing with a big grin on her face and Aaron in her arms.

"Oh, um . . . well, you see . . ." Lindsey trailed off, at a complete loss as to what to say to her friend. She'd never even thought about the fact that Stormy would realize Lindsey had kept a man overnight—her brother-in-law, to be exact.

"Let me guess, you were watching a PG movie and were just so exhausted you both fell asleep on the couch, right?" Stormy said with a laugh.

"Yeah, something like that," Maverick said with a wink that had Lindsey's cheeks going even hotter.

"Or you guys broke the bed in Lindsey's room and Coop and I are going to have to replace everything," Stormy said in the same teasing tone.

"I'm sorry about leaving Princess. See, this is why I shouldn't be a pet owner," Lindsey said as she continued petting her dog. Whether she should or not, there was no way she was ever going to be able to let go of Princess. She loved her far too much to do that now. Even if she had forgotten her the night before.

"I tend to forget anyone and everyone when I have a wild night of lovemaking, too," Stormy said. "What's for breakfast, Mav? I'm starving. Coop had to run off this morning for a board meeting and the baby was fussy last night so I'm crashing your breakfast party."

She went and took a stool at the island.

"It's always a pleasure to cook for beautiful women," Maverick told Stormy as he pulled out another plate. "I'm making pancakes, eggs, and bacon."

"Yum! I haven't had pancakes since before the baby was born. It's either quick meals or no meals. Coop keeps trying to get me to hire a cook, but I just don't want some strange woman invading my kitchen. I did agree to the maid, though. I'm way too tired with the jewelry shop, baby, and husband to scrub toilets," she said with a laugh.

"You could always do one of those meal plans where a chef makes all your meals for the week in one day and then all you have to do is pull them out and heat them," Mav suggested.

Stormy looked at him like he was a pure genius. "*You* are my favorite brother-in-law," she said with a sassy smile. "As soon as I have my new awesome cook, I'm inviting you over for dinner. Well, that is if I can get you out of my best friend's bed long enough to come eat with us."

He laughed, and Lindsey's face turned beet red.

Maverick placed a plate of food in front of Stormy and then cradled Aaron to him with his good arm so she could eat with both hands. Then he came over and sat on the floor next to Lindsey, holding the baby with one arm and petting Benji with the other.

The scene was so domestic—so perfect.

And it scared the living hell out of Lindsey. She had dived in with both feet, and now she wasn't sure she knew how to swim.

CHAPTER
TWENTY-NINE

Maverick slammed down his phone for the tenth time as his call went right to voicemail. He'd suspected Lindsey was avoiding him the day before after not hearing from her for a couple of days, but now he knew it for a fact.

They'd gotten too close. Hell, it scared him too, but she was the one running and ducking for cover. He couldn't allow that. It wasn't what she needed, and whether she was willing to admit it or not, it wasn't what she wanted either.

She was just scared. But if she truly thought she could hide from him, she hadn't learned a single thing about him in the last month—or the last couple of years, for that matter. In addition, Maverick wasn't a man to give up on a mission just because the going got dangerous.

It was time to give some tough love.

Grabbing his sweatshirt, he left his new house. It really was perfect. He didn't feel like he was in a museum anymore. Maybe it was time to bring Lindsey to it. He wanted to be the one protecting her—the one to keep bad things from happening. He was more than capable of that. Though she wouldn't admit to needing protection, she still did. She was vulnerable. However, what they'd shared was magical. It was rare, and he wasn't going to allow her to push him away.

At the end of all of this, he wanted to be her friend, wanted to continue having her be a part of his life. That wasn't typical for him. Sure, he didn't make enemies of his ex-lovers, but he didn't have a desire to stay in contact with them either.

But it was different with Lindsey. She was quickly becoming an essential part of his close-knit community. Besides, she was best friends with Stormy, which meant she wasn't going anywhere. That thought gave him peace, though he didn't think he needed reassurance. Maverick really wasn't sure exactly what he did need. All of this was confusing and new to him.

The drive to his brother's place didn't take him long. He bypassed the main house and went straight to the guest cottage. He found it empty. Pounding on the door anyway, he was about ready to knock it down when he was interrupted.

"Problems, brother?"

Maverick turned with a dirty look toward Cooper. How much did he want to share with him? They normally didn't talk about women—well, not in a respectful manner, at least.

It wasn't that they were exactly crude, but they'd always looked at women as beautiful, desirable, and . . . replaceable. Just thinking that thought about Lindsey made him cringe. She wasn't just any woman. She was special and would make a man a great wife someday. It just wouldn't be him.

That thought sent an immediate pang through him. Picturing her with another man was enough to make him want to put his fist through the wall.

"Hello? Earth to Maverick."

"Sorry, Coop. I have a lot on my mind," Mav finally said, turning to see his brother grinning stupidly as he leaned against the porch rail.

"Yeah, I can see that," Cooper said with a laugh.

"Where's Lins? She's avoiding me," Mav said as he moved away from her door. She wasn't going to just appear even if he knocked down the door. Obviously she wasn't home.

"Guess you didn't exactly wow her in the bedroom, huh? She go running away screaming?" Coop said with a laugh.

"Oh, I wowed her all right. It was the best night of either of our lives. She's running scared."

Maverick wanted to instantly take it back, but it was out there in the open now. He expected a joke from his brother, but his face got all serious as he looked at Mav like he was something on a slide under a microscope. Mav didn't like that look at all.

"Hmm. You're really serious about this girl, aren't you?" Coop said.

"No! I mean, I'm just trying to help her, that's all," Mav said, running his hand through his hair as he began to pace on the wide deck.

"I don't think so, Mav. I remember this feeling when I knew I couldn't live another day without Stormy. You've been hit, brother, and the only way to ease the pain is to just accept what you're feeling," Coop told him.

"I don't know what in the hell you're going on about. We've only been dating for a short while and there's a time limit on it. I've been on a mission to help her," Mav told him.

Cooper laughed—actually laughed at him, which made Maverick glare at his brother. Normally, he enjoyed Cooper's company.

"Oh my poor, unfortunate brother. Love isn't a mission. It's also not something that can be stopped. And it looks like you're officially on this ride whether you want to be or not," Cooper said.

"This is nonsense. Love has nothing to do with how I feel about this girl. Sure, I enjoy being with her, and I definitely want to help her, and we do have passion, but that doesn't add up to love," Mav insisted.

"Yeah, I thought that, too," Coop said with a laugh.

"It's a lot different with me and Lins than it was with you and Stormy. Any fool could see you were head over heels for that woman."

"It's okay. It will take you time to see what's happening."

"Whatever," Maverick said before sending another withering look his brother's way. "Where's Lins?" He was done talking to Cooper.

"She took an extra shift at the hospital. She's been doing that quite a bit the past few days. I don't know, though—today she seemed more nervous than usual. You might want to go and check in on her," Coop said.

Maverick was moving away before he even thought about it. He didn't bother saying good-bye to his brother. He needed to go and check on Lindsey, make sure she was okay. His stress was through the roof as he jumped in his truck and gunned the engine. If Lindsey was upset, then he needed to be there for her.

On the other hand, what if it really was just him wanting her to need him? What if she was perfectly fine on her own and that wasn't something he could accept? Maybe all of this was one-sided and he was too infatuated with the girl to notice. Whatever it was didn't matter, though. He had to go see the girl and nothing was going to stop him from doing just that.

CHAPTER THIRTY

Avoidance seemed to be something Lindsey was too capable of. When the going got tough, she fled as fast as she could. Her feelings for Maverick were too strong, so the best cure for that was a heck of a lot of work.

Lindsey was examining her patient when the new attending came rushing into the room, looking at the man's chart, not bothering to even peek at the person on the table.

"Patient needs a cardiac panel, EKG, and Cath UA. Splint the right arm, and get that wound in the right leg secured. Move it!"

"Umm, Dr. Cullen," Lindsey said as she tried to get the doctor's attention. He cut her off.

"Stop speaking and get on this," he thundered.

Grrr. Attitude. She hated the new attending. "Heard you loud and clear, but—" Again she was interrupted. Sometimes it was difficult to keep her patience. Today apparently was one of those days. Hotshot doctors with attitudes didn't amuse her.

"You will listen when I give an order. You are the nurse and I'm the MD. Do you know how to do your damn job? Or did you just slide your way through nursing school and then forget it all while on vacation?"

Lindsey saw red, but somehow managed to keep from screaming at the new doctor. Yes, she'd taken a few months off, but she was sure he hadn't bothered to find out a thing about her or why she'd needed to take leave. He probably thought she was right out of nursing school with zero brains in her head.

"As I was saying," she said with such authority, it actually stopped the man for two seconds. "The labs and EKG were done before you came in. The resident has already sutured the lacerations and the splint is on. If you bothered to look at the patient, you could have saved us both critical time."

The doctor's eyes narrowed as he tried to decide what to say. His next words didn't get much better. "You should have told me as soon as I came in the room." Of course he was turning the blame on her. She had to count to ten before speaking again, or she just might get fired before she was ready to leave the hospital she'd already decided she wouldn't stay at forever.

"I was trying to tell you, but none of that matters right now," she said with a shake of her head. "I've been with him for the past fifteen minutes and he looks like he's going into respiratory failure. We need to address the internal injuries now."

The doctor pushed on the patient's abdomen and looked at him for all of ten seconds. "You're overreacting. We have more patients in here that need our care. This one is fine."

He began to turn away. Lindsey was furious. She chose to stand her ground. Turning to the resident, who was looking at the two of them, his head whipping back and forth, Lindsey spoke to him instead.

"Get ready to intubate. He's about to crash."

"Lindsey!" the doctor shouted, turning back around.

"Trust me. I know how to do my job," she said as the monitors began going off.

The doctor never said another word as they intubated the patient and rushed him off for surgery. He was too much of an arrogant ass to admit he'd been wrong.

Lindsey dragged herself to the break room and made a cup of coffee, giving herself a few minutes until the next patient arrived. The entire shift had been one of *those* days.

She got in only a few sips of coffee before her pager went off and she had to leave her drink as she rushed back to the ER. A large man was being brought in, apparently an overdose. Panic closed Lindsey's chest, but she couldn't let it win.

This wasn't the same man who'd attacked her, even if he was similar in appearance. He was a patient, and no matter who he was or what was wrong, he had a right to medical treatment.

The paramedic spoke fast. "We have a forty-two-year-old male, approximately two hundred fifty pounds. Apparent heroin drug OD per his roommate, as well as multiple unidentified pills. He was found down in his living room with a needle in his arm, unresponsive. We gave him Narcan en route and he woke up hard and fast, so I recommend using caution with the next dose. I was about to give a second dose, but arrived at your ED before I could administer. We have two eighteen-gauge IVs started and his blood sugar is one eighty-four."

The nurses were already at work assessing lines and placing a tube down his nose and into his stomach so they could administer the necessary medication to counteract the pills he'd taken.

"Let's get some charcoal down him ASAP, and draw a tox screen." Dr. Cullen was giving orders for tasks that had already been done, especially since the nurses had handled patients like this one so many times they could do it with their eyes shut. But no one said anything as they continued working on the man.

"Where is the Narcan?" the MD yelled, apparently wanting the nurses to grow more hands and do everything at once.

"What's Narcan?" one of the new lab techs asked Lindsey.

"It's a med that instantly reverses the effects of opiates like heroin, but it has to be given slowly or the patient can wake up wild and swinging.

"We don't want that to happen," the young guy said just as Lindsey was leaning over the patient to check his monitor leads.

"Never mind, I'll give the medicine myself," she heard Dr. Cullen snap.

Before she could utter a sound, Dr. Cullen slammed the medication into the patient's IV.

Suddenly the man's hand came out of nowhere, grabbing her by the throat. He freed his other arm and began pulling out his IVs and nasogastric tube. Blood and charcoal went spraying everywhere, but it didn't even matter to Lindsey because the room was closing in on her as the patient continued squeezing his fat fingers into her throat.

"Get away from me, you murderous bastards. Stop poking me!" he screamed as his free hand batted at the doctors and staff.

Pure terror was rushing through her, and though she was scratching at the man's hand, it wasn't budging. This was too similar, too soon. Yes, she'd had patients go ballistic before, but her head had always been in the game. She'd never been so afraid.

He turned his head and looked at her as if finally noticing her, even though he'd been gripping her throat for what felt an eternity. "Get me out of here, bitch, now!" he thundered.

"Stop him," the MD yelled as the patient threw Lindsey across the room and onto the emergency crash cart. Her rib cage was screaming in pain as she crumpled to the floor like a rag doll.

She hardly had time to notice her own pain before security and staff were jumping over to restrain the patient to the bed. Although he continued fighting them, the Narcan was wearing off, so the drugs in his system were slowly taking him under once more.

"I want five mg Versed IM in him now," Dr. Cullen shouted.

"You're not giving me anything," the patient yelled, though it was much more muted than a few seconds before.

Although the rest of the staff worked quickly and efficiently, they couldn't help but shoot a nasty glare the doctor's way. He shouldn't have shot that medicine so quickly into the patient's IV in the first place.

Finally, the patient's eyes rolled back and his body relaxed. The security staff got him strapped to the bed. It was a police matter now.

The patient was secured and Lindsey was done. She was grateful for the helping hand that lifted her off the ground and out of the pool of blood that had saturated her scrubs. After thanking the nurse, she walked from the ER, too spooked to stay and watch them fix the damage the patient had caused himself.

"Lindsey!" Turning, she found Maverick standing in front of her with a look of worry in his eyes. "What happened? Where did all the blood come from?"

For a moment she didn't know what he was talking about. Then she looked down and saw that her scrubs looked as if she'd just come from a battle—which, in fact, she had.

"It was an unruly patient. He ripped out his IV," she said as she changed directions and headed to the nurse's lounge where she could get out of the scrubs. Tears were close to breaking, but she didn't want to let them fall. She'd cried enough already.

"Are you okay?" Maverick was right beside her, his hand on her back.

"It just shook me up a little," she admitted.

"I'm sorry." He stopped her and made her face him. She couldn't look into his eyes. If she did, surely she would fall apart.

"I'm okay, Mav. Just—just go home. I still have a few hours left," she said as she reached the door to the locker room.

"I'm not going anywhere. Your face is white, your clothes are bloody, and you're in shock. Let's get you cleaned up and get some coffee. I'm sure the staff will understand if you need to leave," he told her.

She stopped inside the locker room, which was blessedly empty. She refused to look at him. He refused to let her shut him out. His fingers slipped beneath her chin and he raised her face to his. Then she was looking into his panicked eyes.

It was odd, really, but seeing the wild look on his face seemed to ground her. It was nice to know someone was out there who cared so much about her that seeing her like this was sending him off the deep end a little.

She couldn't smile, but she tried to make her voice reassuring as she spoke.

"I can't keep running every time I get scared. This is the job. Things happen. But I really need to get cleaned up," she told him.

He was silent as he looked at her, and then she saw something else in his eyes that nearly had her reeling. She didn't want to analyze it, didn't want to focus on what she was seeing. She pulled away from him. She was finding it difficult to breathe.

"You're so damn strong, Lins. I'm proud of you."

His words were spoken almost reverently. It was giving her more and more strength. This man made her feel stronger and more capable. What was she doing continually running from him?

"I really do need to clean up," she said, her voice almost pleading.

"Okay, sug."

He didn't say anything else, just took her into the shower room and began pulling off her clothes. She was trembling in his arms, but the more she thought about what had just occurred, the more she felt like she couldn't speak.

She knew she should say something—do something, but she couldn't.

Soon, the bloodied clothes were off her, and she was standing beneath the warm spray not understanding how she'd gotten there. And she wasn't alone.

Maverick was with her, his chest pressed to her back as he ran his hands through her hair and down her body, getting every last trace of blood off her. Not knowing when the tears started, she just stood there slumped against him as he took care of her.

"I'm here, Lindsey, right here," he whispered as he rinsed soap from her hair before he pulled her from the shower and wrapped one towel around her while using another to dry her body.

He kept whispering soothing words, and soon the tears dried and she managed to dress herself before the two of them exited the changing area. It all was such a blur, the only thing to focus on was his voice, and the strength of his hands as they'd washed her, taking away the filth that man had left on her. Simply having Mav there, being so kind, being her rock, gave her the sense of peace and security she needed to let go of the terror that had been consuming her.

His faith in her was terrifying, but her need for him was even worse. She knew she couldn't think that way. It only added to the chaos of her life.

"I have to finish my shift, Mav," she said as he walked her outside the building for a breath of fresh air.

He stopped in his tracks, a look of disbelief on his face.

"I think they can give you a pass, Lins. You were attacked."

"If I run now, I might never come back in again, Maverick. I can't run anymore. I'm afraid of what will happen if I do," she told him, praying he wouldn't push the issue. If he did, she wouldn't be able to resist, and then all would be lost.

He tugged her into his arms.

"I don't like this one bit, but I'm in awe of the person you are. Let's at least grab a cup of coffee. You deserve a break before going back into that room," he insisted.

"I can concede to that," she told him.

He held her a few moments longer and then they walked side by side to the small dining area.

The caffeine helped tremendously, and she was able to go back to work. It wasn't exactly with bells on, but it was a start. It seemed that if she just focused on the small stuff, life was so much easier to handle. If she started looking at the bigger picture, that's when she felt like she was spinning out of control.

So she was going to just take it a day at a time. No, not even that. She was going to take it a moment at a time, and then an hour, and work herself up to days, weeks, and months. She wouldn't even think about years yet.

CHAPTER
THIRTY-ONE

Maverick hated hospitals. Really hated them. They smelled bad, and were incredibly noisy. He'd spent a fair amount of time in ERs. That's what happened when you liked to live your life fast and hard.

But nothing was going to pull him away from the ER waiting room on this particular night. When he'd seen Lindsey come out of the trauma room covered in blood, her face white with red and purple bruising around her neck in the shape of fingerprints, he'd nearly lost it.

He should have been there sooner. Maybe he could have prevented it. Logically, he knew he couldn't have done anything. How could he when he didn't know what was going on behind those doors? And as much power as he had around town, he still couldn't get into the sterile area without a reason.

Hell, maybe it was time to break another bone just so he could get back there. He would do that for this woman. That was a humbling thought. Shaking his head, he just had to face up to the fact that he was protective of Lindsey, and he hated that something terrible had happened to her.

Still, he wasn't leaving the hospital without her. Glancing at the clock for the fiftieth time, he sighed with relief. Her shift was over in ten minutes. He'd already sweet-talked one of the nurses to find out where the staff exited at the end of their day.

He didn't trust Lindsey not to try to sneak off without him. And he needed to be with her tonight. He was afraid that a lot of their progress had just been smashed in a several-hour period.

It was okay if that were the case, though, because he was going to be there for her to help pick up these new pieces. He had plans to help her decompress after a trying day at work.

Getting up, he smiled at the nurse who had helped him and was rewarded by her nervous giggle. Why couldn't Lindsey be so easy to mesmerize? His life would be much smoother if she were.

Leaning against the wall near the employee exit, Maverick smiled when he spotted Lins coming out, suspiciously looking around, and then making a dash toward her car. She *was* trying to sneak off.

"My truck is over that way," he called, making her whip around.

"You scared me," she exclaimed, holding her hand up to her heart.

"If you hadn't been trying to sneak away, you wouldn't have gotten frightened," he pointed out.

"I wasn't trying to sneak off. I just didn't know the exact plans. I need to go home and shower and . . . stuff," she said as she began moving toward her car again.

"You can shower at my place. I have plans tonight," he said, easily reaching her and turning her in the direction of his truck.

"I can't leave my car here," she told him, tugging against his hold. "And Princess needs me."

"Stormy is watching Princess," he said. "And your car is fine. It's in a secure parking lot. I'll bring you to get it tomorrow." They reached his truck and he leaned her back against it, boxing her in.

"I don't plan on spending the night with you," she said, gaining some fire in her eyes.

"Well, you should know that my plans for you go all the way to the morning." The soft purr in his voice had been known to drop women to their knees before. Apparently not this woman.

"Just because we spent a spectacular night having lots of sex doesn't automatically mean I'm going to keep on doing that with you," she said, placing a hand on her hip.

She was turning his own words back around on him. Good for her.

"Sex is optional, sugar. There's more to life than great sex," he said with a laugh. "I'm still trying to figure out exactly what that is, but I've been *told* there's more to life, at least," he added.

Then he got the smile he'd been hoping for. Damn! When she smiled, it stole his breath, and made his heart lodge in his throat. Her lips were certainly deadly weapons.

"I still need clothes if I'm coming over. Why don't I just meet you?" she offered.

"Because you'll find a reason not to come. I have sweats and T-shirts you can wear. They'll be baggy, but you'll look adorable. Come on, sugar. Let's be spontaneous," he urged.

She looked as if she were pondering it for several moments, and then he knew he'd won. He could see the curiosity in her eyes.

"I'm not agreeing to all night," was all she said.

Too tempted not to, he leaned in and took her lips, being gentle as he sipped her flavor. He wanted to crush her to him, but she'd had a hell of a day. Tonight, all the way into the morning, was going to be about tenderness and laughter. His libido could take a cold shower for now.

Opening his truck door, he helped her inside, then quickly rushed around to the driver's side. Getting in, he knew what he'd been missing the last few days. It was the smell of her perfume engulfing him.

The hospital smells fell away, and all his senses were tuned into the beautiful woman sitting next to him. He'd never be able to drive this truck again without thinking about her.

He took his time getting home, letting her relax as the two of them looked out at the harbor lights when they neared his place. He was nervous for her to see it. He hoped she liked it. Really, it didn't matter much, he tried to tell himself. It wasn't as if he were asking her to move in or anything, but for some reason, he wanted her to like the place.

They pulled up and he sat there a moment as she looked at the front deck.

"When did you move here?" she asked.

"I just bought the place a couple weeks ago," he admitted.

"And it's already furnished?"

"That was one of the great things about the purchase. It came that way. I only had to move a few items. I got rid of a lot of my old stuff and took advantage of the decorating skills of the previous owners."

"Lucky man," she told him. "It looks beautiful—and very big," she said with a nervous laugh.

"Wait until you see the inside."

He rushed around the truck and let her out, then led her up the steps and to the covered front deck. When he unlocked the doors, Benji and Princess came running at them.

"Princess!" Lindsey exclaimed, true joy in her voice as she dropped down and enveloped the dog. After the day she'd had, he'd known she would want to see her.

"I had Coop bring her over. My housekeeper has been keeping an eye on them, and set a few things up for us," he said, suddenly nervous when she looked up at him with a tender gaze.

"Thanks, Mav. That was really thoughtful."

Suddenly he was feeling as if he couldn't breathe again. He tugged at the collar of his shirt as he took off his jacket.

"Let me show you where you can shower and change. Coop texted me and said that Stormy went ahead and grabbed some of your clothes and sent them over with him. You don't have to wear my baggy sweats after all," he told her.

Her cheeks pinked, and it didn't take long for him to find out why. "Stormy has to be thinking . . ." She trailed off.

"She's thinking you had a hell of a day at work and that we're going to make up for it by having a romantic evening," he said as he kneeled down and cupped her face.

"Okay," she said, but he could see she was still embarrassed.

"Come on. Princess can go with you."

She allowed him to help her back up, and then both of them climbed the stairs with the two dogs close at their heels. After he left her in his bedroom, he waited for her outside. He watched the stars and thought about his conversation earlier in the day with Coop.

Maverick was beginning to think his brother just might be right about how he was feeling about Lindsey. But did it even matter if he was falling for the girl? It didn't change anything. He wasn't ready to settle down yet.

That thought depressed him. On this night he didn't want to feel anything other than happiness, so he pushed it away. He had a few things to prepare for their perfect night together, so he focused on those instead of focusing on tomorrow.

CHAPTER THIRTY-TWO

Lindsey took her time in the shower, scrubbing her body clean. She still felt dirty, though. That man's blood hadn't touched her skin, thankfully, and though Mav had cleaned everything off her, it had been a hell of a day and she was having a difficult time feeling sterile enough.

When Lindsey walked out of the bathroom with the towel wrapped snugly around her, Princess was sitting in wait, her ears perking up.

"Did you miss me today, little girl?" she asked before lifting the dog and sitting down on the huge comfortable bed in the middle of the room. Princess stretched up on her hind legs and licked Lindsey's chin. "I'll take that as a yes," she said with a laugh. "I missed you, too."

Taking a little more time, Lindsey gave Princess plenty of love, which they both obviously needed. She then went over to the bag Stormy had sent.

When she opened it up, Lindsey wasn't a happy camper. There was hardly anything in it at all—a few pairs of skimpy panties, brand new lingerie, and a note that said to stay inside and enjoy herself.

With a growl, Lindsey thought about calling Stormy up and reaming her best friend, but that wouldn't do her any good. She decided to raid Mav's closet instead. At least Lindsey knew Stormy didn't disapprove of her relationship with Maverick. She might be just as disappointed as Lindsey was going to be when their time was up.

When she opened Maverick's closet door, her heart might have stalled mid-beat. It was a woman's dream come true with a huge center island and so many drawers that Lindsey didn't know where to start. Only a small portion of the hanger space was even being used. She went over and ran her hand down Maverick's formal military garments and thought she really wouldn't mind seeing the man all decked out in them.

It took a while, but finally she found a pair of sweats with a drawstring that she had to tighten all the way and a T-shirt that said US Air Force on it. It hung all the way down to her thighs.

Taking a big whiff, she inhaled Maverick's scent, thinking she didn't mind wearing his clothing. She felt relaxed in this room, with his things. Plus, her day had been so draining. She thought about curling up in his bed, but she needed to go back downstairs. He was waiting and had made plans for the two of them. She was curious about what he considered to be a soothing evening.

He'd already done such amazing things for her, she couldn't imagine what he had planned. She hoped it didn't involve going anywhere. As much fun as she'd had playing baseball and being whipped around a racecar track, she was emotionally exhausted at the moment and didn't want to see anyone other than Maverick.

The lights were dim when she came down the stairs, but she could see fine. Princess went off to look for Benji and Lindsey made her way to the kitchen. A full wine glass was sitting next to a candle and a note on the counter.

Picking up the glass, she took a sip of the delicious red liquid before reading the note.

Blow out the candle, grab your wine, and come out the back door. Follow the trail.

Nothing else was written. Lindsey's curiosity was fully piqued. She took the glass and sipped on it while she exited the open patio doors. There she found an illuminated path that appeared to lead to the beach, which wasn't far away. There was a glow at the end of the path. Lindsey set out to investigate.

It wasn't a far stroll through the trees. When the forested area cleared, she found a perfect little oasis. There was a small sandy beach surrounded by a rock wall on one side, and bushes on the other with nothing but water in front.

The area was protected from the wind. In the center of it all was a tent, of sorts.

Maverick was standing to the side of the tent with a rose in one hand, a glass of wine in the other, and a beaming smile on his face.

"What is all of this?" she asked as she stepped near him.

"We're going to enjoy a picnic beneath the stars," he said.

She walked closer and peered inside the tent. A large, comfortable bedlike lounger with a blanket and cushions overlooked a soothing fire and the water. Maverick had a picnic set up on a side table.

"Can we even see through the top of the tent?" she asked.

"Ah, the top is clear and there's a ventilation hole for the smoke. I don't want you getting chilled."

When she entered the tent, she realized it was a gas fire, which she supposed was good. At least it wouldn't burn out or send sparks flying at them, popping their air mattress. She could feel the warmth of the fire. It was as heavenly as the entire setting.

"You really do know how to sweep a woman off her feet, don't you?" she said as he led her over to the picnic area.

"I've never done anything like this for another woman," he told her, the truth burning in his eyes.

"You better quit telling me stuff like that, or I might not let you go," she said, only half joking.

"I might not want you to," he said right back, making those butterflies in her stomach take flight. "I see you found my sweats. What happened with the stuff Stormy sent over?"

His innocent question set her cheeks to glowing. "She didn't think I needed much more than lace and silk."

His eyes rounded before a hungry growl rumbled from his throat. "Hmm. I might just have to insist on you changing."

"Not going to happen," she said before she sat down on the lounger with the cushions.

"A guy can wish, can't he?" he said as he joined her, then immediately began placing items on a plate for her. It was all finger foods, which she loved.

"Did you do all of this?"

Handing her the plate, he shrugged. "I came up with it, but I have to admit that I hired it all out so I could wait at the hospital."

"Have you been watching the Hallmark Channel?" She took another drink of wine, and he topped off her glass. She was feeling much warmer inside and out with the tasty drink. Her worries from the hospital were fading farther and farther away.

"What's that?" he asked. It took a moment for her to remember her question.

"It's a television station with romantic movies playing on it all the time. One of my favorites."

"Well then, I will have to watch it, and see if these men on the shows come even close to being as suave as me," he said with a wink.

"So far, I have to say they don't compare."

"I like knowing I'm in the lead," he told her.

And the thing about it was, they really didn't compare to him. Maverick was the type of man who got under a woman's skin, and then he was there to stay. Even after their dates ended, he would remain lodged in her heart. Lindsey truly hoped she was able to remain friends with him because that seemed better than not having him at all.

"I left the dogs alone in the house, Mav. I completely forgot when I got down here. I don't want anything to happen," she said, suddenly worried about Princess and Benji.

"My housekeeper is up there keeping an eye on them. They won't get into anything," he assured her.

Her last worry put to rest, she closed her eyes for a moment and simply appreciated being on this private beach with Mav, the sound of the water gently splashing the shore, the stars shining bright, and the fire keeping them warm.

"Thanks for all of this, Mav. It's exactly what I needed."

"You can talk to me about what happened—today and when you were attacked. It might help you feel better," he told her.

Lindsey's throat closed as her mind spun. She wanted to share with him, but she was afraid to. She was afraid of opening wounds that were finally beginning to close again.

"I don't think I can," she whispered.

"When you are ready, I'm going to be here to listen," he told her as he stood up and pulled her to her feet.

But he wouldn't be there. That was part of the problem. In a week, maybe two, he was going to be gone again. Sure, she would see him, but it would be only once in a while.

He began rubbing her shoulder, and she immediately started turning into a puddle, ready to melt at his feet.

"I can't think when you touch me like this, Mav," she said, her breath starting to come out in pants.

He leaned his head on top of hers for a moment and she wished she could freeze-frame everything exactly how it was at this moment.

"Do you know what the best cure is for a hard day?" he asked seductively.

"I can imagine what it might be," she said with a chuckle.

"So you're willing to do anything I ask?"

Oh, how his voice was melting her. Even when she wanted to pull back from him, he made it impossible. He was bending her to his will, and she wasn't even trying to fight it.

She murmured an incoherent reply. He turned her around and lightly brushed his lips across hers, then he deepened the kiss while he began stripping away their clothes. "I wasn't going to do this," she told him.

"Don't worry, it only hurts for a minute."

"Hurts? What?"

"Skinny-dipping."

Her shriek as he lifted her up and ran for the water was the only sound that could be heard in the quiet of their perfect night.

CHAPTER
THIRTY-THREE

Lindsey couldn't breathe—literally—as freezing water engulfed her body. When she came up, her mouth gaping open, she was ready to kill Maverick. Before, she'd been so caught up in the romance, so caught up in feeling pity for herself and the warm fuzzy feelings she had for Mav, but now she was ready to inflict some torture on this man who liked to shock her. The problem was she couldn't feel her body.

Finally, a blessed breath of air managed to get down her freezing cold throat.

"How in the world is this helpful?" she shuddered as he pulled her into his arms and kissed her with a big smile on his face.

"There's something about a nighttime skinny-dipping session that frees the soul," he told her as his hand roamed her back.

"I can't feel my body, let alone my soul," she said as she pressed closer, trying to find warmth.

"Just remember that things shrink in cold water," he said as she sought him out.

"Mmm, doesn't feel like anything is very small," she murmured.

Her body was already warming up and apparently his was as well. He laughed before pressing against her, his thickness nice and hard and big for her.

"It seems even freezing water can't inhibit me when I'm in your arms."

"So I have power over you?" she said before shoving off him and diving into the water to swim away.

"Yes, you little minx, you do," he said, as he began to give chase.

They played in the water for a few more minutes before she couldn't take it anymore and she rushed out, running back to the fire and grabbing one of the warm robes he had waiting. She placed it around her freezing body. He threw his on before grabbing her.

"Why would you cover up this delicious body?" he said, lifting her off the ground and moving to the massive lounger, and more importantly, the nice thick blanket.

"Because you froze me."

He set her on the cushions and got all the sand off her feet. Then he brushed off his own feet before the two of them dived beneath the blanket, where he immediately pulled her back into his arms.

"You are so unbelievably beautiful," he whispered as his fingers cupped her face.

"You make me feel it," she said, reaching for him, needing to feel his hot flesh beneath her fingertips. "And you've made my day so much better by doing this for me," she admitted.

"Good. Because I don't think I can say it enough. My entire purpose right now is to make you feel good."

"I'd rather you just kissed me," she murmured as she leaned her face closer to his.

He didn't say another word, but instead pulled her lips the last inch to his. Her mind went blank as she kissed him with a passion she couldn't inhibit. She'd tried to stay away from him and that had only caused misery. Now she just wanted his arms around her and his lips . . . everywhere.

And he more than complied. The dancing fire next to them and the blankets on top had quickly warmed her. His touch against her skin was scorching her. She regretted the robe now.

But he didn't let the material get in his way. He untied the robe and then his magical fingers were moving up along her trembling stomach and up over her breast, pinching her hardened nipples.

She moaned against his mouth and then grumbled when he broke the connection. Soon that grumble faded, though, as his lips trailed down her collar bone and he sucked on the peaks of her nipples, his teeth nipping them, making her groans turn into pleasurable cries.

Before he could move lower, she grabbed his head and pulled him back up to her mouth, kissing him hard as she pushed him over onto his back.

"I was on a mission there," he said when she released his mouth.

"My turn," she purred as she undid his robe and moved down his strong neck, kissing and sucking on his salty skin.

"Mmm. I'm liking your turn," he rumbled as his fingers twisted in her hair, tugging slightly, making her moan against his skin.

She kissed her way down his hard abs, reveling in his strength and taste. She was aiming for his magnificent thickness, but she wanted to take her time getting there, building up the anticipation.

His groans of pleasure encouraged her as she reached his strong pelvic bone and then her fingers wrapped around his thickness, her thumb brushing across the tip where his pleasure leaked out, making her body accelerate to boiler levels.

She had to taste him.

"Come here," he groaned as she moved down a little farther, her mouth inches from his tastiness.

She didn't say anything, just bent forward and ran her tongue along his tip, his tangy essence superb, making her want more. Without further hesitation, she wrapped her mouth around him and pushed down as far as she could take him.

Her spit and his excitement lubed the way, making it easy for her to slide up and down his solid rod of steel. She groaned around him as she devoured every drop of his juices, his groans making her speed up as she pleasured him.

Suddenly, Maverick's hands tugged at her, making her mouth pop off his tasty arousal. He pulled her up his body so that she was straddling him.

She could feel his wet, stiff thickness below her, begging for entrance as she sat atop him, his eyes glowing with heat and desire.

"I want to come inside your sweet center, not your mouth," he growled.

She'd never had sex on top before. It was exposing and she was nervous about it—that was, until he lifted her and pulled her body back down over his erect rod. He pushed upward, sinking fully inside her.

Then there was no thought of embarrassment. A cry of pleasure escaped her as he buried himself so deeply. She truly felt they were one person. His face was a mask of pure ecstasy, which made her want to satisfy him even more.

Her body knew exactly what to do. She gripped his shoulder as she began moving her hips up and down, his thickness sliding in and out of her.

He reached up to grip her breasts, his fingers tweaking her nipples as she continued to ride him. Their panting escaped into the night, floating up to the stars as they consumed one another.

"Yes, baby, just like that," he groaned, and she moved even faster, enjoying every single inch of his manhood as it touched her inner walls.

"Yes, Mav, yes."

Moving one hand down to her sweet spot, he flicked his fingers across her swollen bud and she went soaring into the sky. She clamped around him, her body clenching as tremors ran through her, the pleasure too much to handle.

He grabbed her, pulling her head down to consume her mouth. She felt him pumping inside her, his pleasure heating her up.

When both of them stopped trembling, she laid against his chest, listening to his heartbeat pounding steadily in her ear, the most reassuring sound she had ever heard.

"I don't ever want to stop this," Mav said.

That made her own heart pump even faster. That was something she couldn't even begin to think about right now. It was too much for her overloaded brain.

"You might just break me if we keep having this magnificent sex," she told him, trying to make a joke, but he was in a serious mood.

"I would never break you, sug."

His hands ran up and down her back as he whispered the sweet words. She realized he meant them. He wouldn't ever hurt her on purpose. It just wasn't the kind of man he was.

But he could hurt her. He could hurt her so much more than that man had today at work, and so much more than the man who had attacked her. He could break her heart in two, break her soul.

It was up to her to not let that happen. She feared, though, that it might be too late for her to stop it. The only thing she could do at this point was to love him as much as she was capable, appreciate that he wanted to take care of her now, and live in the moment.

"I wanted to stay out here until morning, so we could watch the sunrise together, but it's getting a bit colder than I was expecting," he said as he continued to rub her back.

"I guess it is a little cold," she said as a shiver rushed through her.

He clicked off the fire, threw the blankets back on the bed in a heap, and lifted her into his arms. She sighed against his neck. She was perfectly capable of walking back up the path, but at this moment there was no place she'd rather be than against his chest with his solid arms around her.

He carried her to his room and laid her down. He made love to her again before he opened the door and let both dogs in to come up in the bed with them.

And that's when she realized she had fallen in love with the man.

She was going to enjoy every minute she had left with him. And when it was time to go, she would take only good memories with her.

CHAPTER THIRTY-FOUR

What is it that people always said? That when you're having a great time, it passes far too quickly, but when you're in misery, it drags on? Lindsey was sure the saying was more than true.

The past couple of weeks had passed by in a blur for her. She was . . . happy. Maybe she was too happy. She and Maverick had been working nonstop on the fund-raiser by day and then spending nearly every night locked in each other's arms. It made her think that maybe, just maybe, he didn't want their time together to end. That's how she felt.

It was foolish of her to want to continue the relationship, but when a person was thinking with her heart, she didn't always make the best decisions. She had a feeling she was going to learn that the extremely hard way.

Even though Maverick wasn't talking about the two of them ending whatever it was they had going on, the reality was that all good stories eventually ended. There was a small nagging bit of her brain that told her some things worked out. Look at Cooper and Stormy. They were in love and so happy it was almost difficult to be around them sometimes.

They were the exception to the rule, though, and she was more than aware of that fact. But if she dwelled on the negative, then she would be letting the positive slip right through her fingertips. That wasn't what she wanted either.

Her coworker, Katie, walked up to her, looking incredibly excited. She waited for Lindsey to finish making notes on a patient's chart and then spoke.

"I am so excited for the fund-raiser you're throwing, Lins. There's been so much buzz in the papers lately."

"Yes, it's been a lot of work, but I've really enjoyed doing it."

"What are you wearing to it?" Katie asked.

"I'm not sure I'm even going," she told Katie. Just because she was chairing the event didn't mean she had to be there. It was a lot of fancy people that she really didn't feel she fit in with. She was one of the workers, not one of the elite.

Sure, her brothers were millionaires, but that didn't mean she was riding along on their coattails. She didn't want to take advantage of anyone else's rainbow. She wanted to make her own.

"You have to come. It's going to be so much fun," the very young nurse said in her usual singsong voice. "Of course, you know that, since you've been in on every little detail."

"It's a bit over the top, actually," Lindsey said with a laugh.

"No way. It's like a real-life ball. How romantic is that?" the girl sighed.

"Are you hoping one of the doctors will ride in on a white horse and slip a glass shoe on your foot?" Lindsey asked her with a smile.

"Only if it's Dr. Stine. That man can slip anything he wants on any body part of me," the girl told her with a giggle.

"Yes, Dr. Stine is a good-looking man," Lindsey admitted.

The new doctor had all the staff drooling, even those who were married or in committed relationships. Lindsey wasn't in either category. So why wasn't she attracted to the successful surgeon?

Maybe because Maverick had broken her. Or maybe it was because she was happy—for now. Either way, she wasn't interested in the new surgeon who seemed to have a minor in flirting.

"Did I hear my name?"

Even though she hadn't been gossiping about the man—not really—Lindsey still felt her cheeks heat the slightest bit as the man of the hour walked into the break room. His killer smile was in place and he sidled right up to the girls.

Katie, of course, giggled nervously and began shifting from foot to foot.

"Yes, we were just talking about what a blessing it has been to have you at our hospital. The patients really respect you," Lindsey said.

"Ah, I thought it might have been about something else." He was gazing right at her, the look of interest clear in his eyes. That was something she needed to nip in the bud immediately.

"Nope. Sorry." She turned to leave, but he gently grabbed her arm. She stopped dead in her tracks, having to control her breathing. Though she knew it wasn't logical, she still didn't like strangers touching her.

"Are you going to the ball, Lindsey?" The intensity of the question shocked her.

"I'm not sure yet," she told him as she tugged firmly on her arm. Thankfully he let it go.

"I hope so. Save me a dance."

She was so shocked by his request she didn't have time to respond. She just nodded her head and quickly fled. She wondered if poor Katie was able to survive in there on her own with the good-looking doc. Guess Lindsey would know if the girl didn't show up soon.

Moving to the reception desk, she sat down and decided to finish her charts. That part of her job she could easily do without. It was boring and took forever. Without the horrific caffeine the hospital provided, free of charge, she would most likely pass out from paperwork.

"I can't believe you left me in there with Dr. Dreamy. Ugh. I went all red-faced and ended up sputtering something unintelligible before I ran out the door," Katie said as she came and perched herself on a corner of the desk.

"You're a nurse, Katie. I would think you would have a bit more control over yourself," Lindsey said with a laugh.

"Well, I know one thing—he sure as heck was flirting with *you*. It's really not fair, you know. You have that sexy pilot guy who comes in here all the time, and now you have the dreamy doctor drooling over you too. Please share your secrets," the girl whined.

"I don't have any secrets," Lindsey told the girl with a laugh. "Don't you have work to do?" she finished pointedly.

"Ugh. Nothing. My patients are good. It's just been so dang quiet in here today."

Two other staff members were walking up as the young nurse said this, and all three of them shot a look of horror her way. It was such the wrong thing to say in the ER. Completely taboo. And they all knew it.

As if on cue, the emergency room doors flew open as two guys carrying another came limping inside, blood pouring from all three of them.

"You had to say the *Q* word," Lindsey snapped as all four medical professionals rushed forward to catch the men before they toppled to the floor.

There was no more time to sit around. They got to work sewing wounds, administering antibiotics and painkillers, and setting a broken wrist. The guys were lucky. They'd been performing some Jackass-style stunts that had gone severely wrong—or maybe right. Wasn't the point of those movies to humiliate oneself while causing the most damage possible? Why would people find that entertaining? Okay, she had to admit, she might have watched it once or twice. But still, it was a terrible pastime.

No sooner did they get their young victims treated than an older couple walked in. Both of them looked one knock away from heaven's door. Each of them complained of chest pains.

"Both of you?" Lindsey asked, surprised. Neither had any color, and their breathing was almost nonexistent.

"Yes, dear," the woman replied, still polite even in her pain.

"What happened?" Lindsey asked as they began running tests on them.

The old man wasn't as polite in his pain-induced state. "We aren't that old, you know. I'm not even seventy yet," he spluttered, completely off topic. What did their age have to do with anything?

"I wasn't trying to call you old, sir," Lindsey quickly said, helping him lie back in the bed.

"Darling, you'll be seventy in two days," the woman pointed out. "I was giving him his birthday present a little early, you see—" Her cheeks turned pink as she looked at Lindsey in horror.

Lindsey had no idea what was going on. "What was the present? Did it frighten you both?" she asked.

Right after she asked the question, Dr. Stine's soft laughter could be heard behind her, and she turned to give him a glare. She didn't find this situation in the least funny.

"I think they were having sex, Nurse Helm," he said before winking at her.

Now it was Lindsey's turn to sport red cheeks. She whipped back around to the elderly couple, who were both looking at the floor. Their tests confirmed they were indeed having heart attacks.

There wasn't time to dwell on the fact that they'd been doing the nasty. It was an image she would never get out of her mind again, not even if she drank bleach. But then again, when was it too old to be having sex? The thought of ever having to give it up in her lifetime wasn't appealing.

"Good for you, Mr. Bardon. Happy birthday," Dr. Stine said after they stabilized the husband and wife. The old man grinned.

Lindsey was free to go at the end of her shift, but the afternoon wouldn't slow down. Nope. All because Katie had uttered the Q word. Lindsey tried not to even think of the Q word while in the hospital.

She left the Bardons and then was pulled into another exam room where a little girl had a bone sticking out of her leg. That was an easy call. She was rushed to surgery. And still more patients came through the front doors.

They had to move through the patients quickly and call in their on-call staff to cover the deluge of people. They saw everything from minor scrapes to fractures and other serious injuries.

But by the time the day was over, Lindsey sagged against the wall as she sipped on an ice-cold Pepsi and smiled.

"How can you smile after the hell we've been through?" Katie asked, her hair sticking out in all sorts of new places, her mascara smeared, and her scrubs filthy.

"Because we didn't lose a single patient. I call that a good day," Lindsey told the girl.

"I will never say that Q word again," Katie said as she looked around.

"That might be wise," Lindsey told her.

"You ladies doing okay?" Dr. Stine asked as he came through the hall door.

"Great, Dr. Stine, thanks for asking," Katie said as she straightened up and attempted to brush back her hair. Lindsey wanted to tell her it was no use. There would be no helping that hair, not ever again.

"How did the little girl's surgery go?" Lindsey asked, finally pushing away from the wall and moving toward the lounge where she could take a rinse-off shower, change her clothes, and get out of the hospital. She would take a lot longer shower after she made it home. There had been too much grime on her this afternoon.

"It went great. She's not even going to have a limp when she heals," he said, obviously pleased.

The man might be slightly obnoxious and a bit too full of himself, but he was an incredible surgeon. She could appreciate that.

"Glad you were here, then," she said before moving toward the lounge door. He grabbed her arm again, an act she didn't like. She would really need to speak to him about boundaries.

"Want to go get a drink and celebrate?" he asked.

She was so shocked her mouth must have hung open. She turned back around to look at him, but didn't quite know what to say. Finally, her brain caught up to her vocal cords.

"I'm sort of seeing someone right now, but thanks for the offer," she finally managed. "Plus, I don't date doctors. It's too complicated."

He didn't seem in the least bit fazed. He just smiled at her and then finally let go of her arm. He took a step away before turning back and giving her the full force of his cocky grin.

"I like complicated. See you at the ball."

And just like that, he disappeared again. Lindsey retreated to the employee lounge and then got out of the hospital as quickly as she could. Her day had been messy. It was time to go home.

Hopefully her personal life would never be quite as complicated as her professional life was. It might not be if it weren't for Maverick. Like she said a couple of months ago, Maverick created complications.

CHAPTER
THIRTY-FIVE

Sitting in the den of Cooper's house, Maverick leaned back in the chair as he threw back another whiskey and cola. His brothers had called a meeting, but he wasn't in the mood for one. He finished his drink, got up, made a refill, and then sat back down.

He'd come to the hospital to take Lindsey out after work and had witnessed the interaction between her and the *good* doctor. His first instinct had been to smash his fist through the doctor's face. But something had stopped him.

Maverick knew his relationship with Lindsey wasn't going to last, but he didn't want to leave her devastated when it was over. That feeling of not wanting her to be alone and frightened had stopped him from killing the doctor, but just barely. Then he'd found himself backing away without alerting her to his presence.

He'd been pissed off ever since.

All he wanted to do was rush over to her place and stake his claim. He'd been doing that a lot lately, making love to her, holding her tight, even sleeping all night with her. He knew he needed to back off, but he couldn't quite make himself let go yet.

Why not?

He'd known from the beginning that it wasn't going to be permanent. His life had been so much simpler before he'd decided to make it his mission to help Lindsey.

"Are you with us, Mav?"

Looking up, he noticed both Cooper and Nick staring at him. How long had they been talking? Who knew?

"Yeah, I'm here. What's so important that I had to drop everything and come over here?" he asked, not even trying to cover up his bad mood.

"Is there something you want to share first?" Nick asked him with a smirk on his face.

"What in the hell is that supposed to mean?" Mav snapped.

"You're in a pissy mood. Not getting laid enough?" Nick said with a laugh.

Mav shot out of his seat and thought about pounding on his brother for a few seconds. He even had his fists clenched as he took a menacing step in his direction. When he saw the delight on Nick's face, he knew he was overreacting and needed to back off. He changed directions and went back over to the liquor cabinet.

"What I do or don't get is none of your damn business," he mumbled as he threw back a shot before mixing another drink and going back to his seat. As much as he'd love to knock his brother around, the liquor was beginning to kick in.

"I thought you wanted to box with me?" Nick said, leaning back as he grinned at Maverick.

"Nah. I'm good now," Mav said. "Just a lot on my mind. Let's get this show on the road."

"Damn. You sure go hot and cold, brother," Cooper said, sitting back and watching the show.

"Yeah, yeah, I know." Maverick was beginning to wonder why he'd been in such a bad mood in the first place.

Then the doctor hitting on his woman flashed through his mind, and he remembered all too well, making his blood pressure rise again. Nope. He pushed that image right out of his head. Lindsey would be much better off without him in her life in the long run. Still, their time wasn't quite over yet. They weren't finished planning the fund-raiser, and he just wasn't willing to let her go. Whatever his reasoning, though, he was still holding on when he shouldn't. Maybe it was really him who needed her and not the other way around.

"Get on with this. I have an early day tomorrow," Mav said, wanting to get out of his own head. He was tired of being in there.

"Our guy has new information on Ace," Cooper said.

That stopped all movement in the room.

"What's he got?" Nick finally asked.

"Ace isn't flying anymore. That's for sure. He's also placed a lawsuit against the family for his trust."

Mav let the words flow through him over and over again as he tried to process the words.

"Why in the world would he want to do that? We all had enough of our own money when Father made that stipulation in his will. Did he blow through it all?" Nick asked.

"I don't know why he's doing what he's doing," Cooper said with a sigh as he ran a hand through his hair.

"Will he win?" Mav asked.

"Does it really matter? The money is his. Do we actually care if and how he gets it?" Cooper asked.

"It's the principle. All three of us have grown up, gotten careers, done things to better our lives," Mav said.

"He won't win unless we all grant it," Cooper told them.

"And what do you want to do?" Nick asked.

Maverick really couldn't tell what his brother was thinking. It was obvious that Cooper didn't care if Ace got the money or not. Nick seemed on the fence. Maverick just wanted his brother back. Now he was worried that if he came back, he wouldn't want to be around the man he'd turned into.

"I just want to talk to him," Cooper said.

"I echo that," Maverick told them.

"And if we fight him, do you think he'll ever come home?" Nick pointed out.

"He might get the money and disappear all over again," Cooper said.

"We can't control him," Mav said with a sigh. "We don't have the right to control anyone." That was a lesson he really needed to learn.

"What has he been doing? Where's he living? What's going on in his life?"

"Maybe I can answer some of those questions."

The boys turned to the doorway and looked at Sherman, who was standing there looking in on them. His expression was sad as he moved into the room.

"Uncle Sherman?" Coop said.

"Is there something we're missing?" Nick asked.

"There's a lot your mother and I have kept from you," Sherman said as he moved over to an easy chair and sat down.

"Maybe it's time you tell us, then," Maverick said.

Sherman sighed. "Your brother was always different, right from the beginning. He was a hothead, but he does have a heart of gold inside. It's just buried deep down. He feels like he's been betrayed and he's not going to listen to any of us."

"Why does he feel betrayed? We were all in that room when Dad's will was read. We were pissed, but we got over it," Cooper said.

"It goes beyond the reading of the will, boys. It hinges on something before that. Some things happened that we didn't tell you about."

"Well, now would be the time to tell us," Nick thundered.

"I won't speak of things about Ace without him here to defend himself. But about a year before your father passed, there was an incident. I don't know if you saw the changes in him then, but that's when it started. It also solidified your father's decision to do what he did regarding his will," Sherman said.

"Why are you even starting this if you aren't going to tell us anything?" Cooper snapped.

"I just want you to know that it isn't black and white. There's a lot of color in there—a lot of hurt. I've been trying to reach out to Ace for years. He's protecting himself and he seems to see us as the enemy."

"None of this is making sense. You're talking in riddles," Mav said, his mood growing more sour.

"I think your brother is in serious trouble. I think he's been there for a while, and I know he needs you boys. He's just too stubborn to admit that even to himself."

The statement made the room go silent as the three brothers looked at each other.

"He knows all he has to do is ask and we'll be there for him immediately. But he doesn't want our help. He wants to be on his own," Maverick said.

Sherman gave them all the look he used to give them when they were younger. It was a look that had quickly put them in their place. Just because they were technically adults didn't mean he wasn't still their uncle, didn't mean they didn't respect what he had to say. They hung their heads as they tried to figure out what to say next.

"We don't just love our family when the going is easy. We love them through the darkest hours. It's our job to show Ace he will never be alone. That's what will make him come home," Sherman told them.

"We can love him and still give him the space he wants," Nick said.

"I know space isn't truly what he wants. I think it's what he *thinks* he needs, but the reality is that he needs his brothers. You'll want to be there for him before it's too late."

"Then tell us what to do," Mav said.

"You'll know. Just be ready when he calls."

With that, Sherman stood up and left as quietly as he'd entered. Mav looked at his brothers and no one spoke. They still felt as lost as when they'd first entered the room.

By the time Mav left, he realized he hadn't solved a single one of his problems.

CHAPTER THIRTY-SIX

Night was falling as Maverick stepped up to Lindsey's door, his heart thundering for some odd reason. He held a single red rose, a bottle of her favorite white wine, and chocolate-covered strawberries, which she had admitted were her guilty pleasure.

He'd been trying to pull away, to make the end of their relationship so much easier to bear, but he couldn't seem to do what had to be done. He cared about her—but more than that, he was drawn to her. It was beyond a physical need—it was an obsession.

After the reading of his father's will, he'd sworn he would never marry. Heck, he'd had no desire to wed long before that reading. But since being around Lindsey, the word *forever* had been creeping into his mind more and more. That wasn't what he wanted. At least he didn't think so. Still, there he was, standing on her doorstep, thinking of no one other than her day in and day out.

Tonight he was letting some of that go. Tonight he was going to make her feel special, cared about, give all that he was able to give to her, possibly even leave a piece of his soul behind with her. That's all he could do in saying good-bye.

Maybe he shouldn't draw it out. It might be better to just cut it off clean, but he didn't think that was the way to do it with Lindsey. If he showed her what she meant to him, then it shouldn't hurt so badly in the end. The transition would be smooth.

He would convince himself leaving her was right.

And the sex was just sex. Sure, it was heavenly—unlike anything he'd ever experienced before. But he was sure he'd had that same thought before. He might not be able to remember having that thought, but that didn't mean he hadn't felt it. His mind was just muddled from being with Lindsey for a while now.

Taking in a long, soothing breath, he knocked, telling himself he was a fool to feel as nervous as he did. It was just one more night the two of them were together—no different than any other time in the past month.

The door opened much more quickly than he'd been expecting. Maybe she too felt something different in the air.

"You're early," she said, a touch of uncertainty in her eyes. It broke his heart a little. She could feel the shift between them. It was more than obvious.

"Because you are a sight for sore eyes. I needed to see you," he said, without even thinking about it. She was wearing a red sweater with lipstick to match, and a long black skirt with a slit up the side, a bit of her thigh on display. His mouth was watering. "Beautiful. You are so damn beautiful."

Her big brown eyes widened before she smiled at him in that way that made him lose control. She opened the door wider to invite him in.

"You look pretty suave yourself, Mav. I don't often see you wearing a tie," she said as he stepped through her doorway.

"It's our first time going to a nice place. I wanted to show you I can be civilized—though I'd rather not do it too often," he told her with a wink before holding out his gifts. "Let's have a toast before we leave."

"That sounds nice," she said, accepting the rose, lifting it to her nose, and inhaling before moving to the counter and grabbing a small vase to put it in. "This smells divine. Thank you."

He hadn't been planning on buying her flowers, but he'd passed an outdoor stand and saw the containers with red roses. The flowers had reminded him of her lips, and he'd just grabbed hold of the one and couldn't put it back.

He had a picture in his head of trailing the velvet petals across her smooth skin. And just like that, he was hard and wanting. It was a good thing they were leaving the cottage. His hunger for her was insatiable.

"Sit down. I'll pour us each a glass," he told her, surprised when she actually listened and moved over to the small living room. She took a seat, watching him as he fumbled with the wine opener.

Were his hands shaking? No way. That was impossible. After a couple of tries, he got the corkscrew to line up and then managed to get the cork out of the wine. He poured them each a glass. He brought them over to her along with the strawberries before taking a seat next to her.

"Where are we going tonight?" she asked as she took a sip of the wine and sighed.

"Italian."

"Yummy." She reached forward and picked up one of the strawberries. She nibbled on its sweetness and let out another sigh. "You're spoiling me, you know."

"Hardly. I want to give you the world, and this doesn't even touch that," he said, realizing he actually meant it. There really wasn't anything he didn't want this woman to have—including himself.

Why did he have to complicate it? And why did he have to have a timeline on their romance? Wouldn't it be so much easier if he just went with the flow and let things progress naturally?

It probably would. But then he might get so involved he wouldn't know how to stop. And though everything seemed nearly perfect at the moment, it wouldn't be in a few months—that was a given.

He pushed those thoughts away as he looked at the beautiful woman next to him. She was perfectly content to sip her wine and delicately eat her chocolate-covered strawberry. He held up his wine glass.

"There are challenges in life, some of which are harder to get up from than others. But you are beautiful, talented, kind, strong, and sexy. Thank you for letting me be a part of your life," he said as he reached the glass toward hers.

"Thank you for helping me to feel like me again. And for showing me that it's okay to live and not just exist," she said before clinking her glass against his and taking a sip.

There was a slight sheen of tears in her eyes that made him want to reach across the small space dividing them and pull her close. But she looked down for a moment and took a few breaths. When she met his eyes again, the telling sparkle was gone.

"Are you ready for a night of romance?" he asked, suddenly in a hurry to get away from the cottage. The intimacy was too great.

"Romance, huh? What about excitement?" she asked with a smile.

"I have more than one layer to me. I've taken you on exciting adventures. Sometimes it's also nice to slow down," he said as he stood and held out a hand to help her up.

The moment her fingers laced with his, his good intentions of leaving for dinner were pushed aside. He pulled her into his arms and tasted her sweet lips. Before he could devour her whole, he pulled back. He moved over to her closet where he grabbed her jacket.

Standing behind her, he helped her put it on, unable to stop himself from leaning forward and running his lips across the smooth skin at the base of her neck. Her scent made his knees tremble.

"I want to take you into the bedroom and kiss every inch of your skin," he whispered before running his lips across her ear.

He felt her shiver against him as she sighed and leaned back.

"I'm not all that hungry," she said.

"Oh, I'm certainly hungry," he replied before turning her and taking one more taste of her lips. "But I promised you a night out first."

With that, he took her hand again and opened the door. When she stepped out and saw the limo he had waiting for her, the smile on her lips made his agony of waiting to touch her worth the wait.

"What's this?" she asked as she tugged on his hand and stepped toward the car. The driver quickly opened the back door.

"I want to spoil you tonight," he replied as he helped her inside.

"You're off to a really good start."

They got comfortable in the backseat before he poured them each another glass of wine. He leaned back, enjoying her look of joy as she faced him. She was too far away, but he figured that was probably the safer position at the moment considering his libido was revved up.

"How do you always know what to do each and every time?" she asked, a glow in her cheeks from the good wine.

"I seem to know how you're feeling and what you need," he answered. It was odd, but true.

"And how am I feeling right now?" she asked in a teasing voice.

His pants tightened as he grew even harder looking at her. The outfit she was wearing didn't hide much from him. Her ample chest was rising and falling as her breaths came out in excited little pants. Her legs were shifting as she squeezed her thighs tightly together.

There was a glow in her eyes, and her lips were moist. She was as excited as he was.

"You're anticipating the night ahead and counting down the minutes until I can strip away that sexy outfit you're wearing," he responded before drinking down the rest of his wine. He needed a lot more to keep his libido in check.

"I guess you *are* pretty observant, then," she said, her cheeks heating a bit more as her eyes drooped the slightest bit in her aroused state.

They arrived at the restaurant just before he lost control and leapt across the seats to devour her whole. His desire for this woman was relentless, and he feared he would never feel this way again about another.

To let her go seemed so foolish, but she wasn't his to keep—no matter how much he might want to change that fact.

CHAPTER
THIRTY-SEVEN

The place Maverick had chosen was small and intimate, the tables lit from above with dim chandeliers, accented by flickering candles as centerpieces. He and Lindsey were led to a table in the back corner, where they would have even more privacy.

He could most likely take her right there or, at the very least, slip his fingers beneath her skirt and make her moan into his mouth without anyone being the wiser.

The thought of doing just that had him walking funny as they were led to their table.

Pulling out her seat, he waited until she was comfortable before he moved to the other side of the table and sat, shifting around until he was somewhat comfortable. Until he was deep inside her body, he wouldn't achieve anything near relief on this night, though.

"Your wine, sir," the waiter said as he broke the silence between them.

"I've ordered ahead if that's okay," Maverick told her as he sipped the wine and nodded his head.

She took a sip of the new bottle and smiled. "It's even better than what we had in the limo," she told him. "I guess you do know what I like more than I do. I don't know if I should be afraid of that or not."

"A man who pays attention to a woman is a smart man indeed," he told her.

"Or he's a man who knows how to get what he wants," she pointed out.

"Is there anything wrong with that?"

The waiter was gone but came back again with a selection of appetizers before he disappeared once more. She took her time to think about his last statement.

"No. I guess not. I've always been around confident men," she began and his eyes narrowed.

"I don't like thinking of you with other men." The instant possessiveness he felt belied his goal of setting her free.

"I was talking about my brothers, actually," she said with a chuckle before picking up a shrimp, dipping it in cocktail sauce, and then delicately taking a bite.

"Well, I guess that's okay, then," he told her. "Your brothers are certainly protective of you."

"Yes, they always have been. That's what happens when you're the only girl out of six children. My poor mother said I was her last chance to get a girl. She loves each of us so much, but she'd wanted a girl for so long. She'd threatened my father that if I was another boy, she was moving away," Lindsey told him.

"I can imagine it would feel slightly overwhelming to be in a home with nothing but testosterone all day," Mav said.

"Yeah. She said she'd always wanted a large family, but she'd planned on only four children. Then when Erik came out, another boy, she got pregnant again hoping for a girl. Of course, she had Seth next, and she told my father her family was full. I was actually an accident. She got pregnant before my father was able to go in and take care of permanent birth control. He did it, though, while she was pregnant with me. She didn't get an ultrasound, saying it would be bad luck. Dad said she cried tears of joy for three days straight when I came out with the right parts."

Mav smiled at her impish look. "It looks like you saved your mother's sanity," he told her. He didn't comment on the fact that she had indeed come out with all the right parts.

"She might have regretted her desire to have a girl, though, because I was a terror child. I started walking at eight months, running at a year old, and I didn't slow down until I hit twenty-one. I got in more trouble than all of my brothers combined," she said.

"Why is that?" he asked.

"I felt I had to prove myself, I guess," she said with another chuckle. "My brothers were huge and everyone loved them. They played sports, had all the girls drooling over them, and were the teachers' pets. I wanted to stand out, and I was never as good as them, so I found other ways to do it."

He was shocked by her statement. Reaching across the table, he took her hand and tugged, getting her to look at him.

"Never say you aren't as good as anyone," he commanded. "You're beautiful, intelligent, and have a huge heart. We all make our own way in life any way we can. Don't doubt for a moment that you are special."

Her eyes shone as she met his gaze. "You've done wonders for my ego, Maverick Armstrong. I'm so glad you decided to make me your mission, even if I was ready to throttle you for it at first."

"This has been more than a mission to me, you know that, right?" he said as his thumb caressed the back of her hand.

"We're friends," she said. He wanted to deny her words. "Friends that have found a pretty smoking hot chemistry in the bedroom," she added.

"There's more to us than that," he said, feeling agitated.

"Let's not focus on that, Mav. Didn't you tell me that tonight is about romance?" she pointed out.

He wanted to argue more with her, but wasn't she right? This night—this entire week, actually—was about him giving her a wonderful time before their time ended. Why was he mad when she was saying the exact same thing?

Maybe because he was having such a difficult time letting her go.

He needed her to walk away from him feeling stronger, more beautiful, and ready to face the world. How was she going to do that if he refused to let her go? She couldn't.

She tugged on his fingers and there was worry in her eyes.

"Are you okay, Mav? Something feels a little off tonight."

He needed to add to her list of qualities that she was incredibly observant.

"Of course," he said, before shooting her the smile she'd told him made her knees go a little weak. "I'm with you, so the night couldn't be more perfect."

He pushed down his odd emotions. They weren't necessary. What she needed from him tonight was his full attention, to be left with only good memories from their time together.

"You're such a smooth talker," she said as the waiter approached.

"I didn't order the main course. Think I can guess what you'd prefer?" he asked, making sure his voice was light.

"So far, you've been spot on, Mr. Armstrong. Let's see if you can keep it up."

She pulled her fingers back as she sipped on her wine and had another piece of shrimp. Mav spoke to the waiter. He was so unfocused right now, it was hard to be away from her touch. It was almost as if she were grounding him to the Earth.

That was a ridiculous notion.

For one thing, he didn't want to be grounded. He was happiest when he was high in the sky, flying at top speeds, only a contrail behind him to show the path he'd just taken. For another, they were good together but didn't *need* each other to survive.

He would have to remind himself of that a lot tonight.

They continued their meal, eating asparagus ravioli, and orzo with roasted carrots and dill, along with another bottle of excellent wine. Maverick could feel the buzz from the liquor, but it was nothing compared to the buzz he felt from simply being in Lindsey's presence as she nibbled and sipped.

"This is so good. You need to have a taste," she told him as she scooped a portion of artichoke cheese dip onto a piece of crusty bread and held it out to him.

Taking a bite from the bread, his tongue swirled across her fingers. He was at the end of what he could handle.

"Delicious," he told her, their eyes locking, hers dilating as his groin flexed.

She leaned toward him, and he pushed the food aside as he took a taste of her lips, her own flavor mixed with those of the food and drink they'd been devouring. Leaning back, the desire was clear in her dark eyes.

"Are you going to be okay, sugar?" he asked as he looked deeply into her gaze.

She was as startled by the question as he was by asking it. They both felt the slight hint of sadness in the air. He had been trying to hide it from her, just like she was doing an unsuccessful job at keeping her emotions from him.

"What do you mean?" she asked, stalling for time.

"I just need to know that you'll be okay," he said. This was by far the most important thing to him, he realized.

She analyzed the question, which he was grateful for. He wanted to make sure she was taking it seriously.

"Yes, I think I will be," she told him and then she smiled.

"Good. I want all your dreams to come true. I want to make sure you don't live in the past and you don't let fears haunt you," he told her.

"You've helped me more than any other person in my life, Mav. There aren't words I could properly say that could ever express how grateful I am to you. And honestly, I'm going to be okay."

"Then why the sadness?" he asked as he gripped her fingers. There would never be a time when the feel of her would get old. Why he was pushing her, he didn't know. They both were feeling a slight edge of urgency and sadness.

Did he want her to say it? Did he want her to tell him that their parting wasn't what she wanted? What would he do if she did say that? Would he stay? He didn't know.

She knew that their time was coming to a close, and she was just as reluctant to see that happen. So why wasn't one of them trying to stop it, he wondered. It didn't make sense. But nothing about their relationship made sense if he were being honest with himself.

"I'm not sad. I've enjoyed our time together," she replied, before looking down, breaking the intense connection between them.

"Life has a way of getting in the way, doesn't it?" he said, attempting a chuckle.

"Why don't we just not think about any of that tonight?" she suggested. She looked back up and gazed at him with a boldness in her eyes he hadn't seen before.

He thought over her words, and didn't see a flaw in them. She was ready for him to let her go, but not tonight. No, tonight was about pleasure, love, and romance.

Tomorrow they could both think about the decisions they'd made in life.

"Dessert?" he asked.

"I'm more than ready for that," she told him, fire burning in her gaze.

They were both on the same slate as to what dessert was going to be.

He didn't say another word, just threw down a wad of money for their meal and then stood up. He needed to get her back to her place. He wasn't letting her out of bed the rest of the night.

CHAPTER THIRTY-EIGHT

In some ways, Lindsey's heart was shattering, but in other ways it was healing. She knew this was her last night with Maverick.

This wouldn't be the final time she saw him, but it would be the last time they were together in a romantic way. Instead of dwelling on that fact, she would embrace it as she embraced him and end their time together on a memorable note.

She'd fought being with the man—hadn't thought she needed him, but now she realized he'd been her savior. He'd helped her conquer her fears. And she'd discovered that she hadn't had to lose a piece of herself if she were with a man.

She would be able to love herself *and* somebody else. Her forever person just wouldn't be Maverick Armstrong.

But for tonight, he was hers—and she was his.

The moment they stepped back into her cottage, he pulled her into his arms and kissed her with both tenderness and passion. Her body rose in temperature as he slowly walked them to her bedroom, not bothering to shut the door. It was only the two of them in the place—in what felt like the entire universe.

Holding her the entire way, the kiss grew more intense as they gravitated toward the bed, neither of them willing to let go of the other. Their lips and tongues mated in possession and need.

Their fingers clutched at the other's clothes as they fought to get rid of anything keeping them from being one. In almost a blur, their clothing was ripped away. Maverick lifted her with his muscled arms before gently laying her on the bed, not breaking their connection for even a moment as he climbed on top of her.

She sighed and panted into his mouth as his beautiful fingers skirted across her skin, touching every single place on her body before delving down to her core. He slipped inside, finding her hot and wet—ready for him.

He groaned against her lips before his mouth trailed down between her breasts, one hand pinching her nipple and making her whimper in total abandon. She squirmed beneath his expert touch.

"You taste so good," he murmured as he licked his way down to her center. Spreading her legs wide, he ran his tongue along her pulsing pleasure. She arched off the bed as he tasted her, teased her, and intensified the flames that were already out of control.

As she reached higher and higher toward her climax, he seemed to know the moment she was about to set sail, because he would move his luscious mouth and temper the flames before going back and doing it all over again.

He seemed to want this to never end, which was just exactly how she felt. Though the build-up was nearly destroying her. She reached into his thick dark strands of hair and tugged on him, all to no avail. He was on a mission and nothing was going to detour him from it.

Whimpering and begging did her no good. He continued devouring her body in endless delight, his groans of pleasure making hers that much better. She needed to touch him, though, and he was denying her that. She was growing more insistent in her tugs on his hair.

Finally, he climbed back up her body, his cheeks flushed, his skin hot and damp to the touch, his beautiful green eyes dark with desire.

Right now, in this frozen moment of time, they belonged to one another. There wasn't a single other soul in the world. It was a connection that couldn't be faked. She desperately wanted to tell him of her love, but somehow managed to keep the words locked in her throat.

Reaching beneath her, he clasped tightly to her butt as he pulled her up against his straining erection, making the heat in her core go even hotter.

"I can't get enough of you," he whispered as he leaned down, their mouths mating again as their bodies molded as one. He slowly slipped inside her, letting her take him inch by precious inch until the connection was solid and complete.

"Then take all you want," she told him, giving everything she had of herself. No matter where life took them, she would always be his. No one would have this piece of her, no matter how much time passed, no matter who she met in the future.

This was beyond lovemaking. This was a merging of souls. She hoped she had changed him too, that he wouldn't be the same ever again. Yes, they would live healthy, productive lives, but she wanted him to leave with a piece of her, just as she wanted to take a piece of him.

Her eyes closed as he began moving in and out of her body, picking up the pace as their breathing filled the air around them. Their desire grew and grew.

"So beautiful," he groaned as he held tightly to her butt and pounded against her flesh. "So tight—hot—wet."

He continued whispering words against her ear as they moved in perfect rhythm against each other, their bodies damp with sweat, hot with desire.

And then she couldn't hold out any longer. In an overwhelming blindness, she exploded, her tight core closing around him as she shook in his arms.

His hot breath rushed out against her ear as he hugged her close and spilled his seed deep within her womb. They both shook as they came down from the high of such intense lovemaking.

Neither moved for what might have been hours as their hearts beat against each other in perfect rhythm. Lindsey knew that when she fell asleep, he would slip away into the night.

And she also knew that he'd made sure she would be okay.

Nothing would make her regret her time with Maverick. Not even saying good-bye.

CHAPTER
THIRTY-NINE

Tossing his flight bag on his bed, Maverick glared at the light on his answering machine, blinking over and over again, telling him he had a message—or a dozen messages.

He'd been in a bear of a mood for the past two weeks. And his damn family didn't want to leave him alone. Mav knew the mood would pass. His behavior wasn't dependent on if he missed a woman or not.

Time would make things better. That was, if his family would just leave him alone. He was back at work, and happy to be there. Hell, he'd just come back from a flight to Oregon where he'd done some low maneuvers that normally would put him in a great mood.

It seemed nothing was putting him in a good mood these days, though.

Mav was always the life of the party, the one to smile when everyone else was scowling. He was the one who laughed when other people were in foul moods. So why in the world couldn't he pull himself out of this constant anger he seemed to be feeling?

It certainly wasn't over a woman—even a woman as amazing as Lindsey.

Moving over to his liquor cabinet, he undid his shirt, letting it hang open as he poured a double shot of whiskey. He threw his head back as he let the amber liquid burn its way down his throat.

Even the fire pouring through him wasn't enough to help. He seriously needed to pull himself together. Looking over at the phone again, the temptation to call Lindsey was almost so overwhelming he thought about tossing the phone through his window.

He hadn't been carrying his cellphone just to avoid the temptation of shooting the woman a quick text, or simply caving in and dialing her up. He missed her—more than he'd ever thought possible.

They'd said good-bye. Sure, it hadn't been a long, drawn-out occasion, but that last date had been their good-bye and they both knew it. She was working full time and he was back at the base most days. They were living their lives.

After taking another double shot, Mav finally moved back over to his phone and pressed the button. He might as well find out what was happening on the home front. No one other than his family was bothering to call him these days. His mood was enough to send people fleeing in the opposite direction.

"It's Uncle Sherman. Call me ASAP."

No other messages followed. Mav didn't want to call back. Didn't want to talk to anyone right now, but he knew from personal experience that if he tried to avoid his uncle, the old man would just keep on pestering him.

The phone barely had a chance to get through one ring when his uncle picked up. Uncle Sherman skipped the usual greetings.

"I left you a message six hours ago. I see where I sit on your priorities," Sherman said with obvious annoyance in his voice.

"I've been at work, Uncle. How are you doing?" Mav said as he moved over to refill his glass. He wasn't flying tomorrow. He could drink whatever the heck he felt like drinking. This night, it might be a lot.

"I'm fine. It's you I've been worried about," Sherman responded.

His uncle had called him every possible negative name when he'd told the old man he wasn't dating Lindsey, that he'd just been helping her out for a while, but their time was over.

Mav was doing better than his uncle over the breakup—not that it was a breakup. You couldn't end something that had never begun in the first place. But Sherman sure was a meddler. He just didn't know when to keep out of other people's business. That was a fact.

"There's nothing to worry about, Sherman. I'm busy working or I would be coming around more," he said, feeling like a broken record.

"There's more to life than just work, you know," Sherman told him for the thousandth time. "I thought you were starting to learn that, had wizened up from watching the example of your older brother. Look how good Cooper is doing with a beautiful wife and son. You're all alone in a big empty house."

"I'm not alone. I have Benji," Mav told him as he moved across the living room and sat down. The dog immediately rushed over to him and gave Mav those sad eyes. Mav was sure Benji missed Lindsey too, or maybe that was all in his head.

"You need more than just a dog," Sherman grumbled.

If Maverick didn't love his uncle so much, he would simply hang up the phone and then unplug it. Heck, he might even think about transferring to another base where he wouldn't have to listen to his family tell him how much he was screwing up.

But as soon as the thought entered his thick skull, it went right back out again. He wasn't going anywhere. This was home and it was where he wanted to be. Even if he would prefer the family leave him alone.

"You're a great kid, Mav. You just need to quit being so stubborn," Sherman said, switching gears.

Mav couldn't help but smile. He guessed it didn't matter how old he got, he still liked to hear encouraging words from a man who was more than an uncle to him.

"Thanks, Sherman, and I wonder where I learned that stubbornness from," he said, the corners of his lips tilting up the slightest bit—a first in the past couple of weeks.

"I might be stubborn, but I'm also wise enough to know when I'm being a fool," Sherman told him. "I want you to be happy."

"I am happy, Uncle. I love my career, and my brothers. I have a great mom who I get to spend time with. What more do I need?"

As soon as he said the words, he wanted to take them back, because he knew for sure that Sherman would have no problem telling him in detail what he needed.

"Stop being a fool and go get the girl. Lindsey is perfect for you and you just walked away. I don't like it one little bit," Sherman said.

"She's not mine. She never was," Mav said with a sigh.

"All you have to do is tell her how you feel and she *would* be yours," Sherman countered.

"How do you know that?" Mav snapped.

"Because I saw the two of you together. And right now, she's just as miserable as you are since you've been apart."

That sentence stopped Mav in his tracks. No one had said she'd been miserable. From everything he'd heard, she was doing great—thriving, in fact.

"Where did you hear she was miserable?" Mav asked. He shouldn't play into what his uncle was saying, but he couldn't seem to help himself.

"I saw her just a couple days ago and she seemed so sad. Not even one of her beautiful smiles was shared with me," Sherman said.

"That doesn't mean she's miserable, Uncle. It might just mean she's tired or had a stressful day at work," Mav told him.

Maverick didn't want her to be upset, but he wouldn't mind her missing him just the slightest bit. He admitted that only to himself.

"Okay, I promise to leave you alone if you come out of hiding and spend some time with your family," Sherman said, once again changing tones.

Maverick was instantly suspicious.

"What do you mean?" he asked, not agreeing to anything.

"There's a get-together in a couple days at my friend Joseph's place. You're invited."

Well, there really wasn't a chance of him running into Lindsey at Joseph's. It might be nice to catch up with old friends.

"Okay. I'll come," he told him.

Mav could practically feel Sherman smiling through the phone. Maverick couldn't find a reason to take back his assent at going, though, even though he knew he was doing exactly as the old man wanted.

"Good, then I won't keep bugging you tonight. I'll see you soon."

With that, Sherman hung up the phone before Mav had a chance to say his own good-bye.

Mav didn't move from his easy chair for a long time, and when he did, it was only to grab a bite to eat and shower before he climbed into his cold, empty bed. Maybe one more visit with Lindsey wouldn't be such a bad thing.

No! He pushed the weak thought out of his head. He couldn't do that to her or him. Another good-bye wasn't what they needed to move on with their lives.

If only that nagging feeling in the back of his mind wasn't telling him that all he needed to feel better was to admit how he felt. It wasn't going to happen. Once again, Mav didn't sleep well at all.

CHAPTER FORTY

The hospital was hopping as Lindsey rushed from patient to patient in an attempt to keep up with the influx of people stumbling in through the large sliding doors. Exhaustion had become a constant for her. Sleep hadn't been coming to her so easily since her last night with Maverick.

Even having Princess beneath the covers with her every night wasn't helping much. She adored her dog, but it wasn't the same as having strong arms pull you in close, making you feel protected from the entire world.

She was getting ready to suture a patient when the new intern turned too fast and cut her arm with a scalpel, making Lindsey's eyes instantly start to water.

"I'm so sorry, Lindsey. I don't know how that happened," the new girl said, her own eyes filling and spilling over as she panicked and grabbed gauze, pushing too roughly when she placed it over Lindsey's wound.

"It's fine," Lindsey told the young nurse through gritted teeth. Lindsey then moved away from the patient so her blood wouldn't get on her. Both the patient and the nurse looked a little freaked out.

"I'll send the other nurse in," she told the woman before turning and walking away, the intern on her heels.

"Go get the nurse," Lindsey told her as she moved to another exam room to see the damage.

She wasn't in there for more than a few seconds when Dr. Stine walked in, his usual good-natured grin on his face.

"Peggy was gushing so much, I couldn't understand half of what she was saying, but I'm assuming from the white face and the blood-covered bandage that you've been wounded," he told her as he placed a hand beneath her elbow and led her over to the exam table.

"I'm fine," Lindsey told him, her jaw set. "She just cut me, that's all. I'm sure it won't even need stiches." Why in the world were her teeth chattering? It wasn't like it was that big a deal. She'd been hurt at work before and certainly hadn't been such a baby. She blamed lack of sleep on her heightened emotions.

"Let me look at it, and I'll be the judge," he told her as he attempted to get to the bandage she was holding in place.

"This certainly isn't a matter for you, Dr. Stine. I'm sure you have patients galore," she said, pulling her arm back.

"My schedule is all clear. You're my patient right now," he said as he took her hand and tugged her arm harder this time.

Dr. Stine still hadn't given up on her even though she'd made it more than obvious she wasn't interested in a relationship. He was the last person she wanted examining her. It wasn't that she was repulsed by him or anything. He was kind, funny, and great looking. It was just that her heart was broken and she really wasn't about to see if she could open that wound all over again with another male.

Without reason, her eyes suddenly filled up and spilled over as she looked into the doctor's deep blue eyes. He gazed back at her with too much understanding. Dang it! Why couldn't Peggy have sent in one of the nurses? She didn't need to fall apart in front of the doctor.

"Come on, doll. Let me see," he said.

This time she let him take away the gauze and then she cringed. The wound was worse than she thought. It was deep, with blood still trickling out and measuring about two inches long.

"This will definitely need stitches," he said before squeezing her hand. He gave her another piece of gauze. "Hold this in place while I get what I need."

"I can have Linda stitch it up," she told him.

"Just lie back and relax. I'm doing it," he said, still with a smile, but his firm voice coming through loud and clear. He wasn't going to allow her to argue with him anymore.

She did what he said and laid back on the bed as he brought over a tray.

The stupid cut was pulsing and she began to understand a little more why her patients would moan and groan so much when the injuries appeared to be minor. There was no way for the medical personnel to get inside a patient's head to know what they were feeling.

Dr. Stine gave her some medicine and a numbing shot before he cleaned the wound. Lindsey tried, but she couldn't keep the tears in. What the heck? She hadn't cried once since Maverick had disappeared out of her life. Not when Stormy constantly asked how she was doing and looked at her in that sympathetic way, not when she'd smashed her toe on her bed post, and not when she woke up from a dream of him holding her only to find herself alone.

So why in the world was she sobbing like a baby from little more than a scratch? She again blamed her lack of sleep on the unusual emotions.

"Now, I know I don't have the gentlest hand in the hospital, but I'm not really all that bad, am I?" Dr. Stine asked. He had stopped working and put a finger below her chin to tilt her head up. She was forced to look into his eyes.

"I don't know what's the matter with me. It doesn't even hurt. I think I just need to get more sleep," she said through sobbing hiccups.

"Do you want to talk about it?" he asked with a sense of knowing in his voice.

"No," she sobbed.

He didn't go back to work, just sat there, waiting. Lindsey was beginning to see why all the nurses were swooning after him. If only she were attracted to the good doctor and could agree to go out on a date with him. Maybe she would begin to feel better if she did.

"Whoever the guy is that let you go is a fool, you know," Dr. Stine said as he finally broke the connection of their gaze and began stitching her arm up again.

"What are you talking about?" she asked, the pain medicine he'd given her beginning to kick in and making her feel slightly loopy.

"I've watched you a lot in the past month, Lindsey. You were almost glowing a couple weeks ago. and then something happened. It's been like watching a lightbulb slowly start to fade."

She was totally confused by that analogy, but he continued.

"I'm not saying you aren't just as beautiful. And if you said *yes*, I would jump at the chance to take you out and show you how a man should treat a woman, but it's more than obvious that your heart belongs to someone else," he said.

There was a smile on his lips, but also a spark of understanding so deep in his eyes that she couldn't help more tears from falling.

"I wasn't in a relationship, not really. I just had a hard time after the hospital attack and my best friend's brother-in-law decided to show me life was worth living again. I knew from the beginning we weren't going to stay together. I guess I've just had a harder time than I thought letting him go," she said.

The damn pain medicine was making her share far more than she should have been sharing, especially with the doctor who'd made no qualms about liking her.

He finished up her stitches, bandaged her, and then leaned way too close into her personal bubble. He brushed his fingers against her cheek, making the tears stop instantly.

"The best medicine for a broken heart is to open it back up again to a real man," he said before giving her his mega-wattage smile. "And I *am* the doctor. You should listen to me."

Then before she had time to react, he leaned in and kissed her. It was a sweet kiss, just a brushing of his lips against hers. Then he stood up and helped her into a seated position. She was so stunned, she had no words.

"I'm being paged, but I want you to sit here for fifteen more minutes. Then I'm going to call your emergency contact to come pick you up. You can't work with the pain meds, and you certainly can't drive."

"Don't call my mom!" she shouted as he turned to leave. "My entire family will show up if they get a call from the hospital," she finished more quietly.

"Okay, who do you want me to call?"

Maverick was her first thought, but she pushed that away. Then she pulled her phone from her pocket and gave him Stormy's number.

"I'm not giving up on you until I see a ring on your finger," he said with an intensity in his eyes that left her speechless.

He walked from the room without waiting for a reply from her.

Lindsey didn't move, not even when Stormy came rushing into the room, worry clearly written all over her brow.

When she found out what had happened, though, her worry turned to merriment, which had Lindsey glaring at her best friend.

"Gotta love newbies," Stormy told her.

"Get me out of here," Lindsey said as her friend helped her off the table.

"You must be the best friend."

Lindsey groaned when she found Dr. Stine leaning in the doorway. This was going to lead to far too many questions from Stormy. She was sort of wishing the intern had gouged her a lot worse, requiring her to stay the night away from prying best friends.

"Yes, I am. And who are you?" Stormy asked as her gaze whipped back and forth between Lindsey and the doctor.

"I'm the doc trying to woo your friend. Who's the guy who broke her heart?" he asked with boldness.

Lindsey gasped. They both ignored her.

"My brother-in-law. And as cute as you are, I wouldn't get your hopes up. I don't see their story ending anytime soon," Stormy sassily told him.

"Until I see a ring, I have a shot," he said with a wink.

Unbelievably, Stormy laughed. "Oh, I really like you, doc," she said with that smile that Lindsey had loved from the moment she'd met Stormy.

"It's always good to get the best friend on your side," Dr. Stine said with a wink.

"That it is. You must have sisters," she said.

"I think it's time to go now," Lindsey interrupted.

"I'm not in a hurry," Stormy said before returning her attention back to the doctor.

"I do have three little sisters, actually," he told her.

"I'll be sure to let you know if things don't work out between Lindsey and Maverick," Stormy told him.

"I'm right here!" Lindsey said as she glared at both of them.

"Yes, you are. Trust me, doll, you're never forgettable," Dr. Stine said before his pager went off and he frowned. "We will have to continue this later."

He then took off running, and Lindsey turned her full fury on Stormy.

"That was so uncalled for," she snapped.

"There's nothing like a little jealousy to make a man crazy," Stormy said in a singsong voice.

"What's that supposed to mean?" Lindsey asked.

They finally began moving down the hallway, Stormy gathering Lindsey's purse and coat before exiting the building.

"It means that I'm going to love telling Maverick about the good doctor," Stormy said as she held her car door open.

If Lindsey weren't already feeling good from the pain medicine, she would have had a snappy comment for her friend. But as she sat down and buckled up, she felt her eyes growing heavy.

She'd give Stormy an earful later. After she'd had a nap.

CHAPTER
FORTY-ONE

Maverick should have known better. Nothing came without a price these days. And his uncle was far too much of a meddler to not try to do something about what he deemed a situation that needed to be fixed.

Even knowing this, Maverick couldn't help but stare at Lindsey as she stood by the fire on Joseph Anderson's private beach and talked animatedly to Stormy. Of course she was at the get-together. Why else would Sherman have insisted on him coming? The old man was meddling.

Some people needed to just leave well enough alone.

Maverick couldn't keep his eyes off Lindsey as she turned and laughed at something Cooper said to her, her chest rising and falling in the fitted summer dress she wore that was showing enough leg to grab the attention of every available male on the beach.

He closed his eyes as he remembered running his hands up those silky smooth calves, across her soft thighs to her hot center.

Snapping his eyes back open, he shifted on his feet. Thoughts like that weren't going to get him anywhere but into a hell of a lot of trouble. But dammit, if just at that moment, a small gust of wind didn't come straight from the heavens and ruffle the bottom of her hem, making the garment flutter a bit higher.

His mouth was watering as he waited to get a peek at her delectable assets—and she had perfect ones.

When the wind died and he groaned the slightest bit is when he heard the chuckle. He turned to find Nick approaching with way too knowing a look in his eyes.

"Enjoying the view, brother?" Nick said as he took a swig of his beer.

Maverick's attention was wrenched away from Lindsey as he focused on his brother.

"Yes, it's a nice night," he said, ignoring the knowing tone in Nick's voice.

"Lindsey sure does look good tonight," he said with a sparkle in his eyes.

"Yes, she's in a great mood too," Cooper said as he joined in the conversation. Maverick hadn't even noticed he'd walked away from Lindsey and Stormy. He needed to be on better alert.

"Yeah, I need to get over there and see how she's doing," Nick said, poking the bear wanting to roar inside Mav.

"Go on and talk to her," Cooper told Nick. "She's been telling us about her baseball game."

"He doesn't need to go and talk to her," Mav snapped before he could stop himself.

"Why not?" Nick asked with too much innocence.

"There's no reason. You just don't need to," Mav growled.

"You aren't interested in seeing her anymore, so I don't see what it matters," Nick told him.

"Dammit, Nick!" Maverick thundered before managing to lower his voice when several people turned their way. "She's off limits." This last bit came out between his gritted teeth.

"Well, are you going to do something about it, or not?" Cooper said pointedly.

"I don't know what you're talking about," Maverick said.

"It's more than obvious you're in love with this woman. If you don't do something about it soon, then you'll regret it because women like Lindsey don't stay available for long," Cooper told him.

"Yeah, and the good Dr. Stine is totally after her," Nick said.

"How the hell do you know that?" Mav asked.

"Stormy told me, and I told Nick," Cooper said.

"What are you talking about?" Maverick was getting a massive migraine.

"Stormy had to pick Lindsey up yesterday from the hospital because she got hurt—"

"What?" Maverick cut him off as his eyes immediately sought out Lindsey to make sure she was okay. She didn't appear to be injured, but as his eyes scanned her from head to toe, he noticed the bandage on her arm for the first time. Maybe if he hadn't been staring at her legs and breasts, he might have noticed sooner. "What happened?"

"It wasn't much. She got cut by an intern, but the apparently fantastic Dr. Stine is the one who patched her all up. He then told Stormy he was going to have Lindsey sooner or later," Cooper said, too much glee in his voice as he shared the information.

"Like hell he will," Maverick said.

At that moment, Lindsey looked up and their gazes connected across the sand. His must have been intense because her eyes widened and her cheeks colored before she ripped her gaze away and looked down.

"Are you going to do something about it?" Nick asked.

"Yeah, I think it's about time I did," Mav said.

He took a step toward Lindsey. They were going to have a talk. Because he sure as hell wasn't going to allow another guy to come in and sweep her off her feet. The thought of such a thing happening made his stomach churn.

All of his pep talks went out the window when he took off for her and touched her arm. She didn't say a word as he led her off somewhere a lot more private. Only when they were away from other people did she turn on him.

"What do you think you're doing? That was embarrassing, Mav," she snapped.

"I want to know what you're doing," he snapped back. "What in the hell is going on with Dr. Stine?"

Her eyes rounded as he asked the question, taking a menacing step in her direction.

"Wh . . . what are you talking about?" she stumbled, but he saw the pink in her cheeks.

"Feeling guilty?" he asked.

That was the wrong thing to say. Her eyes narrowed as she lifted her hand, planting it in the center of his chest to stop him from pressing in closer.

"No. I have nothing to feel guilty about. Even if I were seeing another man it wouldn't be any of your business. We aren't a couple, have never been a couple, and won't be one in the future," she said, her chest rising and falling in her agitation.

"None of my business?" he thundered. "Everything you just said doesn't make sense." He had to take a breath. "If we weren't in a relationship then what the hell were we doing?"

The feel of her small hand on his chest was making his head a bit fuzzy, even if the touch wasn't in any small way supposed to resemble a caress. He'd missed her touch so damn much.

"You were on a mission. That mission ended. Now please leave me alone," she told him, before turning and walking away.

Before she made it two steps, he grabbed her uninjured arm and pulled her back to him, this time making her stumble into his chest. He didn't say another word, just bent down and devoured her mouth, putting his mark on her and making sure she knew he was around.

When he pulled back, she was panting. He leaned forward to kiss her again. She was faster though, and raised her hand, smacking him on the cheek before he knew what was happening.

He released her in his shock, and she stumbled backward.

"Don't touch me anymore, Maverick. You've lost that right," she said and then she turned around and ran, but not before he heard the slight hiccup of a cry escape her throat.

She was hurting and that was all on him. He felt her pain to the very pits of his soul.

That's when Maverick decided he needed to do something about it. He'd let her go and it had only brought both of them pain. It was time to fix that.

CHAPTER
FORTY-TWO

Sherman was sitting back in a nice lounge chair with Joseph beside him as he watched Maverick grab hold of Lindsey and take her off somewhere private. Neither man could hide their grins.

"Looks like those two are sure fired up tonight," Joseph said as he puffed on his cigar.

"Yep. They sure have been foolish these past few weeks, but with his brothers prodding him, it won't be long until Maverick is down on one knee proposing to that girl," Sherman said.

"Why do they always have to make it so difficult? If they'd just listen to us in the first place we wouldn't have to do all this meddling," Joseph said with a chuckle.

"You know you would be bored silly if they made it too easy on us," Sherman said. "Though I have to admit, I've been a little worried. Those two haven't spoken for a while."

"Well, it just gave me an excuse to throw a party," Joseph told his friend.

"You don't need an excuse, my friend," Sherman said. "You love to have all your friends and family gathered close by."

As he spoke, a group of Joseph's grandchildren went rushing past, their giggles filling the air as they chased two puppies.

"Life is far too lonely all by yourself. I don't understand these young people thinking they can make it on their own. Why would anyone want to do that when it's so much better to have the love of your life by your side every single day?" Joseph grumbled.

"Yes. I miss my wife so much still that it brings an ache to my heart when I think about her," Sherman said. "It helps me, though, seeing the boys slowly beginning to find love."

"I wouldn't know what to do without my Katherine. She's the love of my life. If she knew how much I was messing in the kids' lives, she would smack me, though," Joseph said as he looked around nervously.

"Your grandkids are sure growing up fast," Sherman told him.

"Yes, they are. There will soon be a whole new generation for me to get my hands on," Joseph said as he looked out across the beach and spotted Jasmine, who was a true beauty. "She's starting college this fall. I can't believe how quickly the time passes."

"Is there anyone special in her life?" Sherman asked.

"No. She's still too young. I'll give her a few years before I start thinking about great-grandchildren," he said with a bear of a laugh.

"Yes. I still have to help Nick find love, and I desperately want to bring Ace home. That boy might think there's too much water under the bridge, but when it comes to family, you never give up," Sherman told him.

"I agree with you there," Joseph told his friend.

"You've done well with your family, Joseph. I'm glad I've gotten to see how it's grown," Sherman said.

Joseph beamed at him, as he always did when anyone praised his family. There was a reason Joseph Anderson had done so well in life—it was because he was loyal and loving, something that couldn't be said about too many people Sherman knew.

"Thank you, my friend. You're doing pretty well yourself," Joseph told him.

"Are you boys over here gossiping?"

Joseph instantly sat up a bit straighter as Katherine approached them.

"We were talking about what a lucky man I am to have wed you," Joseph quickly said as he reached for his bride and gently pulled her down onto his lap to kiss her lips. "Every day I have with you is one more I thank God for."

"You smooth talker, you," she said, a rosy glow instantly showing up in her aged cheeks.

"I'm just telling it how it is, my Katherine."

"You clearly have gotten yourself out of trouble," she told him with a giggle. "Even though I'm sure you're up to no good."

She looked adoringly at her husband's face, and Sherman could see the love they had for each other. It was a beautiful aura of pure goodness.

"I think I will leave you two alone," he said as he slowly rose to his feet and looked around. He could hear Joseph and Katherine giggling as he walked away to the edge of the water and looked out at the gently lapping waves.

Losing his wife had stolen a piece of his soul, and there wasn't a day that went by that he didn't regret not doing more for her each day they'd been together.

Turning back around, his eyes sought out his nephews.

He found Cooper and Stormy snuggled up together on a hammock, their smiles obvious even from this distance as Cooper snuck in little kisses. Evelyn cradled their baby close to her chest nearby.

Nick was speaking to a pretty brunette over by the fire, her soft laughter drifting across the sand. This nephew was as reluctant as his brothers to settle down, but the boy sure loved to flirt with the ladies.

It wouldn't be long before Sherman focused his attention on him.

Looking across the crowd of people, he couldn't find Maverick anymore—or Lindsey. He sure hoped that was a good sign. Those two were meant to be together and everyone knew it.

With a smile, Sherman made his way up the trails to the huge Anderson mansion. His heart was full, and his body tired. It was time to call it a night.

Tomorrow would be a new day for them all.

CHAPTER
FORTY-THREE

The big night was finally happening. The fund-raiser Lindsey had worked on side by side with Maverick was going off without a single hitch. The party planners had everything taken care of. More money was expected to be raised than in any other previous year, and Lindsey was standing in the immaculate ballroom wearing a dress she felt out of place in, wishing she were any other place on Earth.

Maverick was sure to be there, and she wasn't sure how she was going to deal with seeing him. She'd told herself it didn't have to be awkward, told herself they could be friends. But she had been foolish. It would be impossible to be only friends with the man she was hopelessly in love with.

"You are a vision."

Groaning beneath her breath, Lindsey turned to find Dr. Stine looking pretty dang impressive himself in his custom tux. She wasn't used to seeing any of the hospital staff in clothing other than scrubs. It was difficult to recognize some of them.

"You look great," she told him with an attempt at a smile.

"I'm happy you came. I was disappointed when I thought you weren't going to be here."

"I was browbeat into coming," she admitted.

"I was sort of hoping I'm the reason you decided to make an appearance. Then I might be able to talk you into a dance," he happily responded.

"Dr. Stine . . ." she began when he held a finger up to her lips.

"We're not at work. Don't you think you can call me Jesse?"

She reached up and removed his finger. "I might slip at work if I start it now," she said, but she gave him a smile. He was being very kind to her.

"If you say my name with a little pout at the end, then you can call me whatever you want," he told her, his teeth showing as he chuckled at his own joke.

It took her a minute to get it. Then she actually laughed.

"I'm not playing doctor and nurse with you," she said, feeling her spirits lift.

"But I have the perfect outfit in mind," he promised.

She leaned in and gave him a hug. When she pulled back, she knew there was no chance she was going to date this guy. But she also had a feeling she'd just made a new friend—which in her opinion was so much better than going on a few dates and then feeling awkward around each other.

"Thank you for making me laugh. I can't wait to see the woman who will bring you down," she told him.

For the briefest of moments, disappointment flashed in his eyes, but then his smile returned.

"Whoever the guy is that let you get away is a fool. If he doesn't figure it out soon, then I'm going to have to step up my game," he promised.

"He's definitely figured it out."

She and Dr. Stine both turned to find Maverick standing behind them, looking so spectacular her breath was taken away. She'd seen him in a suit once, but the fitted tux hugged him in all the right places. It gave him a look of mystery she found she wanted to unravel.

He stepped closer, letting Dr. Stine know she was taken. Lindsey didn't even have time to think before he leaned in and kissed her intimately, making her lips tingle. When he pulled back, she was almost dizzy, grateful for the arm holding her up.

"I don't think we've met. I'm Maverick Armstrong," he said to Dr. Stine, holding out one hand while possessively holding her with the other.

"Dr. Jesse Stine," the doctor said, taking his hand as he assessed him.

"Thanks for keeping Lins company, but I've got it from here."

He pulled her away before she had a chance to say anything. It took several seconds before she was able to get her wits about her. Just as Mav got her outside on the private balcony, Lindsey decided to put her foot down.

"That was incredibly rude, Mav. What do you think you're doing?" she asked, taking a step back from him, pulling herself more into the shadows.

This was too much. First he'd made that display a few days ago at Joseph Anderson's house, and now he was doing it again here where a lot of her coworkers could see.

"I don't understand why you're doing this."

Her anger was quickly draining and a sense of hopelessness began to fill her.

"I don't want to be without you, sug," he said as he stepped closer again.

"No. Stay there," she warned before taking in a deep breath. "I know we have great sex together, but I can't do this, Mav. It's breaking my heart," she told him before sucking in more air. "I love you. I love you so much that it hurts me when I see you."

She hadn't meant to tell him that—to guilt him—but it just came out. It was his fault for continuing to bombard her with his presence.

"And I love you, sugar," he said with a smile. He moved toward her with even more assurance.

"What does that even mean?" she asked, not wanting to get her hopes up, but unable to completely squash her dreams either.

"It means that I thought I could walk away, that I thought I would be able to just go on with my life, and we could see each other occasionally and be nothing more than friends. That isn't working for me—and I know it's not working for you. We have something that is so rare and beautiful that we'd be fools to let it go."

He dropped to his knee in front of her and pulled out a box, holding it out.

"I didn't think I would ever want to spend my life with just one person. But from that moment on the beach when I actually looked into your eyes for the first time, I haven't had another thought for anyone other than you. I love you, Lindsey, so much that I can't find joy anymore if you aren't with me. Please forgive my foolishness, and please say you'll marry me."

Lindsey's knees shook as this strong, confident man kneeled before her. It was everything she'd ever hoped for. She wanted to pinch herself to make sure the moment was real.

But that look of fear in his eyes that she might not say yes told her the moment was real—told her that she would have him forever.

"You saved me, Maverick," she began as tears started running down her cheeks. "And there's nothing more now that I want than to save us both," she said.

He took the beautiful diamond from its case and slipped it on her finger before standing up and pulling her into his arms, her feet lifting off the ground.

"I've learned something very important in my time with you, sugar," he said, his lips so close to hers. She wanted the talking to stop, but she also wanted to hear what he had to say.

"What's that, my love?" It was amazing how much better she felt just being in his arms again.

"I've learned that sometimes in life a person chooses love, and sometimes love chooses you. It's not a choice that you get to make no matter what people might say."

"If it's not a choice, then what is it?" she asked.

"Simply put, it's fate," he told her.

And then his lips were on hers and she was in heaven. She cared so much for him. Rather than hide away and live in fear, she could now see the perfection in giving herself to another. What a fool she'd been to not want that. Maverick was her everything and she had no doubt that he felt the same for her.

Fears would never rule her heart again.

EPILOGUE

The sun dipped low on the horizon, illuminating the sea before the Coast Guard Cutter *Orca*. Its bow sliced the calm, frigid seas as it traveled westward. The ship was on routine patrol in the Bering Sea and, being the biggest in the fleet, it was ready to take on any task.

With all the swagger of a helicopter cowboy, Nick Armstrong leaned against the low perimeter railing just beyond the helicopter landing pad and stared out over the darkening sky. A flash of lightning caught his eye as he peered into the ominous distance. A low rumble could be heard, but the storm was at least forty miles away.

"That's one heck of a storm," he murmured under his breath. He was thinking about the time he and his father had been caught in one of Puget Sound's storms during a fishing trip . . .

"Hey, Armstrong, stop staring at the sky and help me finish checking the gear," said his copilot, Gail, startling Nick out of his memories.

Nick turned in time to see Gail toss him a coiled rope.

"I was just taking the time to appreciate the awesomeness of Mother Nature . . . you should try it sometime," Nick said with sarcasm.

"I will," she replied. "After my shift."

Nick snapped out of the moment and fell back into his title, Commander Armstrong of the First Air Rescue Team.

Walking back to the landing pad, he stopped, getting an odd sense of foreboding. Nick had the ability to feel trouble, and it was no different tonight. He took a diverted path up to the bridge, where it was already buzzing with activity. He could hear the crackling of a radio call coming over the speaker.

The unsteady and forlorn voice of a man rang out over the Ops Radio: *Mayday, Mayday, Mayday . . . This is the* Southern Belle *. . . We are at 59 degrees . . . 10 minutes North . . . 146 . . . 47 degrees . . . This is the* Southern Belle *. . . Storm . . . High seas . . . taking on water . . . listing 40 degrees to starboard . . .*

The young radio technician, Seaman Harper, hopped into action, keenly focused on his radio and notepad.

Harper was barely nineteen and fresh out of boot camp. As such, he was showing visible nerves as he responded to the Mayday call, his voice cracking.

"This is US Coast Guard Cutter Orca on 121.5 Southern Belle. Need to know if you are in need of assistance? Over."

"Absolutely! We are going down!"

"Roger. This is the US Coast Guard, understand you are going down, requesting number of persons on board? Over."

Following the last transmission of the Coast Guard dispatcher, the radios fell silent, a sure sign the Southern Belle had succumbed to the storm that was still increasing in intensity over the Bering Sea. Harper finished typing all of the information into the Coast Guard computer, which fed information to the rest of the fleet.

The ship's captain sat still, calm, and quiet, with very little emotion on his face. He glanced over at Nick standing in the bridge doorway and spoke in a low Texas drawl. "Go give 'em hell, Nick."

With the slap of his palm on a big red button on the wall, the general alarm sounded on the Cutter. The alarm rang out with a sound akin to some old World War II siren, the type of alarm you would expect to hear if a nuclear bomb had gone off.

"I guess that's me," Nick said with a smile, his adrenaline already pumping.

He quickly made his way down to the flight crew ready room to suit up. Despite the danger of flying into the heart of a storm over churning, frigid seas that would kill you in minutes should you find yourself in the water, Nick couldn't help but love his job. Maybe it was how beautiful his orange and white helicopter was—an HH60 or Jayhawk, the Coast Guard version of the Army's Blackhawk. Maybe it was just the rush. He didn't care. He loved what he did.

In the cockpit of the Jayhawk, flight computers came online as the helicopter woke up with the whine of turbine engines and turning rotor blades. Gail was ready to go next to him so Nick leaned back, peering behind him to check on the two men in the rear of the chopper, a paramedic and a rescue diver.

"You two buckled in?"

"Sir, yes sir!"

"All right, let's get this show on the road. Gail, call for departure."

With checklists complete, First Officer Gail nodded at Nick and got on the radio to request departure clearance from the ship.

"*Orca*, this is CG6055 ready for departure."

"CG6055, this is *Orca*, wind 3-4-0 at 2-5 cleared for departure. Be careful out there, it's getting rough."

"Okay cleared for departure . . . and you know our motto, we deliver . . ."

The HH60 Jayhawk lifted off the deck of the *Orca* and started a low northward turn to the right. The helicopter whirled from the deck. The dust and spray on the deck from them being out to sea for a week swirled around the men below them. Highly motivated to reach the *Southern Belle*, the craft sped into the darkness.

"This is one hell of a storm," Nick commented as hail began striking the windscreen.

The Jayhawk bounced around as it fought against the high winds. Nick did his best to keep it on course as he scanned the roiling sea below.

"Do you see anything yet?" a muffled voice yelled.

"No, not yet," Nick replied.

It wasn't ten minutes into the bumpy flight when they spotted a strobe beacon and a bright yellow raft. It was just a yellow speck against an evil, dark-blue backdrop.

"I see them over there," Gail shouted as she hit Nick's arm.

"I'll get us into position."

Nick lined up the helicopter over the raft, trying his best to keep it level. The rescue diver lowered himself into the basket, preparing for what was to follow. He gave a thumbs up to the medic as he began going down. The swells were getting bigger and climbing higher. Mother Nature was doing her damnedest to take them all down.

The waves pounded the little raft and slammed into the rescue basket. One at a time, they pulled the four stranded, frozen men out of the raft and into the Jayhawk.

"CG6055 . . . this is *Orca* . . . what's your status?" The captain's southern accent rang out in Nick's headset.

"We're pulling the last one onboard now, sir . . . ETA back to ship, 15 minutes. Need medics and fuel."

With the last rescued fisherman on board, Nick turned the battered Jayhawk back toward the ship.

The lightning was cracking even harder and more frequent as the winds increased. The *Orca* was in the distance, getting hit by the brunt of the storm. Waves crashed against the bow of the ship as it powered through the increasingly white-capped sea. This would make the chopper's landing on the ship that much more interesting.

"Looks like she's pitching about 15 degrees to either side. Hang on," Nick warned as he brought the aircraft back down onto the deck. Setting the wheels on the pad brought a sense of relief to the entire crew. Nick wasn't the worrying type, but this was a storm for the record books.

With the rotor still running, the medics rushed the chopper. They pulled the rescued men out one by one. As the last one was being placed onto the stretcher, he reached out for Nick's arm.

"What about the captain?" he asked, straining to speak.

"What do you mean, the captain?" Nick replied.

"There were five of us onboard the *Belle*. The captain was swept from the raft." The man's grip on his arm loosened as he lost consciousness.

Nick looked at Gail, and she knew what he was going to say. She jumped on the mic. "Control, this is CG6055, were going out for another one."

Nick nodded and pushed up the throttle.

"CG6055, the storm is getting worse. Are you sure you can do this?"

"Sir, there's another man out there. The captain of the boat. We're going to go get him." Nick would never leave a man behind.

The Jayhawk was back in the thick of the storm, disappearing into the torrid sky. It didn't take long before Nick was circling over the remnants of the *Southern Belle*. There wasn't a sign of the captain anywhere.

Beep, beep, beep . . . Nick glanced over at the fuel gauge and it was now reading low.

"We have to go back, Armstrong," Gail said with reluctance.

"I know, I know," Nick responded as he fought to keep the aircraft upright. He didn't want to leave, but he was left with no choice.

Just as he began his turn south, they were struck by a bolt of lightning. Nick grabbed the controls, and for a moment, he was fighting a lost battle. The aircraft drifted sideways into the oncoming swell of a giant wave. The sliding cargo door was jarred loose, swinging wildly open and closed.

"Hold on. We need to pull up, Gail," Nick yelled as he put the throttle to max. The turbine engines screamed as the rotors lifted the heavy craft upward. It was too little, too late. Another larger wave crashed into the side of them, this time filling the back with freezing sea water. To make matters worse, the cargo door slammed shut and latched, locking in the heavy payload of water.

"She weighs too much," Nick exclaimed as he strained to get the now-sluggish Jayhawk up.

Gail jumped on the radio. "Mayday, Mayday, Mayday. *Orca*, this is CG6055, we are going to ditch. I repeat, we are going to ditch!"

"Are you ready for this?" she asked as she handed Nick his survival pack.

"Nope."

A large looming wave crashed down on the aircraft, slamming it into the water. The fuselage tumbled into the swell as it began to rise again. Both Nick and Gail were tossed inside the deathtrap. The crew in back must have lost their mics because they were radio silent.

With one final hit, the front window shattered, allowing bone-chilling sea water to flood inside. There was nothing more they could do. The orange and white aircraft slipped below the surface of the water. The faint glow of the red and green navigation lights became dimmer as it sank deeper into the sea.

"CG6055, this is *Orca*, come in."

There was no response.

ACKNOWLEDGMENTS

This is my favorite part of writing a book. It takes so many people to make the magic happen, and without all of you, I couldn't get it done. Thank you to my pilot friends for looking over stuff for accuracy. You guys so love to talk planes; it's a blast to do my research. Thanks to Stephy for all the help with the nurse info. Thanks to my employees for all you do and for the many hours you put in. I know I couldn't do it without you. The hours we work together are so much fun for me.

Thanks so much to my editors, Maria and Lauren. You are amazing and I love the many ideas you come up with to make my stories so much better.

Finally, thank you to my family. Everything I do is for you. I love you all so much. We are nothing without our friends and family. I can't imagine how lonely life would be without each and every one of you.

ABOUT THE AUTHOR

Photo © 2014 Edward Harr

Melody Anne is a *New York Times* and *USA Today* bestselling author who has written a number of popular series, including Billionaire Bachelors, Surrender, and Baby for the Billionaire. Along with romance and young adult novels, Melody has also recently collaborated with fellow authors J.S. Scott and Ruth Cardello for *Taken by a Trillionaire*. *Turbulent Desires* is the second book in Melody's Billionaire Aviators series.

A country girl at heart, Melody loves the small town and strong community she lives in. When she's not writing, she enjoys spending time with her family, friends, and beloved pets. Most of all, she loves being able to do what makes her happiest . . . living in a fantasy world (for at least 95 percent of the time).